ISBN 978-1-7324643-9-1

Cover Design by Brittany Evans

Edited by Represent Publishing

RP Represent Publishing

Dedicated to all those looking for love, healing, growing, evolving, and trying to find some peace. Give yourself some patience and kindness. You deserve it.

A REPRESENT PUBLISHING ANTHOLOGY

BECAUSE
OF *you*

A REPRESENT PUBLISHING ANTHOLOGY

BECAUSE OF *you*

Ashlyn Drewek • D. Allyson Howlett
Chelsea Lauren • Danielle Merchant

REPRESENT
PUBLISHING

Spirits n' Chai

BY D.ALLYSON HOWLETT

One

He was out there, faded under the streetlight like someone took an eraser to him. All you could make out were the lines of what he once was. Colorless and begging to be seen. A week had gone by since he first appeared on the sidewalk across from my apartment. An entire week and no one noticed him. Except me.

It was a quarter to five, and the sun had already disappeared beneath the bay of this bustling seacoast town. Pushing what's left of my short turquoise hair behind my ear, I chewed at my lip ring as less and less people remained to challenge the cold of the streets.

Tonight was the night. I would go down there and talk to him. Once and for all.

The first day he appeared, I thought nothing of it. It was Sunday, and he was leaning against the green lamp post with his faded dark hair and dull-looking blazer and slacks. It wasn't until I ate some scrambled eggs and had a cup of tea that I noticed how transparent he looked.

As the hours rolled on, he waved his hands while people passed, saying "hello" so loudly I could hear him from my apartment window on the second floor of the gold shop. No one stopped. Not one person. Around 1:00 p.m., he seemed to have given up, and just sat defeated on the curb.

The next day, I headed out for work at the art gallery. It was around noon, and I had my dark fir rimmed pleather coat on with a homemade knit cap to keep the cold out. This was Portsmouth after all, and winters here along the Maine and New Hampshire border were always chilly.

As my dark boots hit the pavement, I spotted him staring vacantly into the street. He must have noticed me looking at him, because his eyes widened as I crossed his path. I immediately looked away, burying my face in the collar of my coat. No amount of arm flailing and shouting could bring my attention to him. I grasped onto the strap of my sloth messenger bag and kept walking as fast as I could.

He didn't stop until I turned the corner and fell against the building, my heart beating one hundred miles an hour and my nerves shot. As much as I wanted to run, I made myself peek around the corner. His features were clearer, but still barely visible. As disheveled as he was, his close shaven beard and slicked back hair appeared well kept. He was Indian, that was clear by his prominent jaw and narrow bridge. But his eyes were dark and down turned, plagued by baseball-sized circles.

On the fourth day, I couldn't take it anymore. Every night, he cried or sang a melancholy song in a language I could only guess was Hindu. Despite my bed being on the opposite side of the window that faced the street, his voice carried like black smoke seeping into the brick of the downtown shops.

I called the police and must have sounded like a crazy person. Or, at least, scared shitless by how shaky my voice was from over-rattled nerves.

When the flashing lights breached my window, I scurried over like a mouse and peeked my nose over the sill. The cop slid out of her car, holding the flashlight by her face. When the light passed over the man, it bounced off of his gray-coated frame, like fog on a rain stained road. I clasped my hand over my mouth as the cop continued looking for someone she would never find.

He was a ghost. An unseen spirit to everyone. Everyone but me.

I spent a day or two trying to decide if this man was a figment of my imagination or if he was actually there. But no amount of contemplation, and Googling every chance I got, could stifle my manic mind.

I barely slept all week. Eating was only a means of survival at this point. If I didn't go down there, I'd probably die from exhaustion or a strained heart from all the anxiety I've been dealing with.

Twisting my mouth into a knot, I grabbed my heaviest knit sweater and faux-fur boots. Before heading out the door, I wrapped my pink leopard print scarf around neck.

Every step down the stairs was agony. My heart beat so loud, I could feel my pulse bulging out of my neck. I couldn't even grip the banister; my hands were shaking so much. No air would pass or escape my lungs.

When I reached the door to the street, I stopped to peer out the tall square window. Light snowflakes passed the pane like seeds in the silent wind. The man sat on the curb, his head hanging between his legs. Even through the streak cleaned glass, I could see the flakes pass right through him, settling on the ground on which he sat.

My hand gripped the doorknob as I finally let myself breathe. *Get it together. You can do this.* I pushed against the door and the man's face shot to focus. Dark eyes watched my petrified form as I somehow crossed the street with sheer unbridled determination.

Two

"**Y**ou can see me?" The man's eyes were frantic, hands cast in front of him, anticipating my answer. His Indian accent came through and it immediately reminded me of my freshmen year philosophy professor. I'm sure he would have a field day with this.

I pulled my hands inside my sleeves, yanking at the stitching to feel its softness. The combination of tingling nerves and the crisp night air sent my bones rattling beneath my skin. Looking right at him, I could see the blue painted mailbox on the corner of the next street. His body was completely transparent, with only a slim veil of gray to show he was even there at all.

"Can you see me? Please tell me you can!" The man ran his fingers through his hair. "No. No. I know you can. I could sense it the first time you left your apartment."

The believability of this entire situation kept my mind in a fog. I couldn't tell if I was dreaming or awake. I wanted to run. As fast as my knock-off faux boots would take me.

Shutting my blue-gray eyes, I rolled my tongue over my chapped lips, landing on the metal of my lip ring. My arm muscles tightened against my body before I allowed myself to exhale a warm, nerve ridden breath. "Yes," I shuddered. "I can see you."

Opening my eyes, the man's face brightened with sudden relief. The corner of his mouth turned up into a smile and his once drooping eyes seemed to jump into his dark, full eyebrows.

"Oh, thank god. Thank god. I . . . I don't know how I got here. Or why this is happening. I was . . . I was in a car and then . . . I was here."

He didn't know he was dead.

I didn't know if I was numb from the cold or from the shock damaging everything I had ever known about reality. But nothing would register except the fact that this man was dead, and I was talking to him. Me. Someone who, up until recently, didn't know what it felt like to be seen at all.

The weight of being the one to tell him twisted my stomach like a wrung towel. Shifting my feet from left to right to help combat the chill, I looked down at the faint snow-covered sidewalk.

"You're . . . you're dead," I whisper loud enough to carry over.

"I'm what?" His voice was stern, like I was a child telling him I flushed his watch down the toilet.

Forcing myself to look at him, I let out a scattered breath. "You're a ghost. Or maybe you're not. Maybe I'm imagining this whole thing."

Every so often, the wisps at the horizon of his see-through form fluttered in the motionless wind. Though he was still, his eyes darted in every direction. I didn't have the capacity to interpret his state of mind. Being told you were dead had to have some sort of impact on your mental health. But he had no body. He was conscious energy, or my subconscious finally coping with the trauma I had avoided dealing with for the past nine months.

"Dead?" he muttered. "No. No. No. No. No. I . . . I can't

9

be . . . dead." His ghostly chest visibly heaved as his hands shook. His gray hue swelled, creating a dark cloud of uncertainty around his ghostly form. As he pushed his hands to his head, the color thickened, crawling like a shadow through the air.

All I could hear were my veins keeping time in my ears. I didn't think it was possible to be so scared and confused at the same time. Taking a step back, I shied away from whatever dark matter he was omitting. The air grew thick with what I could only describe as humidity. It pressed against my lungs and weighed me down, making it harder to move. I needed to get out of there. The longer I stood beneath the streetlamp, the more my internal organs were beginning to fail. Turning around, I made for the door leading up to my apartment.

"No, no! Please don't go!" In an instant, all evidence of despair was sucked from the street, returning it to its still state of winter crispness. The ghost flowed around me like a feather, standing before me, creating a haze between me and my escape.

"*Please*. You can't leave me here." He begged through the worry-filled wrinkles on his forehead and diamond shaped eyes.

The strings of my heart tightened from fear or sadness or both. My awkward introverted tendencies tickled my toes inside my boots, encouraging me to beat it. But I couldn't. This had to be real. Terrifying and sad all at once. I couldn't run away. I could see him. No one else had stepped forward. I did. Why did I?

His swirling aura beckoned me with eerie anticipation. I swallowed the next gulp of air, drying my throat to Sahara Desert levels. "What's your name?" I asked, forcing my lips and tongue to cooperate.

"I'm Krish." His gaze wandered, as if trying to remember. "Yes. My name . . . my name is Krish."

"Krish. Okay." I rubbed my hands together. "It's getting late. I need to . . . wrap my head around this. I'll . . . come back tomorrow." Crossing my arms over my chest, I puffed another heat filled cloud in his direction. It dissipated against his face, almost becoming part of him. I bit through the steady fear to not seem desperate to get away. "Is that okay?"

Krish nodded. "Yes. Yes, that's fine."

"Okay." I glanced back to the lamppost. "Try to get some rest . . . or . . . just relax, I guess." I came back to him. "I'll see you in the morning."

"Yes. Okay." He clutched his arm, rubbing up and down the sleeves of his blazer. "I'm sorry. I didn't mean to—"

"It's okay. Don't . . . don't worry about it." I tried to ignore the numbing cold he unintentionally injected into me by just being there. "My name is Raina, by the way."

"It's a pleasure to meet you." Krish mustered a smile before slowly making his way back to the lamppost. "Have a good night, Raina."

"Good night." I watched him move without making any indentations in the thin layer of snow on the ground. He settled on the curb, wrapping his arms around his legs to rest his chin on his knees. I couldn't imagine what he was thinking right now. Whatever it was, he was damn good at keeping a straight face.

Making a B-Line for my apartment door, I turned the knob to open it. But before I could pass over the threshold, I glanced back one last time. Krish's eyes caught mine, and he managed a simple wave, his face calm and filled with quiet deliberation.

I pushed against the door and fell into the stairway, shutting it behind me as quietly as I could. Leaning against the entrance, I let the tension escape through my lips in a long, drawn-out breath.

This was crazy. So much so that I couldn't be sure if I

believed it. The tingling in my arm began to settle. I grasped my forearm, the slow dissipation absorbing into the soft warmth of my sweater. If this is all in my head, then I ought to win an award for having the most imaginative, whacked out mind in the world. That or be dragged away in a straight jacket.

Three

I didn't have to leave until noon. Looking out my window, Krish stood amongst the bustle of downtown Portsmouth. He swayed back and forth on his heels, hands coming together in a clap before swinging them behind his back. He seemed eager. Eager and unsure.

The rock in my stomach dragged down my appetite. I wasn't ready to engage in a conversation with a ghost in broad daylight. How would I pull this off without someone thinking I was nuts?

I looked at my vintage black cat clock, its eyes shifting from left to right. 11:15 a.m. It took me twenty minutes to walk to the gallery. It was too early to leave, but the more I waited, the more I felt like jumping out the window.

Grabbing my polka dotted water bottle and messenger bag, I threw my coat and boots on and made my way to the stairs. I pulled a small clump of blue hair away from my face, clipping it back against my skull. My chopstick earrings still adorned my lobes from the other day. Usually I changed my jewelry daily, but a ghost was a pretty good excuse for breaking routine.

Krish zoomed across the street as soon as I opened the door. Clasping his hands together, he forced a smile and bowed. "Good afternoon, Raina. So good to see you."

I stood next to him, fishing out my phone and earbuds from the front pocket of my bag. Fitting my buds into my ears, I pretended to shuffle across my phone screen. It was the only way I could survive this.

"What are you—"

"I have to go to work," I whispered, glancing at him. "You'll walk with me."

Krish nodded, though uncertainty plagued his face. "I will try."

"Try?"

"I do not know if I can leave this street. I haven't been able to."

I look around wearily. No one noticed me, which was nothing new but according to plan, at least today. "You crossed the street just now. Maybe you can come with me."

I didn't wait for a response. With a quick step to the right, I made my way down Chambers Street. Keeping my hands in the wells of my jacket pockets, I glanced down the side street before crossing onto the opposite sidewalk.

It didn't take long for Krish to fall in beside me, moving with a smoothness that only smoke could mimic. He did his best to avoid running into anyone who passed us. A few bodies made it through, but none stopped to contemplate or even notice. If they did know, I wonder what their reaction would be.

It wasn't too cold today, but cold enough that every quick huff of breath plumed in front of me. My heart beat steadily. It wasn't as desperate as the night before, but harsh enough that I could feel every beat strike against my ribcage.

"Where do you work?" Krish asked as we waited at the next corner to cross.

"The art gallery on Ceres." I glanced at him, not wanting

to make complete eye contact but not wanting to be a jerk, either.

"I do not think I know it."

The light flashed from the walking man sign, showing it was time to cross. "What do you know?"

Krish sighed, drawing his attention to the ground. I kept my gaze downward, watching his feet walk in tandem with mine. Only I was creating footprints, and he wasn't.

"I remember being in a car. I believe I was driving. I cannot really recall."

Last night, the news of his fate seemed to escalate his new ghostly form. Now, he seemed to have more control. There was still a sense of chaos about him, like a dull ringing not even my ear buds could cancel out. But his color was an ambient gray, with no hints that he would expand into whatever dark form the dead could possess in times of turmoil.

"Do you remember anything before that?" I brushed past a heavily bundled man as we crossed the street again, avoiding a few stopped cars to allow more foot traffic to pass.

Krish caressed his lightly bearded chin, squeezing the impressions of his skin and pulling them downward as his brow furrowed. "It's just a shadow. Like the remnants of a memory. There was a wedding . . . yes. A wedding!" His eyes flashed, illuminating the gray of his spirit. "I was attending a wedding. My family was there. It was for . . . a sibling. I believe? I remember . . . a sister and her husband, carried into a grand hall. But there's something else." His expression shifted downward as uncertainty plagued his eyes. "Something I'm missing."

My eyes watched his deep contemplation. Recounting his last days before his death, it was as debilitating as going to an actual funeral. He didn't seem too bothered by it. Probably because he couldn't remember. How can you miss something you can't remember?

As we moved onto Market Street, Krish caught me looking

at him. Breaking his stagnant concentration, he formed a weak smile. "This must be strange for you."

"Strange? No. Not at all," I muttered. "I talk to ghosts all the time."

"You do?"

My head shook. "No. I was being sarcastic. Sorry. Probably not appropriate, considering the circumstances." My feet came to an unexpected halt. Clenching my eyes shut, I reluctantly turn toward my ghostly companion. "I'm sorry."

"Sorry for what?"

I forced myself to look at him. "Sorry that you died."

Floating in stillness, a few pedestrians traveled straight through him, bending his body in the direction of their stride, but not enough to disturb his gaze. "I'm sorry too."

Curiosity engulfed my mind, but I quickly forced it into submission. There are so many questions I want to ask. All rude and not empathetic. My fingers play with my hair, relentlessly tucking it behind my ear as my eyes shifted from side to side while I deliberated my words.

"You're nervous," Krish spoke calmly.

"Aren't you?"

"I . . . " his voice trailed off, his head dropping to his chest. "I'm not sure what I am." His hands rub up his chest, wrinkling the flaps of his blazer. "Everything I feel is new. Like discovering a new sense. Like . . . " His eyes rose to mine.

That statement sent an unnatural fear into my heart, kicking my adrenaline into high gear. Ghosts may be defined as an energy blueprint of their former selves, but this far overshadows that by a dozen or so nautical miles. I wasn't someone who freaked out about the supernatural. I used to love it as a kid. Breaking into abandoned nut houses, holding seances in cemeteries and dark basements with my friends. You know, normal odd girl stuff.

But this wasn't child's play. This was real. Real ghosts, actual death, real shit.

We continued along Market Street in silence. Questions cycled through my head like social media scrolling. Ceres came into view. The cobblestone street fell along the Piscataqua River, stretching out into the ocean with breathtaking clarity. Boat docks lined the riverbank, the vessels bobbing in the winter water just before the bridge. Krish slowed his stride, taking a moment to stop and admire the scenery. I waited with him, looking out across the border into Maine, watching the whisky clouds speckle the blended red and blue sky.

"Colors are . . . strange things," Krish spoke softly.

I came beside him, adjusting the straps of my bag across my shoulder. "What do you mean?"

"They're alive. Like a pulse. Surrounding everything that breathes."

My teeth clenched as a chill dripped down my spine. "That is unreasonably creepy."

"Yours is blue." His words forced my eyes upon him. With a steady hand, he searched around my circumference like he was measuring something. Carefully, he reached over my head, hovering and wiggling his fingers in the air above. "It's warm. Moving swiftly like a river."

I watched as each of his digits traveled through the empty space. The motion tickled my skin, standing my arm hair to full attention. Every passing second expediting the strangeness building up in my stomach. It tensed my muscles and shortened each sea-salted breath as it entered my lungs.

Meeting my unblinking gaze, a smirk spread across his lips. "It matches your hair."

"Okay." I took a step back, shaking the tension out through my arms. "That was . . . I don't know what that was."

"I'm sorry." He relinquished his hand. "I didn't mean to frighten you."

"No, don't apologize." My hands squeeze my arms to regain the feeling. "It's new. It's just new." I wipe my hands on

17

my jacket and try to seem unfazed. But I'm sure that's not possible at this point.

"I . . . I don't know what to make of this." Krish returned to search the lapping waves of the sea. "Why do I remain? If I am dead, why haven't I found the light?"

My heart sank into my stomach. "I don't know. I . . . don't know why this is happening to you. Or me. To both of us."

He looked back at me, matching my pathetic gaze with his own debilitating disbelief. "Perhaps we must find the answer. Together."

A nervous laugh erupted from my lips. "This is wild."

"I agree." He joined in my uncertain chuckle before settling down in quiet contemplation. "Will you help me?"

My tongue tangled in my throat. I wasn't the type of person to go headfirst into uncharted territory. But I had little choice in the matter. I mean, if the roles were reversed, wouldn't I want someone to help me?

"I'll try." My honesty leaking through my teeth. "That is, I'm doubtful I'll be much help. But I'll do my best."

Krish gave a simple nod, the helplessness slowly leaking from his face. I barely knew anything about this man, but I hoped I wouldn't disappoint him.

We press on, turning onto Ceres. There weren't as many people down this road, since the open sea made the air colder than if we were combing the main streets of downtown. We only managed to travel a few feet before Krish stopped in front of one of the many cafes that littered this seaside town. I watched him vividly study the building as if reliving a memory.

"Have you been here before?" I asked.

"No. I have never been here before. But," he took a hesitant step forward. "Something is here."

I looked toward the wood sided building. It was a quaint little coffee shop, adorably named *Beans n' Cream*; with a painted green and black sign hanging over the double door entrance. I never cared much for coffee, being more of a tea drinker myself. A few round iron tables and matching chairs sat in front, each adorned by a large pale umbrella to stifle the sun. A small fence kept the tables belonging to the establishment.

"Can we go in?" Krish looked at me with unbridled hope.

Shifting my gaze, I stared into the long paneled windows of the cafe. The coffee equipment was shining, with a bronze newness, from behind the long stretch of counter facing the sea. A large chalkboard menu covered the wall beyond the register.

I gulped down whatever moisture still clung to the inside of my mouth. "I need to get to work."

"Tomorrow then?"

I looked toward my ghostly friend, biting the inside of my lip. If I pushed myself any more today, I'm convinced my arms and legs would detach from my body. There was still a lot to process, and I wasn't sure what it all was supposed to mean. Nor did I think I ever would.

Tensing every muscle in my body, I reluctantly nodded my head. "Sure. Tomorrow."

"Thank you." He clasped his hands together. "This is difficult for you. I understand. I appreciate it."

I couldn't believe a ghost was pitying me. Me. I should pity him. He's dead. I'm not. Which is worse? An awkward 24-year-old forced to come out of her shell or a ghost whose only hope of finding closure was that said 24-year-old?

Why a more competent person wasn't chosen to help this lost soul was clearly beyond even supernatural understanding.

"Don't thank me just yet."

"I do not wish to inconvenience you. I—"

"Believe me." I turned on my heels and continued down the street. "This goes beyond inconveniencing anyone. This is so . . . unimaginably out there. I don't think normal rules apply."

A relieved laugh escaped Krish. "Yes. I suppose they don't."

Four

Yesterday went pretty well, considering the circumstances. Krish really enjoyed the art gallery. He spent my entire shift reading up on the artists we had featured this month, giving their work a critical eye. Judging by his interest, he surely was a man of sophistication and culture. On the way home, he talked about what he had learned, asking me questions about past exhibitions and what events we held at the gallery.

I had never met anyone quite so interested in art, aside from those who thought they were better than everyone else. Art was something that shunned me for most of my teen and young adult life. Instead of swooning over boys and playing sports, I was the one sitting in the corner under the bleachers with my sketchbook. Combing over coffee table books at the bookstore. And writing papers about 15th century architecture.

It wasn't until two years ago that I met someone who seemed to mimic my life in every way possible. He fit in so well in the beginning; he was perfect. Until he peeled away the layers of my life, one small strand at a time.

"Do you have an education in art?" Krish asked on our silent walk home.

Shaking my head, I buried my nose into the fuzzy collar of my jacket to stifle the cold. "Sort of. I was going to school for studio arts, but money dried up for my dad. I had to drop out."

"There are ways you can still pursue an education."

"Drowning in debt doesn't sound that appealing."

He smiled, sliding his hands into his coat pockets. "Well, the gallery gives you a window. How long have you been working there?"

"About a year. I run shows sometimes."

"Ah." Krish leaned closer to me, breaking my personal space bubble. "There are more galleries in the world you can aspire to be a part of. Other than this one."

I shook my head. "I'm not a very ambitious person."

But the more we walked, the more I thought about how cool it would be to run an art gallery in Boston or New York. *Me? A curator at a New York City art gallery?* As the thought crept into my brain, my stomach turned on itself. I could never do that, not me. I wasn't meant to do anything like that. I was just something to admire for a little while. Not meant to have an option, let alone make an impact. At least, that was the old me.

"What is wrong?" Krish's genuine concern melted away the memories of my past.

Raising my shoulders, I forced a smile. "What makes you think something's wrong?"

He hesitated, sliding his hands into his blazer. "Your aura. It's changing."

Perfect. There would be no hiding my feelings from him, it seemed. "Guess I can't hide anything from you." A nervous smile breached my lips. "Maybe I'm not supposed to."

"You do not need to tell me if it is too personal."

"No, I—" A rock jumped into my throat to shut me up.

Even after nine months, it felt wrong to talk about it. Like I was breaking the rules. Rules I no longer abided by since leaving him, but still felt tethered to. "I was in a pretty controlling relationship for a while. I wasn't allowed to be myself or ... anything. At all." I looked away from him to try and keep the boulder from escaping. "It was . . . very hard to leave."

"But you did."

He spoke so confidently; I was able to look at him without feeling like I did something wrong. My initial reaction to interacting with a ghost was fear-based, but now that I've spent the day with him, it was strangely gratifying. Refreshing almost. Krish was a spirit of confidence, despite the moments of credited confusion and uncertainty. He was remarkably easy to talk to. Because he was dead? Maybe. Or because he didn't have a choice but to listen to my agonizing past. One I wished I could erase for all eternity.

Five

"What's with the blue hair?"

My entire body tensed hearing Paul's condescending tone. Standing in the kitchen, I put a glass, freshly washed, into the drying rack. I didn't bother to turn around as he approached me. His looming presence casting a shadow over my so-called life. Shoving the nauseous feeling deep down into my gut, I continued to wash the dishes, grabbing another glass as the water flowed over its surface.

"I wanted a change, that's all."

"Is that the new thing now?" He dragged his fingers along the edges of my hair, sending chills down my spine. "You and your trends."

He walked toward the fridge, releasing his hold on me enough so I could breathe without it hurting. "I'll entertain it for now. But you should dye it back before the week is over."

My mind wretched with total disgust. "Why?"

I heard the fridge open, the sounds of shifting Tupperware and bottles shot through me like sharp stones pelting my skin. "We can't go to my parents' house this Saturday with you looking like that. What will my family think of you, seeing you deface yourself like this? A beautiful girl like you shouldn't ruin

24

her looks just because it's popular. I can't have you pretending to be something you're not, not when I'm trying to keep up appearances with my folks."

The sponge dropped from my hand into the sink. I held on to the glass under the faucet, staring at the etching of my name and his along its surface. This was the gift he gave me for our one-year anniversary, marking the day everything about our relationship changed.

Shutting my eyes, I held my lips taut, biting into the soft tissue on the inside of my mouth. The points of my fingers felt hot beneath the running water as the nausea clawed its way up my esophagus. The next words I wanted to say hung at the back of my throat like bird shit on a window. But I had to scrape it off. I couldn't stand the feeling of it lingering on the edge of fear and uncertainty.

"I'm not changing it."

The fridge door shut, and I heard Paul's sneakers pivoting on the linoleum floor. "What did you say?"

My eyes shot open as I turned to face his smug expression. "I'm not changing my hair."

He smirked, tilting his head as his smooth stride carefully approached me. The glass still clenched in my hand; I don't think I blinked once as he came to stand in front of me. "If you don't change it, I'll cut it off while you sleep."

I couldn't move. Let alone breathe. His long spider-legged fingers came up to my face. An arrogant chuckle rumbled from his partially closed lips. "Come on, Raina. I'm only kidding. You know I wouldn't cut off your hair." He tucked my hair behind my multi-pierced ear. "We'll go to the convenient store later and pick out a nice color for you. I'll help you dye it."

He brought his smug face close to mine, his stale breath seeping into my nostrils. "Don't you want me to find you attractive?"

In the blink of an eye, I smashed the glass against his jaw, shattering it into a million pieces across the floor. Paul clutched *his face, reeling as he stepped back from the shards left embedded in his flesh. "YOU FUCKING BITCH!" Blood dripped from the spaces between his fingers, pooling onto the floor in time with the rushing water still escaping from the faucet.*

I turned around, grabbed my bag off the hook, and shot through the door. Running down the stairs, tears poured from my eyes as I heard him yelling down the corridor after me. My heart was in a race with itself, begging my feet to move faster. I didn't stop. I ran. As far and as fast as I could. I ran and never looked back.

I WOKE up in a dry sweat. Air couldn't cycle through my lungs fast enough. Looking out my window, the sun had already risen, meaning it was at least 8:00 a.m. I pulled my crocheted blanket over my knees and wrapped my arms around them. It's been a long time since I dreamed about Paul or anything related to the life I escaped from. I guess talking to Krish about it, no matter how subtle it was, rattled those memories from the grave.

It was a new day. A day without Paul suffocating me into oblivion. I had to be grateful for that. Despite being nine months since I left, I still didn't feel whole. Maybe he took more from me than I thought. If I would ever get it back, who knew. I was pretty content to be this way forever.

I ripped the blankets from my bed and hopped onto the floor. It was time to get moving, away from the bad memories. Nothing beat those away like the notion I had a ghost to host, in a manner of speaking. A ghost who was stuck here until he found whatever he needed to find.

After taking a quick shower and grabbing a bite from my tiny kitchen, I bundled up and shot out the door to join Krish at the corner. He had a welcoming smile as I crossed the street to meet him, throwing my hair into some messy bun pigtails. The second I came beside him, his smile diminished.

"What's wrong?" he asked with an almost melted expression.

"Nothing." I shrugged. "I . . . had a bad dream, is all."

"Dreams are usually a window to something bigger. Do you want to talk about it?"

"Not particularly." We waited together on the corner, letting the light snow pass, or in his case, through. "Come on. Let's get to your cafe."

CAFE FOLK usually kept to themselves. It wasn't the people I was uncomfortable with, but the *amount* of people. Especially in the morning.

Rubbing the sweat from my hands across my black spotted leggings, I shivered in my boots as we approached the door. Raising my hand to grip the handle felt like moving a monster truck tire, but luckily, someone was coming out and graciously held the door for me.

So far, so good.

I smiled as we entered the cafe, absorbing the warm atmosphere of this friendly, caffeine-ridden establishment.

Krish stood right behind me, waiting to advance to the counter. But my feet were glued to the floor. I did experience lapses of nerves in unfamiliar places, but this was different. Maybe because I had an agenda, a reason for being here that was so out of this world, I barely believed it.

"Raina?" Krish's questioning voice coiled in my ear. "Are you going to order something?"

I almost blurted out a response, but held my tongue. A girl talking to herself in the middle of a cafe was not the attention I wanted. Scurrying up to the counter, a glasses-wearing brunette stood ready to greet me. She was wearing a red and gray camo print shirt and tight pre-ripped jeans.

"Hi," she said with a bubbly smile. "What can I get for you today?"

Fiddling with my purple painted nails, I looked up at the chalkboard menu. At my current level of uneasiness, everything looked jumbled and turned upside down. I tried my best to focus, but it was becoming impossible with the added pressure to perform.

The brunette seemed to notice my indifference as she leaned against the counter to peer at the board. "Any flavors you're into?"

Twisting my mouth, I glanced at her. "I'm not much of a coffee drinker."

"We have some great teas. Our signature vanilla chai is our most popular."

"Sure, let's go with that."

She smiled and typed in my order. "What size?"

"Small is fine."

I gave her my cat face debit card, which she took courteously. "Cute card." After a few seconds and a signature later, she handed my card back. "Can I have a name?"

I hesitated, like my name was too sacred to utter aloud. "Raina."

"It'll be right out for you, Raina." I tucked my card back into the slot behind my phone. "By the way," the girl's continued conversation startled me, "love your hair."

A half-smile crept upon my face. "Thanks."

I slipped from the counter and walked to the bar along the window. Finding the farthest stool from civilization, I popped down and immediately pulled out my phone to avoid any further social interactions. Though the barista's comment stuck in my head, lifting my spirits a bit. She liked my hair. And no one chose it but me.

The entire time I was at the counter, I had completely

forgotten about Krish. When he slid onto the stool next to me, I jumped in my seat. Krish didn't seem to notice; not even a blink could break his concentrated stare.

"What's up?" I whispered as I trolled through my phone.

"That man there." He pointed a steady finger. "There is something . . . familiar about him."

Curiosity overtook my need to hide. I followed his gaze to a guy sitting at one of the small round tables, his left side facing us. He had dark, curly hair sitting in a neat mop against shaved sides. A black knit jacket covered his tight arms as he sat hunched over a wafting beverage. My observation traveled down to his legs, which were bouncing nervously in acid-washed jeans and slick ankle-high boots. A few rings glistened against his left hand, complimenting his sand-coated complexion.

It was like Aladdin jumped out of the Disney movie and raided a Neiman Marcus.

With a slight brow raise, Aladdin turned and caught my dull blue eyes. For a second, I admired how deep his eyes were. But only for a second.

"Vanilla Chai for Raina!"

I sprang from my seat, pulling my scarf over my mouth as I approached the counter. Grabbing my tea, I practically ran back to my seat to avoid any chances of me looking at Krish's newfound interest.

Hunkering down, I pushed my drink forward, resting my chin on my arms. Not even gritting my teeth could calm the seething embarrassment dancing in my stomach right now.

"He's looking at you." Krish didn't seem to notice my blatant bashfulness.

"Thank you." I buried my face in my arms. "Did not need to know that."

"Can you go over to him?"

My head shook on autopilot. "No way. No freaking way."

"You must. . . . I mean." Krish lowered his head to my level. "His aura, or energy. . . . It is what I felt yesterday."

"Well, have you seen him before?" I asked without allowing my face to breach the texture of my jacket.

"No. Never. But . . . he is the source." His attention shifted back to the man in question. "I'm sure of it."

I ventured another peek at the so-called chosen one. He wasn't looking our way anymore, just mildly sipping on his drink with an elbow on the table. Even though his leg was still bouncing, it was the only part that looked remotely movable. Tension oozed from his tight posture, clearly trying to keep something from spilling out.

"He looks uneasy." I rose from my hiding place. "I can't just walk up to him. What would I even say?" I took a nervous sip of my chai, which sat appealingly in a large tan-coated mug of frothy goodness. Nutmeg and cinnamon spice floated on the top. The minute it hit my tongue, its rich taste settled the gremlins that ran rampant in my stomach.

Krish retreated against his chair, causing the wisps of his ghostly form to waft at the edges. "Will you try? Please."

A dragging sigh deflated the awkwardness into my warm, steaming belly. The chai really did the trick in calming my unbridled nerves. Maybe I could do this. Or maybe I'd crash and burn on contact.

Krish put his hand on the bar, leaning forward. "If you do and it's nothing, we leave. You never have to return here again. There is nothing to lose."

"Only my dignity," I mumbled under my breath.

That got a chuckle out of him. "You are always this dramatic?"

I stifled a faint laugh at my absurdity. "No. Usually not."

He eyed Aladdin again, drawing my gaze to the restless Arabian knight. "I do not wish to make you uncomfortable. But I must know. What this could possibly mean."

I took a deep breath, swallowing any gremlins down that

were still trying to overtake me. He was right. We were a team. Haphazardly thrown together, but a team nonetheless. If we ever wanted to figure out what this meant, I couldn't let anything hold me back.

I grabbed my mug of chai and took a nice, satisfying gulp. "All right." I returned the mug to the table with a thud. "Let's do this."

Pushing off my stool, I straightened my jacket and turned toward my target.

"Raina, you've got—"

I didn't wait for Krish to finish, as my feet moved in a straight line toward Aladdin's table. My heartbeat echoed with every heel-to-floor stride, rippling the aftershock through my entire body.

Saying "hi" to a guy—an attractive guy at that—was absolutely terrifying. Since Paul, I have never even looked at another guy. I avoided them. Any guy that looked this good was either a complete asshole or too uptight for the likes of me. Now I was forcing one such guy to at least acknowledge my existence. If I told myself two weeks ago I would be doing this, I would have laughed in my own face.

Before I could even think of second guessing myself, I'm standing in front of his table. Planting my boots firmly on the smooth imitation stone floor, I watched as his attention fell on me.

Not a sound escaped as he looked at me with his brow raised and the corner of his mouth slowly drawing upward. I attempted to clear my throat, but it came out more like a squeak.

"Um . . . excuse me?" he said, raising a few loose fingers to grace his nose. "You've got something . . . "

My body went rigid. "What?"

"Something . . . " he scratched his nose, "on your nose."

Somehow, through my tunneling vision, I wiped my hand over my face. I could feel moisture smear across my knuckles.

Pulling my hand into view, I spy some chai tea froth, with a hint of nutmeg, thin against my skin.

"Shit." I don't give him a chance to respond, as I've already burst through the front door and onto the street.

The hair on the back of my neck rose, sending spider sensations into the pit of my stomach. I created as much distance between me and the coffee shop as I could.

I knew I'd blow it. *Stupid, stupid, stupid.*

Somehow, Krish is gliding beside me. "I tried to tell you."

"You could have been more forward."

"We will try again."

"No." I turned swiftly on my heels to face him. "I can't go back there now that I've embarrassed myself!"

"Perhaps you just need a day to—"

"Krish. No."

The graying lines of his form began to swirl and turn outward. "You'd give up so easily?"

"I'm not giving up. I just . . . it's not easy for me to just go up to someone and talk to them like that."

"I understand."

"No. You *don't*. Guys are poisonous. All of them. Fucking poison and should be avoided." My eyes shut. Maybe I was being too harsh, but the gremlins were in full force now. Crawling up my shoulders and whispering doubt into my ears. This was exactly what I was afraid of. The tense, debilitating feeling started to come back. That feeling I had every waking moment of my life with Paul.

I had no clue what kind of person Krish was before he died. But he didn't seem like someone who would allow himself to be caught in a situation like that, doubted himself and his ability to function as a human being.

I could never go back there. It's tainted now. My awkward social graces hungered for embarrassment. It became number 327 in my places to never find myself in again for as long as I live.

I took a deep breath and held it in my lungs for what seemed like an unfathomable amount of time. By the time I released, my eyes fell open to a swirling tornado of darkness slowly reaching into the sky from where Krish stood. He hovered at its center, fists clenched and black gaze focused. I didn't know how to be scared at this point, but the sheer rate of whatever unhinged energy this mass was producing shrunk me down to miniature proportions.

"Krish," I spoke softly. "What's happening to you?"

The moment my words breached the cloud, Krish fell backward like he was trying to keep himself steady. His hands opened and ran through his hair. A harsh exhale extinguishing the void surrounding him, like someone blowing out a candle.

"I . . . I do not know what that was." He closed his eyes, shaking his head as the gray returned.

Biding my time, I waited until there wasn't a single speck of black left contorted around him. "It happened before."

His head twisted toward me, eyes poised at my confession. "It has?"

Pressing my lips together, I tossed my lip ring back and forth to garner some sort of control over this unexplainable phenomena. I didn't want to exacerbate this any longer. I needed to be calm, for him. Maybe my self-doubt and defiance was making him turn into . . . something else. I don't know if that even sounded rational.

"Let's go home," I said, walking up to him as his gaze settled on me. "Take a step back. Maybe try again another day."

"Yes," he whispered breathlessly. "Perhaps that is a good idea."

Six

Not talking about what happened only made being around Krish that much worse. Part of me was afraid I would ignite the black fire again, or whatever ghost hunters wanted to call it. Staring at him from my window, his appearance had diminished. His hair and clothes were disheveled more so than when I first saw him. The bags under his eyes seemed to deepen, making his dark eyes more intense the longer you stared into them.

Feeling like I had to justify myself to a dead guy spoke volumes. Desperation was an understatement. We were both desperate in some way. I didn't know what the situation was doing to him, in his mind or his energy cloud or whatever. But it was clear as day as he sat with his hands hanging between his knees, letting town-goers run through him like a car cutting through a puddle of water, that he was suffering.

I had the day off on Saturday. The weather called for a rocket high of 30 degrees. That's warm for January. A light snow still coated the streets, scattered atop the curb and rooftops of the local businesses.

I threw on a long sleeve black and gray tunic and some knitted leggings. Grabbing a canvas and my watercolor case, I hopped down the stairs and breached the door to the outside world. It was early, so the streets were mostly vacant.

Krish looked at me with sad eyes. Walking over to him, I waved the canvas in my sparkle-gloved hands. "Hey. I was going to head down to the shore and do some painting. Want to tag along?"

He sat against the lamppost and looked away, his once well kept hair lying in disarray. His suit was more wrinkled and stained. The top buttons of his graying shirt were missing completely.

When he didn't respond, I shifted in my stance, bending down to him. "Look. I'm sorry about what happened on Wednesday."

His head dropped even farther into his chest. "I am dead. My life is over. So what does it matter? If I am doomed to remain this way forever, then so be it."

Instinct told me to leave it alone, but I forced myself to reach out to him. With a steady hand, I aimed for his shoulder. I knew I'd pass right through him, but I couldn't think of anything else to do. Instead of watching his graying form dissipate and reappear, it landed. Krish's gaze darted to where I fell, looking into my wide-eyed expression. There was no mention of being able to do this in ghost documentaries or theories of science. My fingers wanted to retract, but I bit through the urge to flee. The surface of his tattered blazer was smooth, despite the visible damage. There was no warmth or cold coming off him. Just a gentle throbbing, like he still had a pulse.

The moment ticked by without much of a reaction. We just looked at each other, each wondering if the other had the answer. I finally drew my hand away, unable to shake the tingling nerves set off in my fingertips. "Okay . . . that was . . . "

"Raina." His ghostly hand took my wrist, pulling us both to stand. "I do not know what's happening to us. But there must be a reason. I am sorry if I have disrupted your

35

life. But," he carefully let go, "I am grateful to you. Truly I am."

The back of my throat began to close. Whatever it was that forced Krish on me either did it for a reason or wanted to watch us squirm. I didn't ask to be haunted by a cultured gentleman. Someone I would never in a million years associate with outside of my profession. He's nowhere on my level, residing on top while I'm scratching at the floor. He had a confidence in me I didn't even have in myself. All because he had to believe I could help find the answer.

I nodded excessively to push any sadness back down. "I know. I'm grateful too. In a supernatural way."

He smiled, pushing his dark hair from his face. "Thank you, my friend."

After a few seconds, I let a stifle of nervous energy out through my teeth. "So, you coming with me?"

"Of course. I would love to."

We headed toward the shore, with the sun slowly climbing above the horizon to meet us. There were a few suitable spots for painting. Having an understanding with Krish, I was far less worried about being caught talking to myself as we made our way down the street.

Krish absorbed my ramblings like a champ. Maybe he was genuinely interested, or maybe just trying to be a good listener. Either way, it felt good. I was talking so much; I didn't realize we were cresting the corner of Market and Ceres. My body went this way so often, autopilot was getting us there.

The light crested the silent roll of the waves as they lapped against the shoreline. If you looked to the left, the iron beamed bridge echoed with a gentle hum from any early bird drivers daring to cross the frigid waters. A few boats dotted the horizon, gearing up for some cold water catches.

We stepped around to the corner, taking a few quiet seconds to admire the morning. The cold sea air tried to penetrate my warm knit jacket, but to no avail.

"Has your art been featured at the gallery?" Krish asked as he settled his hands in his pockets.

"No. The owners say they'd look at my work and consider it. But none of my paintings are good enough."

"According to who?" I glanced as he raised an eyebrow at my pessimism.

"According to my negative outlook."

"Well," he said as we continued our stroll. "How do you know if you don't try? What is the worst that can happen? They say yes, you move forward. They say no, you are right where you were before."

"I hear you, and you're right." I walked backward to face him. "Doesn't mean I'll do it."

"Hey there."

Krish stopped to look to his left. My eyes followed and fell upon the cozy little cafe I had the pleasure of embarrassing myself in just a few days before. Sitting at one of the many round iron tables scattered about the front patio was Aladdin. His hands wrapped around a steaming hot ceramic cup, tall enough to hold more than the amount of caffeine the human body should consume in a day. He looked right at me with a half-smile across his five o'clock shadow. A dark North Face aided his attempt to sit in the wintry morning air. The same ankle boots adorned his feet, complimented by a pair of black speckled jeans. A black and white scarf sat cozily around his neck.

My arms dropped to my sides, standing like a deer in the headlights. I glanced at Krish, who did nothing but wait with a patient expression. Looking down the street, my gaze came back to the cafe. "Were you talking to me?"

Aladdin's half-smile became a full one. "Who else would I be talking to?"

I remembered he couldn't see Krish, and physically, I was the only being on the street. *Of course, he's talking to me.* The realization turned up the dial on my nerves, releasing the gremlins into a proper sweep of my insides. My grip on the square canvas tightened. "Oh."

Aladdin glanced down the road along the shoreline. "Are you in a rush?"

I shook my head, wishing like hell I could lie in situations like this. "No, just . . . out for a little walk."

"Would you like to sit down?" He gestured to the empty seat across from him, welcoming my warm body to take a load off.

My muscles tighten as I chewed on my lip ring. "For what reason?"

Shifting in his seat, he glimpsed to the right before returning to me with a raised eyebrow. "Are you always this cautious?"

"When a strange person asks me to sit with him. Yeah. I better be."

A light, breath-filled chuckle escaped with a flash of his teeth. "You didn't seem to have an issue walking up to me the other day."

I didn't think I could move if I wanted to, but Krish placed a supportive hand on my lower back. Before I knew it, I was sitting across from the Arabian knight, with Krish sitting at the table beside us.

I placed my canvas and paints on the table before curling my hands back into my lap.

"Do you want anything to drink?" he asked in a polite tone.

"No. Thanks. I'm okay." I squished my hands between my legs, casting uneasy glances between Krish and the table's surface.

"I'm Ameel, by the way." He held out a gloved hand, waiting for me to do the polite thing.

I could barely pull mine from my thigh trap, but took his and offered a gesture of introduction. "Raina."

"That's a pretty name." Our hands parted as quickly as

they came together. He wrapped his back around his cup. "It suits you."

"Why does it suit me?"

"Well, Raina. Rain. Your hair is blue. Is that on purpose?"

His observation both surprised and annoyed me. I never put my love for vibrant-colored hair and my name together. Not even my current mermaid shade of blue. I liked the color. And it matched, in a cheesy, childish kind of way.

Self-consciously, I moved my fingers through my hair, making sure it was still tucked behind my decorated ears. "I honestly never thought about it before."

Silence fell over the table. I rested my hands on its surface, pulling at my gloves as I tried to think of something else to say. Ameel tapped the side of his mug, tightening his mouth, unsure how to proceed. A soft draft of sea air mixed with his Old Spice aroma tickled my nose. I could tell he used the Bear-Glove fragrance, because it's the one I most awkwardly sniffed at CVS when I had to stock up on bathing products. I had a bottle in my shower, not gonna lie.

"So," he finally got out. "You're an artist?"

My head snapped back to attention. "Why would you think that?"

"The canvas and paints." He eyed my obvious art supplies sitting on the table.

"Oh." My arm shot out to grab them, slowly sliding them into my lap. "I dabble, I guess you could say. Nothing serious."

"Sounds familiar."

"What?"

Ameel ran his hand over his chin, covering his mouth before leaning back in his seat. "Sorry. It's nothing." His gaze fell to his right, accompanied by a sigh I could only guess was out of frustration or nerves.

Krish leaned his elbows on his knees and watched Ameel closely. I wish I could see what he was seeing right now. If

Krish was picking up on this guy's aura, I bet it was changing colors faster than a chameleon.

My hands pressed into the empty canvas, now secured to my lap. If I put any more pressure on it, I was certain I'd destroy any chance of catching a beautiful morning in paint across its surface.

"So." Ameel adjusted his chair, crossing his arms on the table. "I haven't seen you around here the past few days. Have you been avoiding it on purpose?"

My heart jumped into my throat. He would only say that if he was expecting me to come back here. Waiting for me to resurface so he could interact with me. Had he come every day to see if I'd be here?

"After I embarrassed myself, yes. I have been."

The words coming out of my mouth shocked me to my core. I was proceeding with an escalated bitchiness. Usually I was a pretty friendly individual, but this guy. I don't know. There was something about him I couldn't read right off the cusp. He was dodging, same as I was. We were both skating around something. Mine more obvious, of course.

"I wasn't trying to embarrass you," he confessed politely. Ameel took a sip from his cappuccino filled mug, pressing his lips together to savor the bitter taste. "Why did you come up to me, anyway?"

I couldn't come out with the truth, nor could I think of a good lie. Rolling my tongue over the bottom of my gums, I shifted in my seat. "You wouldn't believe me if I told you."

Ameel popped a grin, his posture straightening in his chair. "Try me."

My eyes narrowed, and my posture tightened along my back. "I'd rather not try."

"Alright. Your walls are up. I get it." He reached behind his neck as he leaned back.

I chanced a glance at Krish, who looked on eagerly like someone watching a film, expecting something to happen.

Settling back onto the table, my hair fell against my cheek. "Maybe I will take that drink after all."

"Sorry, that offer has left the building," he said rather smugly.

My brows skyrocketed upward. "Aren't you supposed to be a gentleman to a complete stranger?"

"Who said you were a stranger? I know your name. You know mine. We're on an acquaintance level now."

"Fine." I folded my arms against my chest and huffed into the cold air, looking toward the sea. "Have it your way."

"What? No fight in the bull? You look tougher than that."

My head snapped back to him. A white-toothed grin smeared all over his dangerously charming face. If he wasn't so nice to look at, I would have left right then, but this wasn't over yet. He was hiding something. Something Krish could only see in his current state of being. But me, I could find a way to pull it out of this guy. Then maybe Krish would be free.

"Tell you what." He leaned forward. "You tell me why you came up to me a few days ago, and I'll get you anything off the menu."

He was playing hardball and enjoying himself in the process. These are the kind of jerks I usually avoided, but this was for Krish. And maybe a chance for me to flex my muscles a bit.

"Alright." I glance at Krish before settling back on Ameel. "I was going to comment on how you looked like Aladdin."

Ameel's hand came up to catch his uncomfortable laughter. "What?" I watched as he continued to find a way to hold himself together.

I kept my Van Damme card in play, leaning forward slightly. "The chai latte, if you don't mind."

Ameel took a moment to settle down, watching the intensity on my face as his expression began to cool. "Alright." Ameel pushed his chair to stand. "Be right back."

Leaving the table, he disappeared inside the cafe. I turned to Krish with unbridled nerves dripping from my fingers. Krish sat up, eager to listen to what I couldn't contain.

"Please tell me you see something." My shoulders flexed up my back as I let some nervous energy out through my teeth. "I don't know how much longer I can withstand his jerkiness."

Krish shifted his gaze, looking everywhere and nowhere at the same time. His mind was working overtime, trying to figure something out by the crease in his brow and the tight fold of his lips.

"What's wrong?"

"I don't know . . . but," he focused on me, "remember when I told you about seeing your energy? Your aura?"

Resting my elbows on my lap with a subtle nod, I waited for him to elaborate.

Krish's tongue rolled across his bottom lip before pressing them down again in deep contemplation. "It's changing. The more you sit with this man, it's becoming something else. Calmer, tranquil. Shifting from a harsh blue. Mixing with his crimson."

This sounded like something out of sci-fi movie, horror, or a combination of both. Hearing him explain what his observations of us were felt like a complete violation of privacy. But he couldn't help it. He was on a different plane of existence. And by the looks of him, as troubled by it as I was.

"Calmer? Nothing about this conversation is calm." I rubbed my eyes, still as confused as ever. "What does it mean?"

Krish shook his head, raising his hands in surrender. "I do not know. But whatever it is, it is strong. Pulling me in like a moth to a fire. I can almost feel its warmth. It's welcoming and . . . quite exhilarating."

"Glad you seem to be enjoying yourself."

"I also remember something."

My reluctant state of being shifted immediately as his

statement sunk in. I straightened my posture, seeing that he wasn't done revealing the clue that was unearthed from this unlikely conversation.

"One. Yes." He eased into the seat. "A ferry. Riding across the Hudson River. The Statue of Liberty in the distance. I'm leaning against the railing, overlooking the water as the boat cuts through the waves. When something catches my eye. Standing at the bow . . . flowing in the forced wind like a feather gliding through the air . . . " He stopped, trailing off into the clouds of his ghostly figure.

I waited for him to continue, but he was lost. Consumed by this memory that he still can't seem to grasp on to. "Krish?"

The cafe door opened and Ameel walked out with my chai in hand. He placed it on the table, careful to avoid any chance of spilling a single drop. "Here you go, Ariel."

I swung my legs back under the table. "Ariel?" The tantalizing aroma of nutmeg and cinnamon was enough to stifle a rise in my annoyance levels.

Ameel sat back down in his chair. "Yeah. I'm Aladdin. So you're Ariel."

I wrapped my hands around my tea, taking in the comforting warmth through my fingers. "I look nothing like Ariel."

"Why? Because her hair is red and yours is blue?"

"Among other things." I brought the mug to my lips, savoring the delicious taste as it coated my mouth. If it wasn't for this beverage, my blood pressure would be through the roof with all this bickering.

"So, do all Middle Easterners look like Aladdin? Is that what you're suggesting?"

I almost choked on my tea, but managed to force it down with a hard swallow. Clearing my throat, I pressed my fist against my chest before making my recovery. "No."

He folded his arms against his chest. "Because that's what it sounds like."

I wasn't trying to be offensive. I meant it as a compliment. Aladdin was my childhood crush since I was 6 years old, but I couldn't tell him that. He definitely didn't act like Aladdin. More like the monkey, Abu. Kind of nice, but also a complete jerk when it came down to it.

"I meant it as a compliment," I spoke calmly, keeping my hands wrapped around my mug to ground myself.

"Well, don't assume someone will take it as that."

"Are you always this argumentative?"

"Are you always so inconsiderate?"

"Wow." I pushed my tea forward and stood up. "Well. Thank you for the tea." Throwing my bag over my shoulder, I gathered my art supplies. "You really know how to make a first impression."

Krish stood with me, his gaze swimming with fixed uncertainty. I wasn't mad. How could he know this guy would be a complete asshole? As much as I wanted to help him, there was no way I was going to sit here and spend my morning arguing with the likes of Ameel.

Before I made it around the table, Ameel stood up. "Wait."

I stopped, eyeing him as he looked toward his right again, rubbing the back of his head with a weary hand.

"I didn't mean to come off as a jerk." His eyes caught mine. "I'm sorry."

My lip curled in the corner of my mouth as I eagerly tapped my boots on the slick concrete. "Thank you. And I apologize if I offended you. That wasn't my intention."

"Can I make it up to you?"

His request forced my eyes to widen. What was the purpose of him wanting to hang out with me? He clearly didn't find my company enjoyable and vice versa. But as he waited for my response, there was a glint of hopefulness in his eyes.

"Why?" I asked. "We clearly don't get along."

He shrugged. "We don't have to."

A defiant *NO* was dripping from my tongue. If it weren't for Krish, I'd kick this jerk to the curb and be done with him. But there was a small part of me that felt more alive bickering with this guy. I was confident. Not afraid that I'd say something wrong. I didn't notice until now, but the moment we started getting into the meat of our conversation, the gremlins in my stomach vanished. Could this all be connected somehow? God only knew at this point.

With a deep sigh, I watched Krish as he waited for my response. He didn't make any gesture or indication that he wanted me to say yes, but I knew deep down, something was pulling him to create this situation. The answers weren't found yet. We barely scratched the surface.

"Sure," I finally said. "Why not."

Seven

"So," Ameel tapped a finger on the table, "you work at an art gallery? That's cool."

We sat inside the cafe, trying to make small talk. It was awkward, not gonna lie. Trying to pull any interest out of this conversation was minimal, at best. This second meeting, or whatever it was, was less tense than the first, at least for me. Ameel seemed cooler, but his leg was bouncing under the table again with an unsteady foot peeking out from the edge.

Krish watched us from the wall, leaning inside the corner like it would swallow him up. I had a hard time looking at him lately. His face was now gaunt, almost like he was decaying right before my eyes.

"What do you do?" I forced my question as I lightly tapped my purple nails against the mug of chai sitting in front of me.

Ameel smirked, adjusting himself in his suave leather jacket. "If I told you, I'd have to kill you."

"Ha," I almost grunted. "You're funny."

"Come on, lighten up." He leaned into the table. "You seem so tense."

"And you're not?" I peered at his neurotic foot. "Your leg hasn't stopped moving since we sat down."

"Nothing gets past you."

"What is *that* supposed to mean?"

I don't know what it was, but Ameel really knew how to push my buttons. Maybe I was being a little excessive in my defensiveness, but it was something I couldn't shut off. This is the most interaction I've had with a guy in nine months. Nine months of isolation, with nothing but my thoughts and my canvas. I had a lot of time to think in nine months, and nothing to show for it. I hadn't been able to change or better myself. Stuck in an endless loop of looking over my shoulder.

He shook his head with a pithy smile. "You don't have many friends, do you?"

My back straightened as I sat up in my seat, taken aback by his brashness. "Excuse me?"

Leaning in his chair, he shrugged against the vertical wooden seat back. "You're the most defiant person I've ever met."

My hand came away from the mug and balled into a fist beside it. "You don't know anything about me."

"I doubt anyone does. The rate you chew people up."

"What is your problem?"

He came up off the seat back. "My problem is having to sit through this conversation."

The pulse behind my eyes blurred my vision. I glanced at Krish, who only stared at us with an almost vacant expression. How much longer did I have to endure this test? Ameel clearly was a complete jerk, and yet, I was forced to sit through his antagonistic attitude and try to get something concrete from this. The thing that Krish so-called saw in him. One more minute and I was ready to walk.

"You invited me." My voice was stern. "I told you not to bother."

"But you came anyway. Why? To act like a little shit . . . "

His face dropped, shrinking back like a scolded child. "I'm sorry. I'm . . . not usually like this."

My fingers relaxed around my mug, ready to throw my guard back up at any moment. "Like what? A complete asshole?"

With a slight nod, Ameel's chin sank deeper into the shadow of himself. "I am an asshole."

The silence that passed between us gave me a chance to come down. I waited for him to recover from whatever emotional crisis he was facing within himself. To get that hair raised with a complete stranger . . . we were both protecting ourselves from the other. I wasn't someone who aired out my dirty laundry to just anyone. Especially a guy like him. The more we sat there, I came to realize how little people knew about what happened between me and Paul. My brother did, but he just got angry. He didn't listen. And Krish . . . but I barely let him peek at the entire Andy Warhol chaos my life had been. What it still was.

"Hey." Ameel slowly looked at me, his face sullen in uncomfortable uncertainty. "Can I tell you something?"

I swallowed hard, preparing myself for some deplorable nonsense. But his eyes were shifting with fear, like this wasn't a joke anymore. Laying my hands flat against the table, I gave myself another moment to deflate. "Sure."

He straightened his posture, looking dead out into the open cafe before bringing his hands together in front of him.

"I dated . . . this girl for a while." He came back for a glance at my patient gray-blue eyes. "Years, actually. We were a couple, not just dating." His shoulders tensed for a second and then came back down again. "She told me she wanted to take the next step in our relationship. Marriage. Kids. Full commitment for the rest of our lives."

Looking down at his hands seemed to save him from his confession for a moment. But the hesitation didn't last much longer. "She was ready for it. But . . . I wasn't. I don't know

48

what it was, but I was . . . scared to tell her the truth. That I wasted her time all those years we were together. How scared I was to take that step, even with her. I don't know. So I fucked it up."

"How?" His gaze rose at my single word. The gremlins were at work again, but it felt different this time. I didn't feel anxious, nervous maybe. Whatever he was about to tell me would bring some sense to all this, somehow. I'd forgotten that people were people, no matter where they came from. Bad things happened to everyone. All of them. I wasn't the only one. I wasn't alone.

Ameel pressed his lips together in hesitation. "I pushed her away. Treated her like shit. I . . . I cheated on her." A nerve-rattled breath shook his gaze to his still-folded hands. "I cheated on her so many times."

His hand came across his forehead, disrupting the smooth-ness of his skin with lines and crevasses of his own making. They folded his brows together, coming back down to land helplessly on the table's surface.

"When she found out, I didn't even bat an eye. Didn't deny it. She left with my ridicule in her ear and tears polluting her face. And I didn't even try to stop her."

Both hands moved against his temples, pressing the clean cuts of his gentleman's haircut. The curls sitting atop his head fell down into his face, blurring my view of his unsteady eyes.

Rolling my lip ring between my teeth, I watched his atten-tion return to the openness of the cafe, lost in the emotion digging up this memory had brought with it. "Did you love her?"

"Does it matter?" His head rolled back to me, more tense than before. "No one deserves to be treated like that. Like they don't matter. Who does that to someone?" He shook his head before settling down between his drooping shoulders. "She spent three years of her life with me, and I tore it down like it was nothing. It wasn't nothing. I . . . I guess it doesn't matter what it was now."

The strings of my heart wrapped around itself, stifling the blood from entering and exiting the chambers that kept my body alive. I bit my tongue to keep my eyes from breaking. A roaring sea of memories crashed inside my skull. He was like Paul. But unlike Paul, he showed remorse. Regret. The hurt was clear in every word spoken and every movement he made. How sorry he was; I didn't think it was possible to be that way.

"Why . . . " I swallowed. "Why are you telling me this?"

"I don't know." He wiped his finger across his nose, sniffling loudly before looking at me again. "You seemed like someone who would understand. Somehow."

My heart was strangled at this point. I did understand. All too well. Only I was on the opposite end of it. I was the victim. Did Paul regret what he did? No. He wouldn't. He enjoyed every second he held me under his thumb. And I let him. Because I was too scared. Even when I smashed a glass against his face and left him reeling, I was petrified. It didn't change how afraid I was. It only made it worse.

A thought popped into my head as we remained across from the other. How did Ameel know I'd understand? Did he know Paul? Did he put him up to this? No. There's no way. Krish brought him into my life, not a psychotic ex-boyfriend.

The entire cafe seemed to close in around me, slowly cracking my bones into tiny fragments left to litter my insides and damage the inner workings of my physical form. I was glad Ameel somberly stared into his cup, watching the steady movement of the liquid as I squeezed my hands in between my thighs to keep myself from shaking. Trying to recover any resemblance of control was impossible. I was there again, standing in the kitchen, allowing my oppressor to suck the life from me with every word.

How could Ameel know? That I was a mirror of the

victim to his retaliation against commitment? It could all be bullshit. Maybe he was an actor playing a part. I couldn't know for sure. It felt genuine, but I couldn't be sure. This is what happened when I dropped my guard for even a second. Whoever it may be, they would find a way to worm in.

There was more being uncovered than I bargained for. This wasn't just about finding out what kept Krish tethered to this life. Not anymore.

Eight

Walking to work the next day, I found myself kicking rocks and stones into the shallow shoreline. It was almost midday, and the sun was shrouded in a haze of whisking clouds, moving faster than the wind could blow. I had my pink and black knit hat pulled over my ears and my leopard print scarf wrapped clumsily at my neck. Fur rimmed boots overlapped my patterned leg warmers, keeping my feet dry if I happened to step into the water.

Krish kept pace with me, his hands in his pockets, hanging like an article of clothing on a clothes hanger. We didn't talk much after Ameel's confession. I had nothing much to say about it, only that I still didn't know what to make of it. Was he being honest? It was easy to believe in the moment, but now that time had passed, doubt spread over it like a pool of blood across a white linoleum floor. Even if it were the truth, no amount of scrubbing could hide what doubt had already embedded in my mind.

"The conversation with Ameel," Krish's voice was riddled with cracks and a hoarseness that matched his diminishing form. "It must not have been easy for him to tell you what he did."

Tucking my chin into my scarf, I pulled at the fingers of my winter patterned gloves. "It's bullshit."

"Why do you say that?"

"Why would he tell me?" I stopped at the bottom of the stone stairwell leading up to the street and faced him. "A complete stranger? There's only one reason for it."

Krish yanked on his hole-ridden blazer. "And what would that reason be?"

Saying what I wanted to say would sound childish. Rolling my tongue over the metal of my lip ring, I shrugged as my arms folded against my chest. "All men lie. It's how they get what they want."

"Do you truly believe that?" Even though I've told Krish bits and pieces of my life before escaping Paul, there was still so much to divulge that I just couldn't dig up. It was buried, and that's where it needed to remain.

"You did not see what I saw," Krish continued. "His aura was in turmoil. Hues shifting and changing with despair and a longing to be heard. This was something he had not confessed to anyone. It was painful for him."

The gremlins stacked bricks and stone along the top of my walls with every word he said. I knew he was probably right, but there was no real way for me to know. Krish could be making it up so I wouldn't abandon this frail attempt at answers. He could be using me, too.

"How do I know that? Because you told me?" I started walking up the stairs, stopping after the first three or four before turning around again. "Look. I don't even know if you're really a ghost. You could be a figment of my imagination. My subconscious trying to force me to break down the walls I built around myself. For good reasons."

"And?" Krish's hand fluttered to the railing and grasped it. "What if I am? What is it you are so afraid to face, Raina?"

I leaned against the railing in my attempt to justify my defenses. "He's just like my ex. Treating his girlfriend like she didn't matter. I didn't matter. I didn't even have a voice! He ran my life and showed me off like some prize he'd won, dressing me up how *he* wanted me to be."

With a quick turn, I made my way up the stairs to the street. My stomach was in knots and nausea soon riddled the back of my throat. Just saying that much made my skin crawl. I hated remembering. I hated having to remember.

"Your feelings are genuine," Krish's voice came from behind me. "That man had no right to take your humanity from you."

As we arrived on the street by the cafe, Krish reached for my arm, turning me around to face him. "But does that condemn every other person from getting close to you for the rest of your life?"

"*Yes.* It does." It hurt to admit that out loud. Ignoring the truth in that statement was easier than facing the fear that created it. I wish I wasn't this way, but it was impossible to wrangle myself free from it. I was still in the trap, writhing and twisting myself to get free. But the more I struggled, the deeper the teeth sank into my bones.

Krish's hand relaxed on my arm, the steady pulse of his presence sent waves of calm through my rattled body. "I understand you are fearful."

"Krish," I whispered as I shook my head. "You don't know anything about being afraid."

His eyes sunk farther into his sockets after hearing my words. Unkempt hair broke free and fell where it pleased. "Perhaps you are right." His hand dropped from my arm. "I am only saying what I feel to be my truth. That is all I have now."

A dense swallow dropped the nausea back down into the pit of my stomach. I didn't mean to sound offensive or accuse him of not having feelings. But no one could understand unless they've walked in my shoes. It was impossible to know how much fear could rule your life unless you lived it.

"Hey." I looked up and found Ameel trotting over to me. He was wearing his usual dark knit jacket and jeans. The curls bounced on top of his head as he came to a halt a few feet from where I stood. "I thought I'd find you here."

Seeing him elevated my blood pressure to almost bursting levels. I squinted, trying to control the urge to scream as loud as I could.

"Look. I can't talk long. I got a work thing. But I just wanted to say I'm sorry for unloading on you the other day."

"It was bullshit." My voice was harsh and accusing, cutting through the air like a knife.

Ameel drew his head back in surprise. "What?"

"What you said. About your girlfriend?" My arms went rigid at my sides. "It was all bullshit."

"It wasn't bullshit." His arms came up with his shoulders. "Why would I make something like that up?"

"I can think of a few reasons."

"Name one."

I could feel my heart beating faster and faster with every passing second. "To butter me up. Make me feel sorry for you. So you can get in my head or pants, most likely."

"Wow," he scoffed, shaking his head. "No offense, but you are the last person I would try that with."

"More incentive. You think I'm easy."

"What the hell is your deal? Is this how you treat everyone you come in contact with? Or is it just me? *Or,*" he leaned in on his heels towards me, "is it a guy thing?"

I twisted my mouth into a knot and tightened my jaw. I could feel a rush of emotion washing over me, drowning my surging anger in the waves of my unbridled despair. With a weary sigh, I hugged my arms to my chest in an attempt to keep myself from falling apart. "I have my reasons."

"Reasons that justify you treating people like shit, huh?"

Ameel's hand came up the side of his head and rested on his curly top. "I guess we're the same in that."

He paced back and forth, from the edge of the street toward the sidewalk. I watched him, still keeping my arms wrapped around me. I could feel Krish standing behind me, and I was glad for it. If I fell, he would catch me.

"Fuck it." Ameel threw his hands up. "I don't know why I bothered. What am I even doing . . . " With a deep breath, he turned away from me with his hands on his hips, staring down the street as a few cars and people continued on with their day. "Whatever." Backing up, he looked at me. "I'm done. See you never, Ariel. Have a nice life."

Nine

We made our way to the gallery in silence. Krish stayed close to me. I could feel his tattered clothing brush against my jacketed arm every now and again. It wasn't a physical touch that I felt, but a chill. So cold and hopeless, it numbed me down to my bones. Gritting my teeth was the only way I could keep it at bay. But as we walked further, I was beginning to be numb to it, like it was becoming part of me.

Walking into the gallery, I was greeted by my boss with a well-groomed smile. My boss was a rather tall fellow, with slicked back hair and a genuine approachability I couldn't explain with rationality. He always dressed well, and his wife, who was co-owner of the gallery, kept up appearances.

I took my place behind the front desk, seeing the stack of papers I would need to go through that day. The gallery was preparing for a spring exhibition, featuring newer artists from all over New England. My job was to make sure all the artwork was shipped and received appropriately, as well as keeping social channels up-to-date with artist information, special invites, and weekly sneak peeks. When the boss was here, he took care of the visitors for the most part, leaving me uninter-rupted in my work. It was a lot to do, but I loved keeping busy.

Krish wearily slumped down on the floor behind my desk, bringing his knees up to rest his head. Straggly dark hair hung down onto his dirtied slacks as a heavy sigh rose and fell from his graying frame.

"Krish," I whispered as I glanced down at him. "I'm sorry."

"You are doing all you can." His gaze found mine. "What more is there?"

My mind wandered to a ton of possibilities, all of which I did not wish to partake in. If I never saw Ameel again, then this was all for nothing. There were no other signs Krish had given me that there was another option.

"I'll find Ameel again." I sighed. "I hate seeing you like this. You're falling apart."

There was no response as Krish sank back against the wall with his eyes clamped shut. I don't think he would admit he was in any sort of pain. Do ghosts feel pain? Maybe emptiness.

"Raina."

My boss's voice interrupted my train of thought as my eyes shot open. He wasn't alone. Ameel's hand slid across the counter of my desk, coming to a stop a foot or so from my computer. My eyes widened with shock as I tried desperately to keep my heart from jumping out of my throat.

"Raina, this is Ameel Javed. He's the videographer who'll be shooting our next exhibition." I heard my boss talking, but I couldn't stop myself from staring at Ameel's polite expres-sion. My boss's brow rose, the corner of his mouth curling into the pockets of his cheekbones. "Raina?"

I blinked a few times before finding my boss's curious stare. The blurred form of Krish popped up in my peripheral view. "Yes. Okay. But . . . don't you usually shoot the exhibi-tions? I didn't know you were bringing someone else in."

"I think it's time for a change, don't you? Give us more to work with now that we have to worry about social media marketing. Besides, we're getting some bigger names this year." He placed a warm hand on Ameel's shoulder. "Raina will take all your information. You'll be working with her directly up until the event."

"Sounds good." Ameel's lips parted to reveal his charmingly alluring smile. "I look forward to working with you."

A cough caught in my throat as I failed to keep my posture steady. "Likewise."

"Well, I'll leave you to it. Why don't you give him a tour of the gallery? It's not as big as others you'll find, but it's got character." With a final glance, my boss left Ameel standing in front of me, his arms rested on the desk as he leaned in toward my computer.

"What are you doing here?" was my gut response once I was clear from prying ears.

He shrugged. "Working. I'm the videographer, or did you miss that part of the conversation?"

"Did you know you were coming here?"

"Yeah, but I didn't know *you* would be here."

My toes began to curl in my boots as I shifted my eyes, not knowing where to focus. Krish looked as surprised as I did, which brought life back into his withering face.

Clearing my throat, I pulled up the contacts for the exhibition and added a new entry. "Well, I need your information."

"It's all on my card."

With a single motion, his hand slid across the counter, landing next to my keyboard. Instinctually, I reached out to take it, landing on the surface of his fingers. My attention flashed to him and we lingered there for a second, neither one moving nor willing to pull away. For some reason, I couldn't think or act. The blood rushing through my veins intensified faster than if I were running a marathon. It kept time in my ears and against my chest, counting down the seconds that we allowed this to continue.

Finally, as if somehow communicating without words, we each drew away from the other. Slowly, so that not an inch of touched skin would go unnoticed. Even though it was only the top of his fingers, they were soft like velvet. His rings breaking the connection between us for only a millisecond, but a millisecond I unconsciously wished I could have back.

I grasped on to his card like I needed it to live, my heart slowly coming back down to normalcy. Ameel's arms came off the counter. He scratched the back of his neck; his once concentrated eyes now scanning the floor for answers. I didn't need him to say a word. Not a single sound to know that he was trapped by whatever it was that had come over us just as strongly as I was.

"Thank you . . . Aladdin," I whispered as I placed the card against my screen, barely able to make out the words.

"Sure."

I typed his information in silence, unable to blink or look at him again. Out of the corner of my eye, he was shifting around. Keeping his feet moving, probably to distract himself. The air was stripped of the usual tension I felt around him. Now it was anxious, scary maybe. Like something we both never wanted to happen, had or was about to.

After inputting all his information, I led him around the gallery, explaining how things would go for the exhibition. My voice was on auto-pilot to his one-word responses. The wittiness and smugness were completely absent from his tone. I, too, could not think of a single thing to fall back on. It didn't help that the closer I was to him, the more my lungs fell short of breath. When the tour was over, I walked him to the door.

"I'll send you more information for the exhibit once I get it all together," I said as straightforward as I could force myself to. "The planning meeting is in two weeks."

"Right, I'll be there." His hands sat in his pockets, head hanging slightly, forcing his eyes to dart upward to look at me.

I wanted to touch him again, but the urge was so unnatural it froze me to the floor. "Listen, Aladdin . . . " I glanced back into the gallery, seeing Krish sitting on one of the benches. His sullen gaze fixed on us. "About before."

"It's okay." Ameel straightened his posture and took a nervous breath. "Don't worry about it."

"No, it's just . . . " My hands started to clam up as I gripped my clipboard. "I didn't mean to call you a liar. I do believe you. I just . . . "

"You don't have to say anything." A weak smile graced his face, rippling the hairs of my arms.

"Okay."

We stood there; me watching him and him watching me. The soft brown of his eyes searching my features like he was admiring a fine piece of art. Nerves shot through me, rapidly expediting the rush of euphoria to my heart. Then he took a slow step forward, narrowing the gap between us. I clutched my clipboard like I wanted it to become part of me, breathing in the Old Spice scent I secretly desired. But then Ameel seemed to catch himself, leaning back toward the door.

"Bye, Ariel."

Faster than my mind could comprehend, he was out the door. As it slowly closed, meeting with the doorframe, I caught a breath in my lungs and held it there.

Walking as fast as I could, I raced towards the bathroom, shutting the door before falling behind it. Krish was already sitting on the bleached tile in front of me, as my head fell in between my hands. Our connection replayed in my head over and over again. I didn't understand it, how this smart-ass had completely derailed me like a love-struck idiot. My heart had yet to recover from emotions I didn't even know I still had. How I wanted to be close to him, touch him, even knowing that he was a lying, rotten cheater.

"Raina." Krish's voice was a breath of the wind. "Raina."

My eyes fell to his. As weary as they were, there was a flash of newness in them. "It was stronger. The memory." His hand came up with weak intent, grasping at the hazy air surrounding him. "When your hands met, I could almost reach out and touch it. What I've lost. It's there. Just beyond."

There was madness in his tone as his hands came on mine. The graying aurora surrounding him began to darken against his closed eyes. His lips trembled, and I was afraid he would fall apart into a thousand tiny pieces. "The water . . . like mirrors catching the sunlight. Cast upon a pale blue. Something at the bow. Beckoning me with precious light. From eyes I cannot see . . . "

His hands began to burn mine. So intensely, my flight response bowed away from him, backing into the corner of the bathroom. No amount of air could quell the need to escape from my racing mind. I watched as his color continued to swell, reaching up toward the intense lights nestled in the ceiling, coating them completely in an ominous haze. He didn't seem to notice I wasn't there, hands still hovering to where he had met mine.

For a moment, I was frozen by the ever-growing darkness that slowly consumed every inch of the bathroom. Darting my gaze from one stretch to the other, I finally came back to the crouched form of Krish, still stagnant in his position and darkening posture. His eyes were a hollow void with nothing left to hold on to.

Biting my lip ring, I lunged forward on sheer willpower. His burning palms met my cold, distressed fingers as I shook them uncontrollably. "Snap out of it. *Krish*!"

Nothing changed. Panic moved my hold to his face, which seemed to come away beneath my fingers. Tossing my hair to the side, I tried to stay focused and not let fear get the better of me. "Krish. It's Raina. Please come back to me. I need you to come back."

The holes where his eyes once were expanded. In less than a second, the form returned to them, shooting open with confused clarity. The fog subsided like he had sucked it back into his ghostly form. His eyes were colorless until the final mist had returned to him, filling the whites with the dark brown he once possessed.

"What happened?" he asked, grasping my hands with such force I thought he'd break my fingers. "What did I do?"

"It's okay. It's gonna be okay."

"Did I hurt you? I . . . I don't remember."

"*Krish.*" The sharp tone I rarely adopted struck focus onto his face. He watched me. The lines of his face deepened and his complexion deteriorated before my very eyes. How I was keeping myself from screaming bloody murder, I had no idea. As terrified as I was, he looked equally, if not more. This was scarier for him than me. *And he didn't know fear. What's wrong with me?* I had to be the one to keep it together. Because he was falling apart.

"It's okay. We . . . " Swallowing the subsiding panic, I tried to keep myself in control. "We'll figure it out. We're almost there."

"We are?"

My legs trembled under my body. I had no clue if what I was saying was true. But I had to lie. To keep him from becoming whatever darkness was trying to take him. I didn't know if I could save him. I didn't even know what *this* was. All I knew is that when I touched Ameel, something happened that stirred the pot of whatever ghost story I was forced to be a part of. It was the only thing I had to go on. Maybe this was the answer. The question was, could I force myself to endure memories I wished I could forget, if only to save Krish's soul from becoming something monstrous.

It wasn't until now that I realized how much I didn't want Krish to leave my side. I took advantage of his presence and what it had given me. I was finally heard, finally recognized.

Everything I've been through, he never pushed it aside or made an excuse for why it happened or how I felt. I couldn't let whatever it was that was trying to destroy him take him away. No matter what. I had to break the pattern before it was too late.

"Yes." I forced a weak smile, which he matched the moment it graced my lips. "We are."

Ten

"Listen." Krish placed his hands on my shoulders, gliding me to a halt as we walked toward the cafe. "I will not ask you to do something you do not want to do."

Gritting my teeth, I bit my lower lip, letting the metal ring slide across my teeth. "It's too late. I already texted him. It's happening."

I spent those last few days wracking my brain over what the next steps were. My mind and my heart were not in sync at all. Logically, I wanted to run as fast as humanly possible from this situation. I have never been so scared and confused in my entire life. Everything was happening faster than I could comprehend. But time was not on my side. If I didn't act now, Krish would die again. Or become a demon. It didn't matter *what* he would become, only that I had to stop it from happening.

And Ameel. As much as I wanted to hate him, I could not ignore the effect touching him had on me. It changed my analogy of his character. Made me want to know more about him. Get close to him, both physically and emotionally. And

65

the fact that he was also acting strange because of it. . . . There wasn't a clearer message that something was happening.

Crossing the sunlit street, we were almost to the shoreline where Beans n' Cream would be waiting for us. Despite the extra layer of sushi printed socks on my feet, I could barely feel my toes. My hands pulled at the loose lumps of wool on my knitted tunic. The tassels of my leopard scarf wafted behind me, animating the quickness of my pace. It was all or nothing. Krish's chance rode on my cooperation, and that twisted my stomach into more knots than I could count.

I stopped just as we were about to enter the cafe. "Krish." I looked at him. "I'm sorry I've been so selfish."

He placed a weary hand on my shoulder. "There is nothing you need to be sorry for, but thank you." His bony fingers squeezed gently. "You are strong, Raina. It is your greatest gift."

My lips rolled back into my mouth, sucking down the sudden emotion from creeping up on me. This was the time where I needed my strength the most.

As we walked through the cafe door, my eyes fell directly on the back of Ameel's head. He turned around the second my entire body was safely on the other side of the doors. My heart skipped a beat as his shining, dark eyes fell on me.

"Raina," Krish's voice tumbled to my ear.

"I'm fine," I whispered after a deep breath propelled me forward. Dark fit jeans matched Ameel's favorite footwear. A white Ziggy Stardust tee sat underneath the unbuttoned folds of his blue flannel. He neatly combed his curls back, but a few strands hung from the sides almost intentionally.

"Hey." He followed me to the chair across from him, which I took with subtle caution. "I ordered your signature chai already."

"Thanks." I slipped my sloth bag over the chair.

Krish hovered behind me, waiting like a cloud of cigarette smoke. I could sense the fear gently wafting from the gray flickers of his haunting. My fingers tapped against the wooden table. I wasn't even sure what I was going to do. Only that I needed to see Ameel and figure out what the hell this was.

Ameel looked at me with an uncertain gaze. A heaviness encapsulated my chest the longer we sat in silence amongst the clinking of ceramic mugs and the light chattering of other patrons.

With a quick sigh, he folded his hands in front of him. "I was surprised to get your text."

I curled my fingers between my legs, almost too terrified to look at him. "Yeah, well. I . . . have to tell you something."

"Is it about the gallery?"

"No." I forced my gaze, even though the gremlins were threatening to empty anything that remained of my breakfast out through my mouth.

"What is it?"

All the nerve endings throughout my body were shooting off rockets across my skin. I opened my mouth, but no words came out. The sounds of the cafe seemed to escalate, making it harder for me to concentrate on anything resembling a conversation. My heart was beating so fast I couldn't count how many times it knocked against my chest.

"There's . . . something following me." My words lingered between us, cementing our uncertainty.

"A ghost."

My eyes widened. "Yes, but it's more than that."

"Here you two go." The barista placed our orders on the table before us. There wasn't enough logical sense left in me to even muster a cordial response. Ameel and I stayed locked in each other's gaze as the barista stepped away from our table. "Enjoy."

Ameel looked down at his wafting cup of joe. "Listen, Ariel . . . " he said with a breathless sigh as his eyes met mine again.

"No. Wait." I didn't know what to make of what was said,

only that there was something I needed to do first before I could fully understand everything that was happening.

"I was with someone." I could feel my hands begin to shake, so I wrapped them around the warm, wafting mug of vanilla chai, watching the cream and cinnamon swirl into unpredictable patterns.

"He was . . . " I swallowed hard, trying to muster up the strength Krish saw in me to help push through this. "He told me how to act. What to wear. I looked how he wanted me to look and did what he wanted me to do. I lost myself in his illusion of what he saw me to be. Lost without a voice of my own."

My eyes wandered up to face Ameel. He watched me intently, hands still folded in front of him, a sharp line replacing his mouth. "I was afraid of what he would do if I defied him. If he'd hurt me or worse. When I finally got away, I thought I wouldn't be afraid anymore. That I'd finally be free. But I'm still afraid. Even more than when I was with him."

Ameel held his last breath tight within his chest. "What's his name?"

My face furrowed in confusion. "What?"

"What's his name? I swear to God, I'll beat the shit out of him."

I shook my head. "No. I . . . I don't want that."

He leaned forward. "Who is he, Ariel?"

"*Stop.*" My hands fell flat on the table. "I didn't tell you, so you could do something stupid. I told you because . . . " I bit my tongue. He listened, but only to what Paul had done to me. Not about what the aftershock had been.

Standing up, I pushed the chair out from under me and grabbed my bag, throwing it onto my shoulder. "I need to go."

"No. Wait." Ameel reached for me as I hurried for the door.

Bursting through the door like a bull, my pulse echoed in my ears, sending a numbing shiver down my spine. Fear grabbed me by the hair and was pulling me as far away from that corner cafe as possible.

It's too much. I can't do it. I can't.

My feet hit the concrete laid staircase leading down to the snow-kissed shore. I never wanted to be invisible, even when I was. But now, I'd give anything to switch places with Krish. To let the darkness take me away and everything I was running from.

Eleven

The water barely rippled, like glass reflecting hints of light that dared to hit. Krish fluttered around me like a tornado, disrupting the stillness of my empty stare at the rocky sand beneath my feet.

"Raina. Raina, please stop."

Shaking my head, I gripped onto the strap of my bag, pulling it tight against my shoulder. "I can't. I'm so sorry, Krish."

"Yes, you can."

"No." I turned around to face his pulsing form. "I'm afraid . . . I'm so . . . fucking scared."

Krish's boney fingers grasped my shoulders. "If you let that keep you in one place, you will miss countless chances that could be something more. Something greater. You deserve to live a life without fear."

Dropping my head, I could feel dry emotion forcing condensation to build up behind my eyes. "It's not that simple."

"You cannot fly if you do not jump."

I looked up into Krish's gaunt cheeks and exhaust laden eyes. "If I don't jump, I won't fall! I won't get hurt anymore."

Krish's hands ran down my arm. "We must fall to understand what it means to live. To be present." His shadowy grip sent a strange, icy sensation into my wrists. "I am sorry for what you had to go through. But you are not alone anymore. You need to let the past go. Jump."

"Never" meant nothing would go wrong. That was what I chose to live by since escaping that life of confinement and fear. If I never let anyone in, I'd be okay. If I never tried, I wouldn't fail. If I never forgave, I would have something to hold on to. But that something was remorse and contempt, all bad things that ate you alive from the inside out. That sounded ignorant and foolish to me now. All because a dead person flipped my life upside down. Because he pushed me to save him by saving myself.

"Raina."

A faint voice barely broke Krish's concentration, but I followed his gaze behind me as he dropped my hands to turn. Ameel stood before me, nerves rattling his fingers as they played in his palms.

"I . . . I didn't mean to say that. If it upset you—"

"What was her name?" My voice shook with uncertainty. I could feel the seams coming apart at my sides. Everything I had kept buried inside me for so long, threatening to pour out.

"What?"

"Her name." I took in a rattled breath. "Your girlfriend."

Ameel pressed his hands together, bracing himself. We waited there, staring at each other as light snowflakes began to trickle down from the sky.

"Raina . . . " Krish's voice trailed off as a fog began to drift across the snow-flurried sand. I didn't need to see what was happening; I felt it like a storm. Krish fell to his knees beside me, the darkness leaking out of him like a waterfall. "I . . . "

The hair on my arms tickled my skin as my nerves re-lived the terror they felt on the floor of the bathroom. I kept my gaze on Ameel, still waiting for something to happen. Not knowing something *was* happening. Beyond anyone's control.

"Melanie." The name fell from his lips like a stone. He let out a nervous huff. "God. I haven't said her name out loud since—"

"Since it happened?"

His body settled. "Yeah."

The darkness leaking from Krish stained the sand beneath my feet. I couldn't look at it. I had to stay focused on Ameel. Or I'd run away all over again.

"Mine was Paul." His name was the trigger I had feared to pull, sending tears streaming from the overflowing sea behind my eyes. "Paul . . . " I hung my head, watching the blackness creep up my boots. But there was no fear. Not after muttering that name.

"I hate you." I gritted my teeth as my hair fell into my face, watching tears crash into the pool of shadows lapping at my feet. "I hate what you took from me. I wish I'd never met you. I wish I'd never fallen in love with you. You broke my spirit. My life it's . . . so broken."

Something collided with me, creating a safety net around my entire person. BearGlove flooded my nostrils, igniting my senses in a warmth I had long since forgotten. Ameel tightened his arms around me, leaning his face against my head, his lips resting inches from my ear.

"I'm sorry. You didn't deserve to be treated like that. Like you meant nothing. You meant everything to me. I just . . . " I could feel his chin quivering against my temples.

"I was so scared. And that's not an excuse. There is no excuse for what I did. You deserved better. So much better. I wish I could take it all back. I hurt you so badly. I just . . . I'm sorry. Melanie, I'm so sorry."

Closing my eyes, I buried my head against his chest, clutching onto him like if I let go, I'd fall into oblivion. My chest tightened as my body relaxed in his arms, using the safety between them as the only catalyst for my strength.

"I forgive you, Paul. I forgive you."

A light burst beneath us, scattering across the sand like a skipping stone. I broke away from Ameel, both of us stepping in opposite directions as the light expanded. It eradicated the darkness consuming Krish's melting form. My hands clutched against my chest as Krish rose from the sand. His once-darkening silhouette refreshed in a now white glow, enhancing his vibrancy and reigniting the youthfulness he once possessed. I squinted as a final burst exploded from him, feeling the shock wave of light pass through me.

When the haze finally dissipated, Krish stood before me, admiring his renewed self with a smile tickling his lips. He looked at me, his handsome face no longer shrouded in gray. He was alive again.

"Krish."

Both of us looked in Ameel's direction, who stood beside a form drenched in blue light. I took a step back as it began to come away, outlining the flow of ebony tendrils against a beautifully crafted profile. A long coral dress pulsed to life, cascading down to a pair of daintily slippered feet. I stared at this now fully embodied woman, who could not keep her brilliantly lit eyes from Krish's astonished gaze.

"Fiona," Krish muttered.

My hands covered my quivering chin as small pockets of tears continued to fall from my eyes. Fiona gave a warm smile as she sailed forward, meeting Krish in-between Ameel and me. Krish took her hands gingerly, as if unsure she was really there.

"Krish." Fiona's fingers reached for his face, gracing his cheek. "I . . . I remember you."

The two embraced, each holding on so tightly in fear that they may lose each other all over again. My gaze darted to Ameel, who stood stoically in awe at their reunion. When he

73

noticed me, he smiled, expediting the pattering of my fluttering heart.

"Your hair in the wind as we crossed the Hudson. How could I forget you? You stopped my heart with a single glance," Krish muttered as he leaned his forehead against hers. "But I've found you."

Krish turned to me with grateful satisfaction as they broke from one another. I didn't hesitate in my stride to meet him, his arms safely cradling me against his now warm, comforting glow. Burying my face in his chest, my tears seemed to pass right through him as he steadied my shuttering frame.

"Thank you, Raina." I looked up at his beaming smile, smelling the sweet perfume of his joy. "You saved me."

Wiping a stray tear from my face, I let the warm spark of his touch refresh my skin. "I don't want you to leave."

Krish brushed my tears away with his thumb as his continued smile came next to my ear. "I will always be with you." A gentle kiss touched down on my cheek. Coming back to meet my gaze, his arms loosened around me. "You are finally free."

I felt my face bend to his, creating a joyfulness inside me I never knew I had. "We're both free." His arms fall, clutching my hands one final time. "I'll never forget you."

"It's time. To live your life now." His fingers slipped from mine as he moved away.

I glanced at Ameel. Fiona was in his ear, whispering something before placing a kiss on his forehead. The action closed his eyes with a quiet serenity, as she came to meet Krish with her hand, ready to accept him.

I stepped back, watching them turn toward the sea. At the shoreline, the dull light masked by the clouds soon parted, giving way to a brilliant pathway to the sky. Krish and Fiona faded into the gently lapping water, hand in hand, sparkling against the sun's rays until there was nothing left but the endless horizon. Silence took hold for a few trailing moments.

I waited, secretly longing for them to come back. But I knew they wouldn't. They'd found the light.

With a shaky hand, I wiped the wetness from my face, sucking in a harsh breath as I turned toward Ameel. He looked at me, both of us unsure what to even do or say. My heart felt still, anticipating the start of something bigger than I had ever experienced.

"When you said ghost at the cafe." I choked up momentarily, letting a few more tears escape. "You meant it."

Ameel nodded, remaining quiet in the aftermath of the moment.

"I don't think they were ghosts." A soft smile graced my cheeks.

"No." His gaze strayed toward the sea. "They were angels." A glisten of sadness fell down his cheek before he lowered his head with a sigh. "You know, you're the bravest person I've ever met." His eyes came up to meet mine, now shuttering like a turbulent sea, at words I never thought I'd hear anyone say.

"So . . . I guess . . . I guess, I'll see ya."

He started to walk away, the back of his head slowly becoming the worst sight I could ever see. For a second, I couldn't move or speak, but I pushed for it. Because I wouldn't let anything hold me back. Deep in my mind, I knew it wasn't love. But I needed Ameel. In what way, I wasn't sure. This experience brought us together, two people who would never have done so on our own. I wanted to find out why, and I hoped to Krish he wanted to find out, too.

"Ameel." The call of his name from my lips stopped him, and he turned around to face me. "Do you like . . . breakfast?"

A grin flashed across his face. "Yeah."

I pressed my hand into my palm. "Would you like to . . . go get breakfast with me tomorrow?"

His smile grew, flashing his pearly whites in my direction. "Yeah. I'd like that." He gestured with his head down the street. "You heading to work?"

I nodded softly. "Yeah. In a bit."

"I'll walk you. If you don't mind—"

"No. I mean, yes." I scurried over, taking a stand beside him. "I don't mind." Impulse allowed me to take his hand in mine, matched with little resistance. "Thank you."

"For what?"

"For . . . everything."

My smile matched his own as I moved to release his hand. But Ameel's grasp caught mine, keeping me tethered to him. "You don't have to let go. If you don't want to." I laced my fingers between his, stepping in closer, unable to pull myself from his dark eyes as the snow continued to fall around us. "Shall we move on?"

"Yeah." I leaned into my first step with him beside me. "I'm ready."

Wither

BY ASHLYN DREWEK

One
Zane

They say discretion is the better part of valor. Hiding in the children's section of the library, however, I wasn't so sure.

Clutching a stack of board books to my chest like they would shield me from the woman hunting me, I peeked out again through the shelving to see where she was. It was absolutely ridiculous. I knew that. I might not have looked like it, but I was a grown man and I was literally hiding amongst children from a woman half my size. But size wasn't a detriment to Oksana. Nothing was.

Stalking through the aisles like a feral cat, her sharp eyes swept to and fro, taking note of every face and discarding their entire existence. And unfortunately for me and everyone else in the library, she wouldn't leave until she found the one she was hunting for.

Mine.

"Do you have any books about dragons?" a tiny voice asked behind me.

I nearly jumped out of my skin and whirled around, taking in the pint-sized boy with a shock of red hair. "Dragons? Wh—what kind of dragons?"

"I don't know," he replied with a shrug, reassessing me with a bored expression. "That's why I asked you."

"Right." Oh my God, Zane! Get it together! "This way."

Offloading the armful of books onto the shelf, I made a note to come back for them later and led him over to the display of medieval fantasy books.

"Yeah!" As soon as he spied the books, he darted ahead of me, grabbing the one with a giant black dragon on the cover. He didn't waste any time flipping through it, chattering away to no one in particular about his thoughts on each and every picture or odd chapter title.

I couldn't help but smile, watching him with a sense of pride. Being a librarian wasn't the most exciting job in the world, but it was moments like that—where you watch a kid get *so* engrossed with a book they forget the outside world exists—that made the paltry salary and dust allergies worth it.

After the kid wandered away with his book, I lingered in the children's section a while longer, straightening the discarded books and tossing blocks back into the bin.

"There you are."

I froze in place. The hair on the back of my neck stood on end like a mouse that had been caught. Pivoting slowly, I forced a smile to my face. "Oksana. Nice to see you."

"I was beginning to think you changed your schedule on me again," she said with a faux pout, sauntering forward and sliding her fingertips up and down the strap on her gym bag, as if it was an enticement of some sort.

"Esther's the one who makes the schedule, not me," I said, hoping my excuse sounded good. At the very least, I managed to seem equally disappointed. I mean, it wasn't a lie. Esther *did* make the schedule. But she happily changed my hours to whatever I needed, like pushing back my start time to avoid Oksana's yoga class in the studio next door. Esther also accommodated my last-minute requests for random days off whenever I saw Oksana loitering outside my apartment building.

"I wish that old hag would stop messing with you," Oksana said, brushing a wrinkle out of my shirt and smoothing the dark blue fabric over my chest.

"She's not a hag. And she's not messing with me." A frown pulled at the corners of my mouth, for her rude remark and the fact I was two seconds away from flinging her hand off of me.

Thankfully, Oksana retracted her hand so she could toss her long, black hair over her shoulder. Batting her lashes, she smiled sweetly. "Have you had lunch yet? I'd love to go check out the bistro down the street."

"I can't. I'm the only one here today." As if to prove my point, I sidestepped her and headed toward the circulation desk.

"Oh, perfect! I'll bring it to you and we can have a picnic."

"There's no eating allowed in the library."

Oksana pouted again, linking her arm through mine and walking with me for three measly steps. "Zane, you're going to have to stop playing hard to get."

"I'm not playing hard to get, Oksana," I said, gently disentangling myself from her and rounding the desk for some more distance, even though I doubted a little swinging door was much of a deterrent. "I'm gay."

"That's what all the pretty boys say."

Sighing, I closed my eyes. Over the course of being acquainted with one another, I'd told her—repeatedly—I was gay. I didn't know why she didn't believe me, nor did I know what I was going to have to do to prove it. Although, I was pretty sure I could make out with the first random guy that came through the door and she still wouldn't believe me.

"Oksana . . . " I opened my eyes and cocked my head. "I really have a lot of work to do."

She glanced around the library and the handful of patrons scattered throughout. Arching a dark brow at me, she smiled nonetheless and ran a finger down the front of my chest. "You can't avoid a date forever."

"You don't want to date me. I promise."

"Yeah, you're right," she said, perching on the edge of the desk. She leaned on one arm, conveniently pushing her cleavage into view beneath her barely there sports bra. "I don't want to date you. We're going to get married one day. I can feel it." I started to protest, but she kept going, a wistful look in her eyes. "Just picture it. Us in one of those cute little houses in the historic district; you taking over as the head librarian here; me running my photography business. We can have lunch together every day and pick our kids up from school. Oh, Zane. They'd be so beautiful! With your bone structure and my coloring?"

"My bone structure?" I quirked a brow at her.

"Excuse me," an elderly woman huffed behind Oksana. "I need to return these."

Oksana glanced over her shoulder at the woman and scoffed. Before I had to tell her to get off the desk, she slid off on her own accord and gave me a dazzling smile. "I'll see you tomorrow, Zane."

"Have a nice night," I mumbled, already dreading the next shift.

As soon as she walked away, the other woman stepped forward and thunked a stack of random books on the desk. "Have you thought about getting a restraining order? Or maybe a different job?"

I pretended not to hear her and flipped through the books, scanning them into the system for the return. Except, none of them had a recent due date. "Some of these haven't been touched in over a year. Are you sure you checked them out at this library?"

Furrowing my brow, I looked up at the woman for the answer and gasped like an idiot. She was gone. There was absolutely no trace of her in the lobby and I knew for a fact she hadn't walked out since the front door was right next to the desk and no one had gone out since Oksana.

"So weird . . . " I shook my head and moved the stack of books to the cart to be shelved later.

Underneath the last book was a section of the newspaper, folded up with a giant, scribbled circle around one of the ads.

Curiosity more than anything prompted me to pick it up and see what the woman had circled with such enthusiasm.

It was a job posting.

More specifically, it stated:

PERSONAL ASSISTANT.

Personal assistant to an author needed for six-month contract. Responsibilities include research, typing, editing, attending meetings, and personal errands. Nondisclosure agreement required. Room/board provided along with weekly salary. Email: markabner@abnerandsons.com

A weekly salary was obviously nice, but throw in room and board? I could actually save up some money *and* learn from a successful author. Maybe one day it would help me publish a book of my own, but more importantly, this meant I could finally have enough money to take care of my dad.

While the ad didn't say which author the job was for, there were only a handful of likely candidates in this part of the country with the kind of prestige that would necessitate an NDA. Most of them were based in or around Chicago, according to their bios, which meant it was highly unlikely for them to be looking for an assistant this far in the western suburbs. Still, it could be the opportunity of a lifetime, depending who the author was. And either way, it was a guaranteed break from Oksana.

I emailed them immediately.

Two
Gerulf

"You're late," I snapped as soon as the door to my office swung open. I didn't bother turning around to face the tall, skinny man ambling in. I could see him just fine in the reflection of the glass window.

"I was handling another matter," Mark Abner replied. He hesitated for a moment, glancing between me and the chair in front of my desk, as if trying to decide how rude it would be to sit while I was standing.

"What other matter?"

"Your agent called."

"You mean my agent or my backstabbing bitch of an ex-fiancée?" I shot back, not even giving him time to answer. "What could she possibly want now?"

Mark ignored the question. "They've already extended your contact by six months, despite not having a rough draft. I don't know how much longer I can hold them off. It's already been two years. You have to give them *something*."

"What do you want me to do? The words won't come! And having her breathing down my neck after she knows goddamn well what I've been through isn't going to help!" I clenched my fist against the windowsill, doing everything in my power not to punch through the glass. Although at this point, what were a few more scars to add to the collection? "*She's* the reason I'm in this situation in the first place!"

"I know. Ok? That's why I've taken the liberty of hiring you a personal assistant. Again."

"You what?!" I whirled away from the window that time, staring him down with one furious eye as I closed the distance in long strides. "What did I tell you the last time?!"

"He's a writer. He can help you—" He flinched with my rapid approach, but remained where he was, clearing his throat. "Don't fight this, Gerulf. You need help. *Real* help. Help no one else around here has been able to give you. You've fired the last six assistants without even meeting them. Just *try* to give this one a chance!"

"I don't 'need' anything, least of all some stranger poking around in my life!"

"He's already signed a Non-Disclosure. And he idolizes you. He'll do whatever you say."

"Wonderful. Just what I 'need,'" I snarled, stalking away from my traitorous lawyer and back to the window. "Some sycophant trying to wheedle their way into my good graces so I'll read their fucking book or give them a favorable review. As if I don't have enough to deal with already."

"It doesn't really matter what you say. It's a done deal."

"The hell it isn't! Contracts are broken every day."

"Then go tell him yourself. He's in the library."

Rage flooded every cell in my body. Goddamn him! He was calling my bluff, thinking I'd be too scared to show my face to someone outside these walls. Well the joke was on him because I was pissed off enough to do it.

Storming away from the window, I cut across my office and yanked open the heavy door. It banged against the wall, echoing throughout the house.

I heard Mark scurrying behind me as my steps thundered down the hallway to the library. Throwing the double doors open, I marched inside and scanned the enormous room for any sign of this new interloper.

He wasn't hard to spot.

The first thing I saw was a mass of curly brown hair skimming narrow shoulders. Warm brown eyes landed on mine, followed by a smile that lit up his whole face—a smile that didn't falter even when I stopped abruptly, my jaw slack. For a split second, I didn't know if he was a *he* at all. With his high cheekbones and plush lips, he was nothing if not beautiful.

I hated him.

On the flip side, if *he* was horrified by *my* appearance, he didn't let on. I didn't even catch a glimmer of disgust. He wasn't a writer then. He was an actor. A gifted actor, I would begrudgingly admit, with a face that was too pretty to belong to a man.

"I'm Zane, Zane Beaumont." He rushed forward the rest of the way, sticking his hand out. "It's such an honor to meet you. I'm a massive fan of your work. And I just wanted to thank you for the opportunity to—"

"Shut the fuck up and get out of my house."

He blinked, his hand dropping and his smile finally fading. "Excuse me?"

"Get out!"

Maybe he was deaf. Or dumb. There had to be some sort of explanation as to why he just stood there, mouth agape like a damn guppy.

"Sir, the tea is ready in the solarium," Gilroy said from the doorway, as if I wasn't seconds from throwing this intruder out the window, onto the front lawn.

"I don't want any fucking tea!" I snapped at him, as much for the interruption as for letting Mark bring someone into the house without my permission.

"I was speaking to Mr. Beaumont," Gilroy replied loftily.

Zane glanced between the butler and me, clearly trying to decide who he should listen to.

Fury and humiliation warred inside me. Before I came completely unhinged, I spun on the ball of my foot and headed for the door. Something solid slammed into my left side. I stumbled to my right, turning my head fully toward the left to see what the hell I ran into.

Gilroy was in the midst of regaining his own footing. He straightened and smoothed down his tie, offering me a small nod. At least he had the forethought not to try and muster up some lame excuse or give any verbal acknowledgement whatsoever of our collision.

It didn't matter that my entire left side was a giant blindspot; I should have apologized to him since I was clearly the one at fault. Instead, I swept through the doorway, rubbing my shoulder and cursing everything about this miserable day.

Three
Zane

Wow. They say you should never meet your heroes and I guess they were right. Gerulf Prince was *nothing* like I imagined.

When I pulled up to the gates of the massive house in the middle of nowhere, I thought my GPS was obviously off. But whoever answered the speaker box told me they were expecting me and buzzed me through.

The house was straight out of a fairytale—a large, castle-like structure composed of red brick and half-timber framing. It had a turret. A *turret*! And so many chimneys sticking up out of the roofline I lost count.

It felt weird parking my car next to a fountain in the circular drive, but I didn't know where else I was supposed to put it. It's not like I saw a garage somewhere. So I crossed my fingers and hoped for the best.

A severe-looking man in a black suit answered the door and led me through the house in silence. Literal suits of armor lined one hallway and some of the ceilings were painted with cherubs and chivalric scenes from the Renaissance. The house obviously wasn't *that* old, but the way it was designed and decorated definitely made you forget you were living in the twenty-first century.

My silent tour guide led me to the library and introduced me to another man in a suit. "Mr. Abner, Mr. Beaumont for you."

"Thank you, Gilroy," Mr. Abner said with a smile, shaking my hand. "Thank you for making the drive on such short notice. Please, sit."

I forced myself to stop staring at the floor-to-ceiling walls of books and focus on my interviewer. "Thank you for the opportunity."

"Yes, well, you might not be thanking me by the end of it," he said with a chuckle. "If you wouldn't mind signing this first, then we can begin." He slid a piece of paper across the coffee table and set a heavy pen on the page.

"What is this?" I asked, scanning the long legal explanations beneath a title that clearly said *Non-Disclosure Agreement.*

"An NDA. I'm afraid it's necessary for all of the staff. Are you a reader, Mr. Beaumont? Or a writer?"

"Zane," I replied, scribbling my name at the bottom and handing him the agreement and his pen. "And yes, to both. I graduated with my master's degree in library science in May, but I haven't published anything of my own yet. Just a couple short stories in some anthologies."

"Wonderful. Have you heard of Gerulf Prince?"

"Have I—yeah! Yes! I've heard of him. He's . . . " I couldn't even find the words since I was still trying to pick my jaw up off the floor. I was in Gerulf Prince's house. Gerulf fucking Prince!

To say he was a literary genius was something of an understatement. Worldwide recognition, shelves full of awards, and millions in royalties. There wasn't any genre he couldn't tackle. That's partly how he made his name—blending tropes and sub-genres, churning out twisty plots and characters with such complexity you'd swear they were flesh-and-blood people. The world was eagerly awaiting his next release, a historical thriller set in late nineteenth-century Chicago. So far, no one knew anything about it except the buzz generated by the press about why it was taking so long. It was bound to be another award winner, they said.

Then again, I imagined he'd had a hard time since his car accident. Two years ago, the literary world was devastated to learn he nearly died while vacationing in Switzerland. Reports said he'd been hospitalized for months.

Any information about him sort of dwindled to nothing after that until he made headlines last year. Someone at the publishing house leaked the title of his book, *Loss of Twilight*. There wasn't any sort of synopsis or even a cover design to go with it. The book nerds spent months theorizing what it could possibly be, but no one knew definitively. If things went well, I'd be at the center of it all. The bookworm inside rejoiced.

"I'm sure you know about Gerulf's accident," Mr. Abner said, continuing after I nodded. "Some of the rumors were, unfortunately, true. He was badly injured, and that has led to a delay in writing. He's under contract and if he doesn't give them something, he's facing dire legal consequences. Now, money he can handle, as you can see," he said, gesturing around the massive library. "But with a legal battle comes publicity and Gerulf is adamant no one sees what has happened to him."

"What happened to him?" I asked quietly.

"Superficially, he's scarred very badly on the left side of his body. When the car crashed, his side took the brunt of the impact. He was impaled on part of the door, causing a variety of nerve and muscle damage. He also lost the use of his left eye and learning to adjust to monocular vision has not been easy for him. Which is where you, potentially, come in.

"He needs someone who can do the writing for him, take his dictation and make it into a story. He can't work for long periods of time anymore without getting debilitating migraines, so this would relieve some of the pressure. Likewise, you'd also have to proofread what he's already done before it's sent to the editor. Run errands for him, take him to appointments, read books. Whatever he needs to help make his life easier so he can get this damn book finished."

I nodded. Honestly, I'd pick up his dry cleaning if he wanted me to and do it with a smile. Anything to help one of my favorite authors accomplish his next project. "Yeah. Absolutely. I understand."

Mr. Abner went over a few other details and asked about my background, the usual back-and-forth interview questions. At the end of it, he smiled and laced his fingers together in his lap. "One final question, Zane."

"Of course."

"How do you handle conflict?"

For some reason, I immediately thought of Oksana. I hedged, trying to decide how best to answer him. Finally, I went with the truth instead of trying to sound suave. "I don't. I try to find a way to diffuse the situation. Cooler heads prevail, right?"

His smile broadened. "Excellent. I'd like to officially offer you the position." He withdrew another contract and slid it across the table. "The terms of your employment, along with the salary and a list of other benefits."

"Really?" I blinked and gave myself a mental slap for sounding like a complete moron. I mean, it had been a good interview, but normally you had to wait days or weeks to hear back from a company. Although in this case, they were clearly making an exception.

"Yes, really. Time is of the essence. I need you to start right away."

"Yes, of course. I mean, thank you! I don't know what to say." A split second after I said it, I realized I should have probably looked at the contract before agreeing to anything.

"I hope you say you'll take it."

Flipping through the pages, my eyes nearly bugged out of my head at the salary listed. There were more zeros on that number than I'd ever had on a paycheck in my life. If I saw this thing through, I'd have enough money to help my dad *and* some left over for a nest egg. Only an idiot would turn it down.

As soon as I signed the contract, Mr. Abner excused himself to go find Gerulf. He instructed me to wait in the library and said he'd just be a minute. I heard him mutter, "Hopefully," under his breath as he scurried away.

I'd been confused by that, but after meeting Gerulf Prince in the flesh, I understood what his lawyer had been trying to tell me without explicitly telling me. I couldn't even begin to fathom what Gerulf been through, but the jury was still out on whether or not that entitled him to act like a dick to a perfect stranger.

After Gerulf stormed out of the library, I was left quaking in my shoes, stunned by both the abrupt dismissal and, well, *him*.

I'd be lying if I said I didn't notice what he looked like. How could you *not* notice? The man on the back of his books was striking—dark hair, tan skin, a face chiseled to perfection, and pale eyes that somehow pierced your soul from a simple photograph.

But now I knew why no one had seen in him in so long.

The right side of his face still belonged on a magazine; the left, however, was more suited to a horror book. A nasty, jagged red scar ran vertically down the left side of his face, splitting his dark brow and slashing across his left eye, leaving it an unsettling white color. There were other deep scars on his left cheek, disappearing into his hairline and down into the collar of his black button-up shirt. Just below his jaw, there was a patch of marbled skin, leftover evidence of some sort of burn.

Beyond the vanity associated with such disfigurement, I'm sure it was painful. And who knew how the loss of his eye really impacted him on a day-to-day basis, aside from the migraines and inability to work independently. I mean, I imagined it was pretty bad if he had to resort to hiring a PA to finish his novel. Then again, maybe *he* didn't since *he* was extraordinarily pissed when he came into the room.

"If you'll follow me," Gilroy said, reminding me I was standing there like a dope.

My heart sank. Each step I took toward the door felt like I was slogging through quicksand. I didn't want to go, but I wasn't going to stay when I clearly wasn't wanted either.

Instead of leading me to the front door, Gilroy took me to another part of the house I hadn't seen on the way in.

"Where are we going?" I asked, staring at the paintings lining the hallways. They were a mix of landscapes and portraits, adding to the air of old sophistication the house exuded, almost like it was caught in a time capsule.

"The solarium."

"But Mr. Prince wanted me to leave."

"If you're going to work for Mr. Prince, you'll have to learn to navigate between what he *says* he wants and what he actually needs."

"Isn't that, like, insubordinate?"

"Perhaps. But in this house, the ends justify the means."

Um . . . ok. Pretty sure I'd never read *that* in any HR handbook. "Why did Mr. Abner hire me?"

"You would have to ask Mr. Abner," Gilroy replied with a bored tone.

"I'm just saying, it seemed like a bit of a . . . shock to Mr. Prince. It didn't seem like he knew what was going on."

"Mr. Prince is not used to having guests anymore. He will come around. Hopefully."

Gilroy opened the door to an all-glass room filled with a variety of potted plants and greenery. A fountain built into the brick wall of the house gurgled quietly. Dozens of red rose bushes perfumed the air. Some climbed up white trellises while others spilled out of concrete planters. A black wrought iron table and chairs sat in the center of the room, a tea cart positioned next to them.

"Enjoy your tea, sir."

"Uh, thanks." I gave him a fleeting smile and walked through the door he was holding.

Alone again, I looked around the solarium as I made my way to the table. Easing into the chair, I helped myself to a cucumber sandwich and took a tentative bite.

The fact that two of Gerulf's employees used the word "hopefully" when discussing the outcome of this contract didn't exactly give me warm fuzzies.

I had no idea what I was going to do now. Gilroy heard the order for me to leave, yet he brought me here. Would I stay for the six months anyway? Knowing Gerulf didn't want me here? Or would I collect my salary and go? I'd signed a contract with the lawyer and *I* certainly wasn't the one who broke it.

As tempting as it was to walk away with a good chunk of money for doing absolutely nothing, it didn't sit well with me. It didn't matter that Gerulf had millions, and I had none. Taking his money without actually earning it was tantamount to stealing, no matter how good of a reason I had.

Two tea sandwiches and a cranberry-orange scone later and I still didn't have an answer.

The door opened again. I jumped to my feet, fully expecting to see Gerulf barging through it. Except, the elderly woman who wandered in was anything but terrifying.

"How's it going, love?" she asked with a smile, walking right past me and touching her fingers to the teapot. "Would you like me to bring more?"

"No, I'm fine. Thank you."

"Sit, sit." She flapped a hand at me until I followed her instruction.

"I'm Zane," I offered lamely, even though I didn't know if it mattered at this point.

"Mrs. Potter, the housekeeper. You just let me know if you need anything at all during your stay."

"Stay? But Mr. Prince—"

"Yes, I heard. The whole house heard. Never mind him, dear. He's always had a dreadful temper and I'm afraid it's only gotten worse since the accident. You'll just have to learn to ignore it."

"So you think I should stay?"

"Of course I do. He needs the help."

"I know. Mr. Abner said his literary agent is threatening to sue him if he doesn't produce a rough draft in the next six months."

She laughed and waved me off. "Oh, I'm not talking about that wretched woman. I was talking about Gerulf's craft. He lost his muse, you see. We've all tried to help him get it back, but I think it's going to take another writer to reach him."

"Oh, I'm just a librarian. Not an author."

"I didn't say another author. I said a writer." She smiled and patted my shoulder, heading for the door again. "Use the bellpull when you're finished. Gilroy will take you to your room."

"But I don't have any stuff with me. I need to go home and pack a bag or something." If I even decided to stay. The jury was still out on that, too.

"Well, make sure you come back in time for dinner. Chef's got a pot roast on that you don't want to miss."

"Oh, but I still don't—"

"Just run home and get some of your clothes. We have everything else you need right here." She closed the door behind her, literally shutting the door on our conversation—if you could call it that.

I watched her leave, brows furrowed, trying to make sense of everything she'd said. How did she know I wanted to be an author, anyway? Was she eavesdropping on the interview? For some reason, I wouldn't have been surprised. And what did she mean they had everything I needed? That was weird, considering Gerulf didn't seem like the type to host long-term guests. Or maybe she meant they'd send someone to the store to pick up some stuff.

Strange as it was, I guess I had my answer.

At the very least, I had a feeling the next six months were going to be interesting.

Four
Gerulf

The pain started before I even opened my eyes, an excruciating thumping on the left side of my head. It was probably from all the shouting. I knew better, and yet, I did it anyway. Because no matter what I said, my staff seemed to think they knew better than I did. I felt like a child again—yelling at the top of my lungs for my parents' attention, only to be continuously ignored until my imagined orphanhood became a reality.

Since I could only deal with one tragedy at a time, I shoved Mom and Dad to the back burner and focused on the more pressing issue. Rolling over, I snagged one of the pill bottles off the side table and unscrewed it. I tossed a couple pills back and swallowed them down with a glass of water, waiting impatiently for them to kick in.

I laid there for at least another half hour, listening as the house came alive around me. I knew breakfast was ready from the faint smell of coffee and bacon floating through the air. As much as I wanted to stay in bed, I knew I had to get up. Moving was crucial. Agonizing, but crucial.

Heaving myself out of bed, I stumbled into the bathroom, once again confronting the giant blank space above the marble sink. The dark blue wallpaper had faded over the years, except for the patch of perfectly preserved color where the mirror used to hang. One of these days I was going to have to make a decision about what to do with it—either re-wallpaper the whole bathroom or hang something else up, like a painting.

Pain started creeping up in my head again, so I quit thinking about the fucking wallpaper and the reason I had to concern myself with interior design in the first place.

I didn't need a mirror to be reminded of how hideous I was. I could feel it, deep in my bones where they'd broken and healed and in the tight, unforgiving scar tissue on my face. Perhaps if I'd been ugly before the accident, it wouldn't bother me so much. Vain as it was, I knew I'd been handsome. I prided myself on it. Everyone knew it didn't matter how brilliant you were—unless your brain came wrapped in a pretty package, no one cared. The world wasn't nice to unattractive people and there were plenty of studies to prove it.

My face had opened dozens of doors to me; got me meetings with top literary agents and publishers, landed me coveted TV and magazine interviews, and of course made me a darling in the society pages. And I loved it. I loved the attention. Because for the first time in my life I was getting it—people *noticed* me.

They still noticed me now, but not in the way I ever wanted. That car crash had ruined everything. Absolutely everything. In the blink of an eye, I lost my career, my fiancée, my identity.

Technically, I was still an author.

Technically, my fiancée was still alive, just waltzing around as my *ex*-fiancée and bitch of an agent.

And, yeah, I had a pulse, but what good was that when children literally cried when they saw me? Other than the requisite doctor's appointments, I didn't leave the estate. It was easier that way. Until my oh-so-helpful lawyer took it upon himself to hire yet another person I didn't need nor want in my life. At least that kid would be on his way back to Chicago or wherever they scrounged him up from.

Once I was dressed, I headed down to breakfast, navigating the stairs carefully. I couldn't even remember how many times I'd tripped or actually fallen down them. Depth perception was a real bitch when you only had one eye to work with. That was yet another thing taken from me prematurely —any semblance of dignity.

Heading into the dining room, I stopped immediately when I spied a mop of brown curls.

"What the fuck are you doing?" I asked, marching up to the man as he speared another piece of French toast on his plate.

"Having breakfast," he replied with a smile that was entirely too fucking chipper. "Good morning, by the way."

"I told you to get out! Do I have to call the police and have you thrown out?"

"Um, there's a note from your lawyer," Zane said, motioning with his fork toward my place setting. "He said you might want to read it before you call the police."

Seething, I stomped to the end of the table and snatched the letter off my plate.

Gerulf,

He'll be paid his full salary plus a generous severance package if you terminate his contract before the six months is up. It will cost you a small fortune. I'd advise you make good use of your time with him and try to keep your temper. You can't afford a lawsuit if you hit him.

— Mark

Crumpling up the letter, I threw it to the ground with only a minimal growl. Goddamn him! Goddamn *both* of them!

Mrs. Potter swept in the door, carrying a fresh tray. "Good morning, sir."

"Is it?" I snapped.

"I made all of your favorites this morning," she replied with a smile as bright as Zane's, like co-conspirators. Setting the tray down next to my place setting, she lifted the silver dome and began removing more plates—French toast, eggs, bacon cooked the way I liked, and fresh-squeezed orange juice to go along with the cup of black coffee.

I still didn't make any sort of move to drag my chair out from the table. "So I see. This wouldn't be some sort of attempt at placating me, would it?"

"Never, dear. Sit and eat before it gets cold."

"I think I'll take my breakfast in the solarium." I slid a glare in Zane's direction, noting he'd gone silent since Mrs. Potter arrived. Even his silverware had stopped moving and he sat there, as still as a statue, watching us like a tennis match.

"I'm afraid that's not possible," Mrs. Potter replied.

I glared at her, arching the brow above my good eye. "Why not?"

"The gardener is power washing the floors."

"Then the library."

"Oh, I'm afraid Lisette is dusting."

I folded my arms over my chest, trying to keep my blood pressure from spiking through the roof. "My office?"

"Itzel is cleaning the windows."

"Then send all of this to my room!"

"Of course, sir, but today is the day Gilroy changes out the—"

"Enough of your nonsense, woman! If I can't eat in peace in my own house, then I won't eat at all!" I sidestepped her and marched out of the dining room again. I really didn't have a destination in mind; I just wanted to get away from the two of them and their curious stares, like they were both waiting for me to explode. Which . . . I nearly did.

Itzel opened the door to my office, took one look at me, and promptly slammed it shut again. It didn't matter since I bypassed it, *and* the library, and continued down the hall. I threw open the side door and walked out into the morning sunlight.

Closing my eyes against the harsh light, I followed the sound of gravel crunching beneath my shoes and headed for the gardens.

Did they think I was oblivious to what they were doing? Somehow they'd all gotten it in their heads I needed help. I didn't. I didn't need anything, except to be left alone. To not have everyone fawning over me and trying to do things for me like I was completely inept, or scheming behind my back like I was a fucking moron.

In case they all forgot, *I* was the one under contract to write the fucking book and I'd write it when *I* was damn good and ready. Faye and the rest of the vultures at the publishing house could rot in hell as far as I was concerned. I lost my eye and some motor function on my left side; I didn't have a goddamn lobotomy!

Veering off the main gravel path, I followed a smaller one to the rose garden. Their heady scent hung in the air, combined with freshly mown grass. I stopped and cradled a dark red bloom, morning dew clinging to the velvety petals. Try as I might to find some beauty in this pathetic world, I came up empty, even in the presence of my mother's majestic garden.

They were heirloom roses, she told me. It meant they smelled better than modern rose bushes and were hardier, able to survive the inevitable winter. Since it was still summer, they were in full bloom and would remain so through the fall. But soon enough, all of the petals would wither and fade, like everything else in life.

I sank onto a stone bench and considered the roses in front of me. *Loss of Twilight* needled the back of my mind, begging for inspiration, a sentence or two. *Anything*. But I had nothing. Whatever plot I'd formed once upon a time was gone, along with any sense of passion for the project.

Stewing in my bitterness, it wasn't long before I heard someone else coming down the gravel walkway. I didn't bother turning my head. Hopefully, it was one of the gardeners, who would keep walking and leave me the hell alone. It was bad enough I'd already been chased out of my damn house by a doe-eyed boy and Mrs. Potter's half-brained idea of setting up a playdate for me.

The footsteps changed direction. Instead of continuing on their way, or turning back for the house, they headed straight for me.

"Go away," I snarled, still not bothering to turn around.

"I brought you some breakfast," a soft male voice said. Zane. As if the day couldn't get any worse.

"Apparently you missed the part where I said I'm not hungry."

"No, you said you weren't eating. That's not the same thing." He kept walking, undeterred by the danger he was putting himself in. I could strangle him in this garden and no one would know. I could snap his neck like a twig and turn him into fertilizer. Smash his forehead into the stone bench. I could do whatever I wanted and make him disappear in the blink of an eye. I wrote about murderers for a living—I was quite literally capable of anything if I had a mind to. Whether or not my body was capable of carrying it out was another matter.

Zane set the items on my left, something metal and something like crinkled paper. After a split second, he snatched them up again and moved them to my right. A thermos and something wrapped in brown paper, reminiscent of a sandwich. "Sorry about that," he murmured, stepping back and shoving his hands in his jean pockets.

"Sorry about what? Staying when your presence isn't

welcome? Taking my money when I didn't offer it to you? Or is that a pathetic bid at expressing sympathy for me? Tell me, Zane"—I couldn't help but snort at his name, though I had little room to talk—"what are you so *sorry* for?"

"For putting your breakfast on the left. It won't happen again."

I got to my feet slowly and took a step forward. We were eye-level with one another, but even with my physical disadvantage, I could still overpower him easily. He was like a reed, tall and thin and seconds away from breaking in half.

He held his ground, his pointy chin tipped up. His big brown eyes narrowed and his jaw clenched, but he squared off anyway. It was like watching a puppy get mad at an older, bigger dog, desperate to prove themselves.

"It won't happen again," I repeated, fixing him with a glare, "because you're not staying. Get your shit and get out."

"Respectfully, I was hired to do a job and I'm going to do it."

"Is that a fact?"

"That's a fact."

"You're pretty brave for a twelve-year-old."

He smirked. "You're not as scary as I'm sure you'd like to think you are."

My hand flashed out, seizing him by the throat. I hauled him forward, giving him an up close and personal view of the left side of my face. To my surprise, he didn't look at it. He yelped and clung to my wrist, but his gaze remained focused on my good eye.

"Am I scary now?" I asked between my teeth.

The muscles under my hand constricted with a swallow, but he shook his head. "No."

"Go ahead. Take a good look at the monster. Get it out of your system. Sate the curiosity."

"You're not a monster." He said it with such conviction I was tempted to believe him, but ultimately I knew better.

People said all sorts of conciliatory things when confronted with the threat of physical harm.

I considered him for another moment, the way his breathing hitched and how warm his fingers were wrapped around my wrist. Not once in all the time he stood there did his dark gaze divert to the left side of my face. I could count on one hand the number of times I'd been met with *that* reaction instead of the customary staring, gasping, or whispering. As much as I hated him and hated the idea of someone new and unknown in my house, he wasn't the most miserable human being I'd ever encountered in thirty-seven years. I suppose that was saying something.

"If you want to be useful, go get my laptop," I said, shoving him away from me.

He stumbled backward, touching his throat instinctively. Swallowing, he gave a terse nod and disappeared the way he came.

As soon as he was safely out of earshot, I laughed at the absurdity of it all. This kid wouldn't last the week.

Five
Zane

Mrs. Potter said Gerulf had a "dreadful temper," but that little stunt back there seemed a couple of steps above "dreadful." More like murderous? Unhinged? I mean, I knew he'd been through a lot, but Jesus! With how hard he grabbed my throat, I wouldn't have been surprised if he left bruises.

Scurrying back to the house as fast as I could, I let myself in the side door and came to a screeching halt in the hallway.

I had *no* idea where I was going.

A long hallway extended to my left, lined with suits of armor and closed doors. To the right, it seemed like it was more of the same except for an ornate clock set on an end table.

The clock seemed familiar, so I headed in that direction. Looping around the perimeter of the house, I walked straight into a formal living room or something that basically served as a dead end.

"So much for that," I muttered, trudging back the way I came.

I wandered for what felt like hours, opening the unlocked doors and giving the rooms cursory glances before moving on.

Gerulf said he wanted his laptop, which meant it was probably in the library or an office or something. Maybe even his bedroom, although *that* was an area I was definitely steering clear of.

By some miracle, I made it back to the library.

One of the maids was still dusting, humming along to herself as she wiped down the antique books.

"Excuse me?" I cleared my throat and took a step closer.

She stole a glance at me but didn't stop cleaning. "Oui?"

"'We'? Oh, right. You must be Lisette." I took another step forward and extended my hand, retracting it again when she simply held up the dust rag as an excuse for not shaking. "I'm Zane."

"Can I help you with something?" she asked, her voice accented but not entirely unfriendly. If anything, she sounded as bored with me as she was dusting hundreds, if not thousands, of books.

"Uh, yeah. Actually. Mr. Prince told me to bring him his laptop."

That got her to stop. She arched a blonde eyebrow at me. "His what?"

"Laptop?" I pantomimed typing, hoping it would help. "Computer?"

"I don't know what you're talking about."

"Portátil? Shit, that's Spanish. I'm sorry." Then again, how different could romance languages be?

Her pouty red lips pursed together and she propped a hand on the curve of her hip. "I know what a laptop is. I'm saying he doesn't have one."

"Then what does he use to write his books?"

"A typewriter," she replied with a smirk. Giving me a once-over, a look somewhere between pity and annoyance crossed her face. She shook her head and went back to dusting.

"A typewriter. Great. That's just . . . great." I raked a hand through my hair and pushed the mass of curls away from my face. Struck with an idea, I hurried over to the bellpull by the fireplace and gave it a tug.

Moments later, Gilroy appeared. He glanced around the library with a furrowed brow before turning his attention to me. "Was there something you needed, Mr. Beaumont?"

"Do you know where Gerulf keeps his typewriter?"

"His office, sir."

"Can you please point me in that direction?"

"I shall take you myself." He pivoted on his heel and walked out.

I hurried after him, following him down the hallway and trying to memorize the way as we walked.

"How are you adjusting to your new role?" Gilroy asked, his hands clasped primly behind his back.

"Well, he'd rather starve than eat in the same room as me, he tried to strangle me in the garden, and he told me to fetch a laptop that doesn't exist. I'd say things are going great," I muttered.

Gilroy chuckled quietly. "You've lasted longer than the others, I'll give you that." He stopped in front of a closed door and gestured toward it. "It's on the desk."

"Great. Thank you. Is there a tray or something I can borrow?"

Gilroy considered me for a moment and inclined his head. "I'll be right back."

As soon as Gilroy returned with a large wooden tray, I took it with a smile and expressed my gratitude before stepping into Gerulf's office.

"Ok, asshole," I muttered to myself, hefting the antique typewriter off the desk and setting it on the tray, along with a stack of blank paper, a notebook, and a couple pens to be on the safe side. "I can play your game."

By the time I schlepped all of his stuff out to the garden, I fully expected Gerulf to be gone, to have come back up to the house or disappeared farther into the gardens since he knew I was on a fool's errand. Surprisingly, he was still on the same bench where I left him. The paper wrapping, I noted, was balled up and the thermos was actually in his hands.

"Did you find it?" Gerulf asked, lifting the metal cup to his lips as if it would hide his smirk. He didn't even bother looking in my direction. Smarmy bastard.

"Sure did," I replied with an acidic smile if he happened to glance my way. He didn't—not until I stopped directly in front of him and he was suddenly eye-level with the type-writer. "Where would you like it?"

He recoiled from the machine in his face before letting his gaze drift upward to mine. Slowly, he tossed his head to the side, indicating the bench next to him.

I gave him a curt nod and set the tray down. "Now what?"

"Feel free to scamper back to wherever it is you came from, kid."

"I'm twenty-four." I crossed my arms, realizing a second too late it completely undermined my rebuttal. Rather than uncross my arms and risk looking even more petulant, I held my ground. I was used to being dismissed; people had been doing it my whole life for one reason or another. I was too scrawny, too pretty, too nerdy, too everything a boy *shouldn't* be. Age (and height) helped somewhat, but the point of the matter was I was used to proving myself to people who didn't think much of me. So if Gerulf thought he was going to run me off with a few snarky comments and waste my time, he had another thing coming.

"Do you know how many books I'd written by the age of twenty-four?" he asked, cocking his head.

"Published or unpublished?" I shot back.

The corner of his mouth lifted in another smirk. "How many books have *you* written?"

"None. Yet."

"Uh huh." He dragged his gaze down my body, pausing at my feet before darting up, like he was measuring my worth through sight alone. "And yet you seem to think you're somehow qualified to help me with mine?"

"Your lawyer seems to think I'm qualified."

"My lawyer is an idiot."

"You hired him." Good one, Zane. Stoop to his level *and* insult him. Brilliant.

Gerulf set the thermos to the side and got to his feet slowly, fixing me with a pointed look. Considering me from head-to-toe again, he sidestepped me and moved down the garden path, leaving everything on the stone bench.

I bit my lip, cursing him silently. Why did someone so brilliant have to be such a fucking asshole? Exhaling a slow, steady breath, I tossed the crumpled wrapper onto the tray and wedged the thermos next to the typewriter.

"Are you coming or not?" Gerulf's voice called out.

When I looked up, he was watching me from across the garden with a scowl.

Snatching a pen and notebook, I stuffed them both in my back pocket and hurried after him before he suddenly changed his mind and told me to beat it.

I'd barely caught up to him when he resumed walking. Well, limping. It wasn't noticeable with each step, but every so often, he'd wince and his hand would drift to his left thigh. I let it go the first couple of times, but eventually I blurted out, "Should we take a break?"

"You can't be tired already," he replied, walking onward, his back ramrod straight.

"I'm not, I just thought . . . I don't know. We've been walking for almost an hour and you haven't said anything."

"What does my silence have to do with your lack of endurance?" He arched an eyebrow to punctuate his condescending retort.

"I don't—" I blew out a breath. There was no way in hell I was going to point out my concern for his well-being when he was being so stubborn. And mean. "Why did you want me to come with you if you weren't going to talk?"

"Can't handle the thoughts in your own head? Is that why you don't like silence?"

Oh my God! I was going to kill him. An hour ago, he was the one strangling me and now I was on the verge of strangling him by the row of neatly trimmed boxwoods.

"Listen, I am *trying* here. I'm not some freeloader, ok? I *want* to help you. That is what I'm being paid to do. So if you want to use me as a whipping boy for six months, then fine. But spell it out for me so I know what to expect."

He stopped finally and turned half-way to look at me. "You're a strange individual."

"Look who's talking," I shot back.

"Tell me. Was being insubordinate on your list of qualifications?"

"Maybe if you'd bothered to look at my resume, you'd know the answer to that."

"I don't 'bother' to look at much of anything these days. Too much strain," he replied icily. "So why don't you dazzle me with your illustrious achievements?"

"I majored in English Lit at the University of Chicago and got my master's in Library Science. Graduated with honors, both times, *while* working to put myself through school. No, I haven't published a book, but I've had short stories published in literary magazines and anthologies across the world. And yes, one of these days I will get to my novel, but that's the least of my concerns right now."

"I'm positively awestruck." Gerulf sniffed and pivoted on his foot, carrying on down the garden path. As soon as I caught up to him again, he continued speaking in his eloquent —read: arrogant—manner. "Though I *am* curious. What is your grand strategy in waiting to work on your manuscript? Going to write it all in your head before you bother putting it on paper?"

I made a conscious effort to unclench my jaw when I answered. Though, I suppose it was easy for him to be haughty when he had a Pulitzer on his mantel, and I most certainly did not. "There *is* no strategy. I don't have time right now."

"That's nothing but an excuse."

"A bit hypocritical, don't you think?"

"Oh, I have the time, as you can see. Plenty of time."

"Then what's *your* excuse? Why isn't *your* book finished?"

"Because I don't want to fucking write it." He sliced a glare at me out of the corner of his good eye.

I'm sure it was meant as a warning to shut up, but I kept going regardless. "Why not?"

"I would ask you if you're writing a book with all of these questions, but I already know the answer is 'No.'" God, even his smile was sarcastic. Stunning and derisive all at once. Like the roses he seemed so fond of—beautiful, but full of thorns.

If I was ever going to get through to him, I needed to stop playing his juvenile games. Maybe if I focused solely on work, he'd realize I *was* a professional and I *was* trying to help. "Why don't you tell me what it's about. Maybe I can help."

He looked disappointed that I didn't rise to the challenge. I figured he was going to go back to ignoring me, but after a moment, he actually answered, minus the causticness. "A psychological thriller set in Chicago in the 1890s. Murder, betrayal. The usual."

Well, that didn't sound like the basis of an award-winner like everyone claimed. But, as with every book, it was the execution that mattered more than the simplicity of the trope. "Who's the murderer?"

He shrugged, staring out ahead of us and giving me absolutely nothing to work with.

"Ok. . . . Who is the victim?"

"Some guy. I don't know."

"So why is he murdered? For money? Revenge? Power?" I

113

was grasping at straws here, and when he shrugged again, I wanted to throttle him. "You had to have written down *something* for the publisher. Everyone has been buzzing about this book for *years*."

He stole a glance at me, the smirk back on his lips, like he knew how frustrated I was. Maybe, deep down, he shared the same frustration. "That's because Faye leaked the title, thinking the pressure would make me write faster."

"Who's Faye?"

His quiet laugh was closer to a snarl. "My fucking agent and former fiancée."

"Oh." Well, that must have been awkward. . . . And I'm sure it did not help his current situation *at all*.

"So, you see, this project has been cursed from the get go." Coming to an abrupt halt, he faced me with wide eyes. "Cursed!"

"Cursed?" I blinked at him, trying to connect the dots in my head.

"Give me. Give me the pen." He waved impatiently at my hip, where the notebook was sticking out of my back pocket.

I did as he asked, handing the items over with a furrowed brow. He snatched them out of my hand and started scribbling immediately. "Get an idea?"

Gerulf waved me away before turning and continuing on his walk. He was still writing, muttering to himself like a crazy person.

I wasn't sure if I should follow him or stay where I was. With the way he was favoring his left leg, I felt like I couldn't leave. Yet, he most definitely shooed me like a gnat.

In the end, I opted to return to the rose garden and wait for him there. He'd have to pass by on his way back to the house, so I figured it was a good spot to hover. And if he fell, or something, maybe I'd hear him yell.

About an hour later, Gerulf appeared on the garden path, *still* writing as he walked. He paused now and again to apparently argue with himself before burying his nose in the notebook, the pen darting back and forth over the page.

"Bring the typewriter," he said on the way by, not even slowing down.

I scrambled to my feet and grabbed the tray, hurrying after him. Whatever limp he'd had was practically gone and he disappeared with far more speed than I would have anticipated.

Maybe this was a good thing. Maybe this little burst of creative energy meant the next six months wouldn't be so terrible after all.

Six

Gerulf

The following morning, Zane's brown puppy eyes widened when I slapped a notebook on the dining room table next to him, nearly upending his cup of tea.

"Type that, and when you're finished, come find me," I said, pointing at the notebook in question.

He reached for it slowly, like it might bite him, and thumbed through the pages. "This was a brand new notebook."

"Yeah. And?"

Tucking a long, brown curl behind his ear, he went back to the beginning of my messy scrawl and settled in, apparently content to read right there instead of waiting until he was finished with breakfast. "These aren't just notes. This is . . . this is the story."

I couldn't help but roll my eyes. "Glad to see that master's degree really paid off."

Zane frowned up at me but refrained from further comment. Considering how feisty he was yesterday, I was surprised he didn't snap back with something. Surprised and a little disappointed, honestly. Maybe I needed that back and forth banter to get my brain working again.

But since I couldn't do anything else until he did his part, I left the dining room and retreated to the library.

That's where Zane found me a couple hours later, a stack of typed pages in his hand. He held them out to me with a blank expression, but I didn't miss the way he fidgeted as he stood on the opposite side of the antique desk.

"What?" I asked, knowing I'd probably regret it in two seconds.

"Nothing."

I stared at him, head cocked, waiting for the real answer.

"I think you should change the villain," he said in a rush, pinkness immediately flooding his pale cheeks.

"I'm not paying you to critique it," I replied, tossing the pages on the desk and leaning back in my chair, meeting his gaze head on.

"No, you're paying me to help you. And I'm telling you, the villain would be much stronger as a woman."

My brow furrowed as I considered the point. I wasn't opposed to the change, but I needed more—a valid reason as opposed to shaking things up for the novelty of it. "Why?"

"Because no one ever suspects them," he replied with a small shrug. "Society underestimates their capacity for evil. Leave red herrings for the first guy, Neal, like you already have. But July? The maid? Make her the real killer."

A feather could have knocked me over with the realization he was right. On more than one account. Why didn't I make the connection sooner? *Me*. Of all damn people!

He must have taken my silence for disbelief, because he hurried to my side and angled the papers toward himself, flipping through them quickly. "You've already laid the groundwork. See here?" He pointed out a passage as he spoke. "She's spiteful and vicious and hates the Chandlers. She serves them because she has to, but in her mind, she's superior. When the footman pointed out her lack of education and manners? Look how she reacted. She's vile, even though she tries to hide it."

"Get out," I murmured, taking the stack of papers back from him.

The warmth in his brown eyes disappeared. "But I—"

"Out!" I pointed at the door to emphasize the order and turned my attention to the papers.

Scribbling like mad on the back of the typed manuscript, I couldn't help but feel the weight of Zane's gaze on me as he made his way to the door with the speed of a snail. If he was looking for a pat on the head, he wasn't going to get it. I had a fucking book to write and I couldn't afford to be distracted anymore than I'd already been.

As the days wore on, we fell into a similar pattern. I would write by hand and deliver the pages to Zane to transcribe. He would return them to me as soon as he was done and stand around, shuffling his feet, waiting for me to practically beat his opinion out of him.

Until finally one day, he set the stack of papers on my desk and tapped them, offering his unsolicited thoughts. "I'm sure you're used to hearing it by now, but this is brilliant, Gerulf."

I made a face at him. "What are you talking about?"

"This. This story. These characters. The darkness is . . . insidious. When I first heard about this book, I thought it was going to be violent in an overt sense, in a way that we're used to. But this is worse. It poses the question: what do you do when you don't even feel safe in your own home? Where do you go? And what happens when that evil follows you? I think it's going to resonate with people more than they realize."

"You're just happy I made July the killer."

A flush spread across his cheeks and he looked away. "I

mean, I stand by that suggestion. I think it's part of what makes this book so good. Because it's unexpected." When his gaze returned to mine, a strange sensation fluttered through my chest.

Pride, that's all it was.

Taking a compliment—a genuine compliment from a flesh-and-blood person as opposed to critics' and bloggers' sycophantic praise. A compliment from someone who had read hundreds, if not thousands, of books. Someone who made it their mission to inspire a love of reading in others. Someone who had no idea where the story was going, but was already confident of its ultimate success.

I cleared my throat and forced my attention to the stack of fresh pages in front of me instead of him. "Thank you. You can—"

"Get out. I know," he said with a definitive nod.

"I was going to say 'stay.' If you want. I know you've been dying to properly catalogue the library."

His lips curved into a small, wary smile and his gaze was full of suspicion, like he was waiting for me to yank the proverbial rug out from under his feet. "You mean it?"

"Just try to keep it down. I, um, have this. To do." I picked up my pen and tapped the manuscript. "I can't be distracted."

"You won't even know I'm here." Zane pressed his hands together in barely contained happiness and backed away from me slowly. Once he was a few steps away, he spun on the ball of his foot and practically sprinted to the far end of the library, his chestnut curls bouncing on his shoulders with each step.

"Focus," I hissed at myself, dragging the papers closer and forcing my gaze downward to the task at hand instead of watching Zane float around the library like he was on Cloud Nine.

Seven
Zane

P er the contract, Sundays were supposed to be my one guaranteed day off, but given the fact I was perpetually on thin ice with Gerulf, I didn't push it. Knowing how much he generally despised my existence, I didn't want to give him any reason to fire me. So when he announced one Sunday I needed to drive him into the city, I was less than thrilled but went and got the car anyway. It's not like I could say "no." Besides, I was more irritated with the fact I wanted to be in the city anyway—just not with my boss.

Perceptive as ever, in the seconds it took me to nod in acquiescence to his request, Gerulf's good eye narrowed and he stepped closer. "Is that a problem for you?"

I shook my head mutely. I'm sure Papa would understand why I wasn't there, if he could understand anything anymore.

Apparently I wasn't convincing enough, since Gerulf brought it up again as we got on the tollway, headed eastbound.

"Any other time I ask you to do something, you do it without hesitation. Today, all I asked is that you drive a car to a city you used to live in and you're acting like I kicked a puppy right in front of you."

I tightened my grip on the steering wheel, trying to figure out the best way to phrase it without leading to more questions. "I just thought I would have the day off."

"Why? Did you have plans?"

"Maybe."

"Doing what?"

"It doesn't matter."

"I'd beg to differ. It seems to matter very much, considering how sullen you look."

"I'm not sullen."

"And now you're defensive."

"Do you scrutinize everyone this way?" I stole a glance at him out of the corner of my eye, not the least bit surprised to see he was watching me like a hawk. He always did. Whenever I was within his line of sight, it's like I could feel his gaze taking in every detail, every movement, no matter how small. At first it was unnerving, but then I started recognizing traits of myself in his main character. After that, I was simultaneously flattered *and* even more confused about where I stood with him.

"Only the people living in my house," Gerulf replied matter-of-factly, bringing me right back to the argument.

"I've never heard you question Mrs. Potter like this."

"Because Mrs. Potter doesn't lie to me."

I snorted and rolled my eyes. I wouldn't say "lie" was the right word, but she and Gilroy seemed to treat Gerulf more like their child than their employer—meaning they placated him and omitted upsetting truths, like trying to soothe a toddler on the verge of a tantrum. All in the name of keeping his blood pressure and his pain levels down, or so they told me.

"I'm not lying," I huffed after a minute. "I wanted to see my dad today. That's all."

"To do what?"

"Oh my God." I shot him another look. "What does it matter?"

He shrugged. "Just wondering what a twenty-something wants to do with their father on a Sunday that has him so crabby."

"First of all, you're one to talk about crabbiness. Second of all, it's none of your business. Just picture whatever you did with your dad."

"I didn't do anything with my dad."

"What?"

"My father was too busy to 'do' things. He was always working. And then he died."

"What about your mom?"

"Dead." He leveled an unamused look at me. "Want to ask about my grandparents?"

"No, I get the drift," I replied, adding, "I'm sorry," after a few moments. "My mom died too."

We fell into silence after that. It wasn't entirely uncomfortable, but I also didn't feel the need to break up the uneasiness by asking questions. I trusted he'd tell me where we were going the closer we got to Chicago. And he did.

He directed me to a vast medical complex surprisingly near my dad. Like, on the opposite end of where I needed to be.

"I shouldn't be long," Gerulf said when the car rocked to a stop in the circular drive outside a surgeon's office. Tugging up the hood on his black sweatshirt, he stole a glance at his watch. "Maybe an hour."

"Do you mind if I go to the hospital side? You can text me when you're done."

"Are you ill?"

"No . . . " Shit! I shouldn't have said anything. I should have just gone and made sure to come back before he was done and we'd never have to have this conversation.

"Then why are you going to the hospital?"

"You're not going to let this go, are you?"

He made no move to get out of the car and simply stared at me.

"My dad's a patient there," I mumbled, gripping the steering wheel tighter and refusing to look at him.

"Why couldn't you just say that?"

"Because I didn't want to get into it with you, ok? You already hate me. I don't need to give you anymore ammunition or have you questioning my dedication to this job."

"I don't hate you."

"Well, you don't like me," I said, finally letting my gaze slide to his.

He considered it for a moment before shrugging. I thought maybe he was going to keep arguing, or at least half-heartedly attempt to try and convince me I was mistaken. Nope. Without another word, Gerulf opened the car door and got out, closing the door on my incredulous scoff.

"He's unbelievable. Absolutely un-fucking-believable." Rolling my eyes, I pulled away from the curb and circled around the outside of the hospital.

Sadly, over the past few months, I'd been here so often I could make the trip blindfolded. Through the lobby, make a quick stop at the gift shop, up the elevator, and two right-turns to get to where I needed to be.

"Hi Papa," I said as I entered, with only the usual whirring and beeping sounds to greet me. I pulled the withered bouquet out of the vase by his bed and tossed it in the trash. The inside of the vase had gotten all scummy since the last time I'd been here, so I gave it a cursory rinse in the sink before refilling it and arranging the fresh roses.

"I'm sorry I haven't been around a lot lately," I said, leaning over to kiss his forehead, mindful of the scarred skin on his face, before easing into the chair next to him.

"This new job has taken up more of my time than I originally thought, which I guess is both good and bad. I'm actually learning a lot of what it takes to be an author. It's not as glamorous as people probably think it is. I'm pretty sure helping you file patents was easier." Running my palms over my knees, I settled in the chair. "You won't even believe who I'm working for, though. I can hardly believe it sometimes. Gerulf Prince! You know, the guy who wrote *Outside the Storm*. I think that was the only book I could get you to read that one summer. Then you wouldn't stop talking about it." I chuckled and shook my head at the memory.

"I hate to break it to you, Papa, he's an asshole. I mean, maybe he hasn't always been, but he certainly is now. I guess you can understand. Accidents tend to change people . . .

"His house is amazing, though. And he's *so* smart. He's kind of like you, actually. He gets these random ideas out of nowhere and then bam! He's off and running and I can barely keep up. He writes everything by hand now and I do the typing for him, since he can't do it himself anymore.

"There's something really interesting about seeing his thoughts come out on the paper, like when he scratches out words and rewrites stuff, or when his writing gets sloppy because he's going so quick. It's a different side of him. I thought it would make him happier, though, to be writing again. It's like he's going through the motions, but I don't think his heart is necessarily in this story.

"I don't know," I sighed, blowing off my own observation. "I'm no one. Literally, no one. I don't know anything about what it takes to be an author, let alone one at his level. Maybe after all this time he doesn't get excited by writing anymore."

I steered the conversation away from Gerulf and told Papa about Mrs. Potter and Gilroy and all of the other servants at Gerulf's house; how incredibly inviting they'd been, as if they were trying to make up for our employer's never-ending brusqueness. I talked about books and the weather, any random topic to fill the silence and let him know I was there, in case he could hear me somewhere inside his coma. And once again, I somehow circled back around to Gerulf.

"I don't know what else to do, Papa. I really want to impress him, but I'm starting to think that's impossible. He's probably the most frustrating person I've ever met." Shifting forward with a groan, I propped my elbows on my knees and buried my face in my hands. "I wish you were here to give me some advice."

"Are you about finished?" a voice said from the doorway. Not just any voice. Gerulf's voice.

Bolting upright, I looked in horror at the doorway. It was indeed Gerulf and not some figment of my imagination, like I'd desperately hoped.

Leaning against the doorframe, hood up and arms crossed, he stared at me with a blank expression.

"Fuck . . . " I squeezed my eyes shut and opened them again with a grimace. "How long have you been standing there?"

"Long enough." Double fuck.

"You said it was going to be an hour," I said, swallowing my nerves.

"It was going to be, but that was before I told Roger to fuck off and left."

"The surgeon?" I gaped at him. "The surgeon who made a special appointment for you on the weekend so you could avoid people? You told him to 'fuck off'? Just like that?"

Unperturbed, Gerulf nodded. "Yeah. Just like that." His attention moved from me to my father. He pushed off the doorframe, making his way closer to the bed. "What happened to him?"

"There, um, was an explosion. At his workplace. He's an inventor. I mean, an engineer. Whatever. Anyway, he was down on the production floor working on some prototype. I guess there was a buildup of gas or something in the air and all it took was one spark from static electricity." I glanced between my father and Gerulf, wondering what he was thinking.

The similarity between them wasn't just the fascinating way their brains operated—their disfigurement was as clear as day. While Gerulf had angry, jagged scars, Papa was covered in burns. Practically every part of him had been caught in the blast.

The doctors put him in a coma to recover, and once he came out of it, they were supposed to begin the painful process of skin graphs. But it had already been two months, and he wasn't showing any signs of improvement. None of the doctors had the nerve to tell me what I already knew—my father was dead. The machines were the only thing keeping his body alive, and it was going to be up to me to turn them off. Or whenever the insurance decided to quit paying for his care.

"I'm sorry," Gerulf said quietly, his gaze downcast. "I didn't realize you were dealing with this."

"We're all dealing with something, right?" I tried to crack a smile to lighten the oppressive weight in the room, but I'm pretty sure it looked more like a wince.

Clearing my throat, I got to my feet quickly and stuffed all of my emotions back inside where they belonged. Crying like a baby in front of my boss was *not* something I was prepared to do.

I said goodbye to my dad and hurried out of the room. Gerulf was right behind me, each step of the way. Part of me expected him to try to say something optimistic in the elevator or in the car on the way home.

He didn't.

He didn't because there was nothing optimistic *to* say. I knew the statistics, and he probably did too. Injuries that bad? A coma that long? It was only a matter of time.

Little did I know that time would come the following morning.

Gerulf and I had just sat down to breakfast, his latest stack of papers between us with two pens so we could make amendments as we talked, when my cell phone rang.

"It's the hospital," I said, staring at the caller ID, a block of ice forming in the pit of my stomach.

"Answer it," Gerulf said, glancing pointedly at the phone.

I shook my head and shoved it at him. "You do it."

"Zane, no! I—"

"Please?" My lower lip was already trembling, along with the phone in my hand.

Relenting with a sigh, he set his fork down and took my phone, answering it before it went to voicemail. "No, it's not," he said, cutting a quick glance in my direction. "He's here, but indisposed. I can take a message."

My throat seized and no amount of swallowing would get it to loosen. As soon as Gerulf's gaze dropped to his plate, I knew. It was *the* call.

Pushing away from the table, I slapped a hand over my mouth to keep the sob inside and got to my feet. I stopped at the far end of the dining room, far enough away for privacy but still close enough to hear what Gerulf was saying.

I tried to keep my ragged breathing in check by staring out at the gardens beyond the window. It was a dull, gray day. Wind howled against the glass. The leaves outside were falling like snow, swirls of red and orange and yellow. The gardens were mostly dormant, hunkering down for the coldest, darkest part of the year. I guess I was too—bracing for the coldest, darkest part of my life now that I was well and truly alone.

A warm, solid hand slid over my shoulder, squeezing gently. "I'm so sorry, Zane."

Tears slipped down my cheeks, but I didn't dare turn around. If I did, I'd end up sobbing hysterically on the floor for hours and I couldn't risk this job. Not now. Now that I had nothing else going for me and not when we were so close to being finished.

"If there's anything you need—"

"The food is getting cold," I said, dashing the tears away with the edge of my sleeve. "And we have a busy day. A lot of work to do."

"Yeah. We do." Gerulf gave my shoulder another squeeze and retreated across the room.

I expelled a shaky breath and wiped my eyes again before I rejoined him at the table. Funeral arrangements and assets and lawyers—all of it could wait another day. It would *have* to wait another day, until I could come to terms with this new reality.

I'd always joked with Papa that books were my life, but it was never more true than in this moment, when I had nothing. Helping Gerulf finish his manuscript gave me a reason to keep going, trivial as it was. It was a lifeline in a sea of uncertainty, a lighthouse to give me direction, when all I wanted to do was close my eyes and let the water swallow me whole. Once upon a time I'd cursed Gerulf for being an insufferable asshole, and now, I thanked God I had him, even if I'd never tell him that. Ever. Not in a million lifetimes.

Eight
Gerulf

"I think I can fit one more," Zane said, dangling precariously on the rolling library ladder and trying to wedge another book onto the top shelf.

"This is not how I typically spend New Year's Eve, you know," I said, looking up at him and trying to feign my exasperation. It wasn't really that hard. My idea of ringing in the new year was to be tucked in bed by ten, leaving the celebratory nonsense to the rest of the world.

Zane's idea of a good time, apparently, was finishing his pet project in the library. It was finally catalogued "properly," according to him, despite my best efforts at stalling him. Because once this last stack of books was shelved, he'd have nothing else to keep him here. There was only one chapter left in *Loss of Twilight* and his contract was nearly up. He'd go from a daily presence in my life to . . . nothing. A constant companion turned into a ghost. The thought left me with a strange heaviness in the center of my chest.

"You mean you don't have a private firework show for the staff and bust out your best champagne?" Zane grinned down at me from the top of the ladder, his face half-obscured by his crazy, curly hair.

"You realize when you fall, I'm not going to catch you, right?" Nevertheless, I tightened my grip on the ladder, hoping I had enough strength to at least keep it steady for him.

"I'm sure that has more to do with your poor nerve endings and not your feelings toward me," he replied with a chuckle.

"Considering you've been on my last nerve since the moment I met you, I'd say they're one and the same."

Laughing softly, he climbed down the ladder. I shifted to the side to make room for him, but held on in case it tried to roll away. His fingers grazed mine on one of the rungs on his way down. The movement was so quick, the barest trace of a touch; I wasn't sure if it had happened at all until I looked at Zane's face. Crimson flared along both cheeks and he diverted his eyes. "Sorry."

"It's ok," I replied, watching him descend the rest of the way. Instead of walking away, he stood at the base of the ladder and snuck a glance at me.

"I don't think I've ever properly thanked you, by the way," he said, shifting on his feet.

"For what?"

"Making this time of year a little less lonely without my dad. I know you know what it's like. So I appreciate you helping me . . . adjust. To a new normal."

"Well, I'm technically paying you to be here, so. . . . It's not like I did you a favor." Jesus, it was hot in here. Why did Gilroy feel the need to turn the heat all the way up *and* light the fireplaces?

Zane's cheeks flushed deeper, especially after he lifted his dark gaze to mine. "Wow. Way to make me sound like a hooker or something."

"If anything, I'd say that makes you an escort. Unless you were planning on putting out . . . then that might qualify." Oh my God! Clearly, the filter between my brain and my mouth had ceased to function in the last ten seconds. I blamed the heat. It must have short-circuited something.

The shocking part, though, was the longer I thought about it, I kind of didn't care about my blundering banter. Flirting? Jesting. I'd call it jesting.

Whatever it was, I was struck with the sudden desire to see how scarlet Zane's skin could get. It had been an increasingly amusing pastime for me, especially since his father passed. I made a conscious effort to cut back on the curt remarks and dismissive tone and swapped it for *this*, giving him a hard time with just enough sarcasm, so he knew I was joking. And it worked. He still had moments of sadness, but for the most part, he went back to being the bright-eyed, pain in my ass he was on Day One.

For his part, Zane was torn between laughing and sputtering out some sort of defense, looking anywhere *but* my face. "I mean—I don't recall reading that in the job description . . ."

"That wasn't a 'No.'" I watched his expression carefully, wondering when exactly I'd lost my mind and why I cared what he was really thinking—or feeling.

"Well, it wasn't a 'Yes.'" Zane stole another glance at me, immediately looking away when he saw my gaze was still fixed on him.

"So it's a 'Maybe'?"

"It's a bad idea," he said softly, shifting his weight from one foot to the other and leaning against the ladder, still not looking at me. "Even hypothetically."

A pang of rejection hit me right in the gut, harder than I thought was possible anymore. Somehow the teasing had turned real and the rebuff had heat prickling along the back of my neck. "Because of this?" I gestured vaguely to my face.

"Because you're my boss," he replied without even missing a beat. His gaze lifted to mine again, sadness lingering in his dark eyes. "And because I know better than to want what I can't have. Chasing straight guys never ends well."

"Zane, I—"

The rest of my words came to a screeching halt as the library doors slammed open, banging against the wooden paneling on the walls. The all-too-familiar sound of high heels clicking on the polished floors unleashed a tidal wave of fury inside of me.

Zane and I both turned toward the blonde bitch sauntering into the library, completely ignoring the fact Gilroy was hot on her heels, chewing her out for not waiting in the foyer like she'd been told.

Shedding her fur coat, Faye tossed it at Gilroy's face with a smirk. "Be a dear and hang that up."

He looked at me for further instructions, but I was too enraged to speak, so I merely nodded.

"Who's this?" Faye asked, setting her lecherous sights on Zane. "An intern? No, no. I'm guessing a caretaker. Right?"

Before Zane could answer, I stepped between them, as if it would somehow shield him from her toxicity. "He's no one. Want to tell me what the fuck you're doing here?"

"Still have a temper. What a surprise," Faye replied with a dazzlingly vicious smile. I couldn't help but notice one of the absurdly expensive bags I'd purchased for her was swinging from her elbow as she crossed her arms beneath her breasts, pushing them up even higher under her emerald dress, as if that trick still held any appeal.

"I'll, just, um . . . yeah." Zane pointed at the door as he eased toward it. He exchanged a long look with Faye on his way by. She bit her lower lip suggestively; meanwhile, he made a face at her and quickened his steps.

The minute Zane shut the door, she dropped the sex kitten act and rolled her eyes. "Don't act like you're not happy to see me." Her blonde hair shifted over her shoulder as she tilted her head, her lip curled. "Well, as much as you can see, anyway."

Even though glaring didn't have any effect on her, I did it

anyway, my hands instinctively balling at my sides. "Once again, Faye. What are you doing here?" I repeated it at an insultingly slow pace.

"Maybe if you'd pick up a phone once in a while, I wouldn't have had to come all the way out here. But since you couldn't do that, here I am." She shoved a hand into her purse and rummaged around, unearthing a stack of papers folded in half with a rubber band around them.

"I told you, stick to buying books, sweetheart. You don't have the talent for writing," I sneered at her.

Her shrill, mocking laugh was like an icepick in my eardrum. "Oh, Gerulf. Witty as ever. Glad to see that accident didn't fuck up your brain as much as your face."

"You fucking bitch."

"Save that fight for court, Ger." She smashed the papers into my chest and shoved me for good measure. "You're going to need it."

I didn't have to read beyond SUMMONS to send my heart rate into overdrive. "You're suing me?!"

"You're damn right I'm suing you!" Folding her arms over her chest, one hip popped to the side, full of self-righteousness. "The past two years have been hell for me!"

Spiking the paperwork on the floor, I stepped over it to close the distance between us. "Hell for *you*?! Can you even hear yourself?"

"Oh, here we go. Trying to play the victim again?" She uncrossed her arms and shoved me in the chest even harder than before. "No one is going to buy that, Gerulf! No one!"

Undeterred, I advanced on her again. "Look at what you did to me!"

"*You* were driving," she shot back, shoving me backward as if to emphasize her insult. "You did it to yourself!"

"You yanked on the wheel, you crazy bitch! You're lucky we're not dead!"

"I wish you were, you miserable bastard! You cost me my

job at the agency by being a selfish asshole, refusing to turn over your goddamn manuscript! Now I have nothing because of you!" She lunged forward, slamming her fists against any part of me she could reach, punctuating each word with another strike.

Normally I could take her attacks, but every time her rings dug into my left side, pain surged through my ruined body. Half the time that side was numb and refused to function the way it should, and yet when it came to pain, everything was magnified. How the hell was that fair?

I turned my face away from her flailing and tried to grab her wrists. As soon as I got a hold of her, I pushed her away from me as hard as I could.

She stumbled backward on her heels, crashing into one of the sofa tables. Grabbing the table, she steadied herself; her face contorted with rage. Before I even realized what she was doing, she picked up one of the porcelain figurines and hurled it at me.

I had just enough time to shield my face. It bounced off my shoulder and plummeted to the parquet floor, shattering.

Another one came right behind it. Down the row she went, launching each and every one of my mother's antiques at me. Some broke against my body, others waited until they hit the floor.

"For Christ's sake, Faye!" I winced and hid my face as another figurine sailed through the air. God knows I couldn't afford to lose the other eye. "Enough already! You've made your point!"

"Fuck you, Gerulf!" Instead of taking the wind out of her sails, all my words seemed to do was infuriate her more. She'd run out of figurines, but she was by no means finished.

Snatching the vase off the end of the table, she stormed over to me and swung it as hard as she could at my head. I threw my arm up, trying to block it, but my reaction was too slow. The glass shattered against my skull at the same time I heard Zane shout.

"What the fuck are you doing?!"

I blinked away the stars and looked up as he ran over, anger and confusion written plainly on his face as he wedged himself between us. I thought he was protecting Faye from me until his arms wrapped around my torso and forced me backward, *away* from her, making himself a barrier.

Before Faye could lunge for me again, Gilroy appeared and seized her from behind. She shrieked like a banshee and tried to free herself, but Gilroy held on, wrestling her toward the door.

"Call the police," Zane shouted at someone. "And an ambulance!"

"No," I said with a shake of my head. Pain flared in my skull and I immediately regretted the movement. "Don't call anyone."

The confusion on Zane's face was immediately replaced with outrage. "Look at you! She needs to be arrested!"

"Just let her go." I pressed the heel of my hand against my head and sucked in a sharp breath, dropping it immediately. My palm was streaked with blood. Why did head wounds have to bleed so much? The only positive was that it was on the side that was already hideous.

Faye continued to scream at me, even as Gilroy forcibly removed her from the library, then the house. It was more of the same: cursing my existence; wishing I was dead; hoping I'd die alone and miserable in this house. Once upon a time, I'd confused her anger with passion. The accident had given me clarity into what a fucking abusive bitch she was, but it was too late to do anything about it. I'd already put up with it for years—pressing charges now seemed like a moot point. I just wanted her out of my life for good. Thankfully, it sounded like I got my wish now that the people at Lumière Literary Agency finally got sick of her shit too.

"Come sit down," Zane said softly, taking my elbow and gesturing toward the couch.

"I'd rather go upstairs. I don't want to be here when they come clean up this mess." I cut myself off before "*Again*" slipped out. God knew the maids had their fair share of cleaning up shattered glass of all sorts after her rampages—lamps, bottles, windows, and now priceless antiques.

Zane nodded and steered me around the debris field. Bits of glass and porcelain still crunched beneath our shoes, but for the most part, we avoided it on our way out of the library.

"What a fucking mess," I muttered.

"Don't worry. Lisette is already on her way."

I wasn't talking about the library, but I wasn't going to correct him either. Squeezing my eyes shut, I leaned against him as he guided me up the stairs, one arm wrapped securely around my waist.

Nine
Zane

"Don't lay down yet," I said, kneeling quickly to slide his shoes off before he inadvertently got glass in his sheets. "And the shirt," I said as I got to my feet.

"Not a fucking chance."

"Seriously?! You probably have glass embedded in the fabric. Plus, you're bleeding. But go ahead. Ruin your million-thread count Egyptian cotton sheets."

"They're eight hundred," he countered with a glare.

"Take your shirt off, Gerulf!" It probably wasn't the best thing in the world to be yelling at him after yet another head injury, but there was no other way to get him to listen to reason. Maybe if he wasn't so stubborn, this could have gone a lot smoother.

Huffing, he did as he was told. *Finally*. Wadding up the shirt, he threw it to the side and immediately crossed his arms over his chest, cementing his gaze to the floor.

It wasn't a mystery why he'd wanted to keep his shirt on. At one time, you could tell he'd been built, but much like his face, the left side of his body was also disfigured. It was more than scars, though. His left shoulder and bicep were clearly mangled, like all of the muscle had been cut away, leaving him with only lumps of skin and bone down to his elbow. His torso was crisscrossed with scars—burns and surgical, evidence of his own skin grafting. Some parts were the same color as the rest of him, but others ranged from dark red to an alarming purplish hue to stark white scar tissue. It looked painful, even now.

I didn't let my gaze linger, just long enough to determine he wasn't bleeding from his body. "Don't move," I said, holding up a finger and darting into the master bathroom.

Rummaging around in the cabinet beneath the sink, I grabbed the stuff I thought I'd need and piled it onto a hand towel before snagging a washcloth from the linen closet. As I wet it under the faucet, I stared at the wall in front of me.

The wallpaper was a patterned navy, so dark it looked black with the lighting. But it wasn't what *was* there so much as what *wasn't*. There wasn't a mirror. Doing a quick mental scan of the house, I suddenly realized there weren't *any* mirrors in any of the rooms. Not in the front entryway, not in the parlor, not in the guest room I was staying in. None.

The revelation made my heart hurt even more for him.

Wringing out the washcloth a bit, I scooped up my supplies and returned to Gerulf's bed, setting them down on the nightstand.

Blood had ceased trickling out of his hairline, leaving macabre trails on his skin. That was good, but there were smaller spots on his face that glinted every time he moved.

"Shit. I think there's glass in there," I said, rifling through the first aid box for some tweezers. Tipping his chin up with one hand, I angled his face away from me and went for the biggest chunk first.

He uncrossed his arms, allowing me to move closer to see what I was doing.

Plucking out the piece of glass with the tweezers, I wiped it off into a wad of gauze and kept going. Every so often, a muscle in Gerulf's cheek twitched, but he was otherwise silent throughout the whole process. I'm sure after everything he'd been through, this was a cakewalk.

"Are you ok?" I asked quietly, removing the last shard from his forehead.

"I'm fine."

"You should still call the cops." I set the gauze and tweezers down and picked up the washcloth, wiping away the spots of blood as they bloomed on his skin.

"It's not worth it."

"She's psycho, Gerulf. She could have really hurt you."

"She already did. That down there was just . . . " He sighed and shook his head. The fact he didn't even want to argue was alarming. The man *lived* for arguments, for snappy comebacks, and sarcasm as thick as molasses.

"Did she really cause the accident?" I asked, trying to keep the emotion out of my voice.

"You were eavesdropping?" His head turned toward me, his good eye narrowed, until I pushed it back the other way so I could clean the blood out of his hair.

"When she's shouting loud enough for the whole house to hear, I wouldn't call that eavesdropping." I was totally eavesdropping. I mean, I happened to be standing near one of the vents down the hall that also happened to more or less echo everything being screamed in the library. When glass started breaking, Mrs. Potter told me not to interfere, that Gerulf would be even more pissed at *me* than that psycho in stilettos. He could be as pissed as he wanted, but there was no way in hell I was going to stand there and *not* do something.

After a stubborn moment of silence, Gerulf sighed. He practically wilted in front of me, exhaustion replacing his usual bravado. "Yeah. We were in the Alps, on our way back to the resort from dinner. Arguing. Shocking, I know. I don't even remember what had her so pissed off. I guess it doesn't matter. She started hitting me, and the next thing I knew, she grabbed the fucking wheel. I threw her off, but it was too late. I overcorrected, and we rolled. And kept rolling, right off the road and down the side of that fucking mountain.

"I took the brunt of it. I was trapped for . . . I don't know. It felt like forever. I was pretty much crushed on that side, which wasn't good, but then a fire started to spread. I don't remember anything after that, just pain and gagging on the smell of burning plastic. Mark said they thought I was dead when they finally pulled me out.

"I couldn't even leave Switzerland; I was in such bad shape. Mark stayed with me for a while, then he brought Mrs. Potter over. She took care of me until I could fly home." He squeezed his eyes shut and swallowed thickly.

"Where was *she* at?" I didn't even want to say her name. I knew I couldn't do it without snarling like some deranged guard dog.

He chuckled and swatted my hand away from his hair so he could look up at me. "That bitch flew home the next day and practically cleared out my bank account. She told everyone it was for my treatment. So imagine my surprise when Mark told me I was fucking broke. Oh, and the engagement was off. She left me a voicemail. Whoa! Watch it!"

"Sorry." I jumped and moved the washcloth away from him, setting it on the nightstand. I hadn't even realized I was squeezing it so tightly until I spotted the drip marks on his pants.

"So that's why I have to get this book finished," he continued, letting his gaze drift away again. "The money from the advance is gone, to pay my medical expenses. If I don't deliver, they'll take me to court to get the advance back, plus money that I don't have for punitive damages. And now she's trying to fucking sue me for pain and suffering from the accident."

"She can't do that!"

"It's America. She can and she did." He looked up again, his brow furrowed. "Why are you so mad?"

"Because it's bullshit! She can't do that to you and keep getting away with it!"

"It's America," he repeated slowly. "She *can* and she *did*. No one believes a man when he says his fiancée smacks him around or when she jerked the steering wheel. They take one look at us and one look at her and decide it can't be true."

"It shouldn't be that way."

He stood and shrugged, as if there was nothing else to say on the matter. I didn't know where he was going or what he was planning on doing once he was vertical, but my sappy little heart derailed whatever he was about to do.

Without even thinking, I took a step closer and wrapped my arms around his neck, hugging him as tightly as I dared. I mean, the line between personal and professional was already blurry, so who cared if this obliterated whatever was left?

For months I'd smelled traces of his cologne whenever we were near each other, a dark spiciness that suited his wealth and attitude perfectly. But up close, like this, I got the unfiltered version. His scent, the warmth of his skin—it all stoked feelings inside of me I should *not* have for any straight guy, let alone my boss.

Predictably, Gerulf tensed against me. "What are you doing?"

"You seem like you could use a hug," I answered truthfully.

"I'm not—I don't—I don't hug, Zane. People don't—"

"Just accept the hug, Gerulf."

He cleared his throat, but at least he quit arguing. For all his flirting or teasing or whatever it was earlier, he sure did clam up when actually presented with human contact. I couldn't help but wonder how long it had been since anyone *had* hugged him. Or simply touched him, beyond what was required for his numerous medical appointments.

I don't know how long we stayed like that; me holding him and him barely even breathing as he stood there. Awkwardness and self-doubt crept in with each passing minute until I was thoroughly convinced Gerulf would fire me as soon as he got over the shock of forced human contact and that all of his earlier teasing had been just that. Teasing. Trying to get a rise out of me since he'd backed off a bit on the sarcasm front. And I was an idiot to think it was something, anything, else.

Forcing myself to pull away, I was surprised when I didn't get far.

Gerulf's hands touched my waist, so lightly I almost thought I was imagining it. Gradually, his hands moved further, until his arms were entirely around my waist and our bodies were pressed together in a proper embrace.

I tried to squash the feelings inside and cram them back into the box they belonged in, but the longer we held each other, the more they came rushing out. When his lips grazed the side of my neck, the truth hit me like a freight train.

I loved him.

I didn't want to.

I didn't plan to.

And yet, I did.

I loved his brashness, his cutting sarcasm, his brilliant mind. I loved his pride, his independence, and the way he was when it was just the two of us, when he finally let his guard down.

Our chests rose and fell in tandem, like puzzle pieces slotting together. "Gerulf . . . "

He turned toward me, caressing the side of my face. "Yes?"

"I need you to fire me," I whispered.

A small crease formed between his dark eyebrows. "Why?"

"So I can kiss you without feeling guilty."

"Zane." He cleared his throat softly, and my heart seized, refusing to start again until he spoke. "You're fired."

The words had barely left his lips when mine crashed against his. He threaded his fingers through my hair and angled my head for a deeper kiss. I melted against him, not caring if this was right or wrong. All I cared about was right in front of me.

Ten
Gerulf

The next morning, I woke up to something I never thought I'd see—Zane, asleep in my bed. If I wasn't looking at him, if I couldn't feel his skin against mine, I would have thought I was dreaming. There was no way someone like Zane could ever want to be with someone like me. Yet there he was.

My initial happiness withered until only fear remained.

What would he say when he woke up?

What would he *do* when he woke up?

Would he leave? Was he serious about that whole firing thing or was it supposed to be symbolic?

Was this a onetime thing? A novel way to usher in a New Year? Or worse—a pity lay?

I thought he enjoyed it. He *seemed* to enjoy it. The end result told me he enjoyed it. But what if it was all for show? Oh, God! What if he was doing this for blackmail? He knew about Faye, though. And he was smart enough to know you couldn't squeeze blood out of a turnip. Unless he was counting on future royalties, like that bitch was.

I nearly jumped out of my skin when his hand slid over my chest.

"You know you look angry, even while you're asleep?" Zane murmured as he shifted closer, burying his face in the side of my neck.

"Now, how would I know that?"

"God, you're grumpy in the morning." Still, it didn't deter him from pressing himself along the length of me to get as close as humanly possible.

The central question in my brain came out in a rush. "Did you mean it last night? Or was it jus . . . " A mistake? A game? Boredom? I couldn't even say the words. *Any* words. Mainly because I was afraid if I said them out loud and he said yes, I'd feel like an even bigger idiot than I did already for thinking this would be something it never could.

"Hey . . . " Zane propped himself up on an elbow and caressed the side of my face. His fingertips ended up tracing the jagged scars in my skin, but I couldn't tell if it was on purpose or just because of how fucking big and hideous they were, making them hard to miss. "What's the matter?"

I pushed his arm out of the way and sat up, but he didn't let me out of bed. He grabbed onto my bicep—the one that *wasn't* mangled—and used it to stop me, dragging himself forward so he was right behind me.

"Gerulf, wait. Did I do something? Or say something wrong?"

"No. Of course not."

"Then talk to me."

"Things are different in daylight. *People* are different. The choice you made last night—"

"Last night was perfect," he said softly, reaching for my face. I yielded under his touch, allowing him to turn me so he could meet my gaze. "Don't second-guess it because the sun is up. And please don't push me away. Not now."

"How can you stand to touch me? To see me? Like *this*?"

"Like what?" His dark brows dipped as he ran his thumb along one of the scars on my face. When he reached the end, he let his hand drift to my shoulder and down my left arm, back over to my torso and the patchwork of skin and scars. "I see *you*, Gerulf. I don't know who you were before and I don't care. *This* is the version of you I fell in love with." He squeezed his eyes shut and swore under his breath, retracting his hand. "I'm sorry. I didn't—that wasn't—what I *meant* to say—"

As soon as I processed his exact words, I caught his face between my hands. Pulling him closer, I pressed my lips against his, silencing whatever ridiculous apology he was going to try and make for *my* insecurities and silencing whatever ridiculous doubts lingered for either one of us.

Pieces of my heart unfurled themselves in the wake of his words, pieces I thought had shriveled up and died years ago. Turned out they were simply dormant, waiting for the warmth of an overdue spring.

Never breaking the kiss, Zane shifted forward into my lap and nudged me to lay down. Once I was reclined beneath him, his lips trailed off to the left side of my face, kissing my scars with zero hesitation.

Caressing his jaw, I turned him toward me again so I could look at him in daylight. His pale skin contrasted with the flush in his cheeks and the darkness of his long, curly hair. It was his eyes I focused on, a dark brown so warm and guileless in a world of artifice. And when he smiled? Soft and knowing, with a quiet confidence I'd leaned on more than once over the past few months? How could this be anything *but* love?

"I love you too," I said, in answer to his unspoken question.

His smile brightened as he leaned down, kissing me.

IT WAS mid-morning by the time I managed to stumble down the stairs to what was surely a cold breakfast. I didn't care. For the first time in *years*, I could say I was happy. I'd eat lukewarm pancakes and rubbery eggs and drink cold coffee for the rest of my life if I got to experience this feeling every day.

Mrs. Potter appeared in the hallway as soon as I hit the bottom step. Wringing her hands together, she looked like she was on the verge of tears. "Sir, there's a problem, and I didn't want to bother you with it, but I don't know what else to do."

My happiness evaporated in an instant. "What's wrong?"

"It's Mr. Beaumont. He's . . . he's gone!"

I blinked, my brow furrowing. "What do you mean—"

"Gone!" she repeated, practically shouting the word. "He always comes down for breakfast promptly at 7:30. Without fail. Even on the weekends. Even after his father passed. Chef has it timed perfectly. So today, when he didn't come down, Gilroy went to his room to make sure he was alright, and he's gone! The bed hasn't been slept in and there was no trace of him!"

"No trace of who?" Zane asked, materializing at my side, his damp hair smelling like my shampoo. "What's going on?"

"Mr. Beaumont!" Mrs. Potter threw her arms around his waist and hugged him tightly. "We thought you'd left! We thought something happened!" After a moment, she shoved him away with a scowl, all concern for his welfare gone in the blink of an eye. "Where have you been? We have searched this whole house up and down for you! *And* the gardens, despite the foot of snow out there!"

"I, um . . . " He shifted awkwardly next to me, flushing. "I was, um . . . "

"With me," I finished. To solidify my point, I laced my fingers through Zane's and waited for Mrs. Potter to put two and two together.

"With you? But—" Her confusion was immediately replaced with a delighted shriek as she squeezed an arm around both of our waists. "I'm so happy! Oh, we need to celebrate! Forget everything else. We need something special for today." She whirled away from us, hurrying down the hallway, yelling for Gilroy and the cook to get the champagne.

"You realize she's going to tell the whole house, right?" Zane asked with a laugh.

"I have a feeling they've already been talking about it. They're not as sly as they think they are." I tugged him forward and slipped my other arm around his waist, pulling him up against me.

"Yeah, no. That kitchen is straight out of Downton Abbey with all the gossip flying around."

"Then let's give them something to really talk about." I grinned before pressing my lips to his, one hand tangling in his hair.

Kissing me in spite of a smile, Zane twined his arms around my neck and let his body mold to mine, as if by instinct.

A door opened down the hall. There was a small gasp and a giggle, and the door closed again. Lisette, if I had to guess.

We broke apart with a laugh of our own.

Zane reclaimed my hand, and we set off for the dining room at an easy stroll. "Are we going to finish your manuscript today?"

"No."

"No?"

"No. I fired you, remember?" I shot him a glance out of the corner of my eye, smirking.

"It's daytime now. You can rehire me."

"Only to fire you again when the sun goes down?"

"Yeah. Exactly."

"I appreciate your attempt at professionalism, but that ship has sailed."

"Meaning?"

"You're fired and you're staying fired," I said, making sure there was zero trace of humor in my tone.

A scowl crossed his face. "Gerulf."

"I'm serious. Do you know what a sexual harassment lawsuit would do to me? I can't afford to get caught having sex with my assistant, violating God only knows how many labor laws. Literally. Cannot afford it." I finally cracked a smile to let him know I was kidding.

Zane scoffed and rolled his eyes. "I hope you have a good severance package, then."

"I think you'll be pleased."

"I hope so. Or you're getting a one-star review on Indeed."

"Ouch! One star?"

"Author is an asshole. 0/10 do *not* recommend working for him."

"Well, there goes your reference."

Laughing, he grabbed the front of my shirt and pulled me in for another kiss, one bound to make the staff buzz even more if they saw us.

Epilogue
Zane

Six Months Later

A s soon as the delivery truck rumbled away from the front step, I was out the door in a flash. I snatched the package off the ground and tore into the cardboard on my way back inside, kicking the door shut behind me.

It took everything in me not to completely open the package. But this was Gerulf's book baby. It was only right *he* was the one who got to see it first.

"The proof for *Loss of Twilight* is here," I said as I walked into the library. Gerulf was sitting on one of the antique couches next to the fireplace, staring at nothing. I eased onto the cushion next to him, frowning. "Are you ok?"

He blinked himself out of his reverie and nodded. "Mhmm. Did you open it?"

"No. I mean, I opened the box for you, but I didn't take it out." I held the package out to him, but he pushed it back toward me.

"You do it."

"It's *your* book."

He leveled an unimpressed look in my direction until I sighed and set the box in my lap so I could open the cardboard flaps. Pulling out the brown packing paper, I fished the book out of the depth of the box and turned it over.

Staring back at me on the front cover of a hefty six-by-nine hardcover was my name. Zane Beaumont.

The title was sandwiched between *both* of our names. In the same font. Same size. Same central location. As a co-author. Gerulf Prince *and* Zane Beaumont.

"Gerulf . . . " I didn't even know what I wanted to say. All I could do was stare at my name, in print, gleaming up at me from an actual published book.

"This book wouldn't have happened without you," Gerulf said, squeezing my thigh gently. "You saved my career, Zane. Hell, we both know you did more than that. But this was the only thing I could do to show the world how special you are."

A swirl of emotions radiated through me—happiness, shock, love, more shock. I threw my arms around his neck, hugging him tightly before claiming his lips in a kiss I hoped conveyed all of those feelings, along with my gratitude.

After spending every day with this man for almost a year, he was still finding ways to surprise me. First as my cantankerous employer, who wanted absolutely nothing to do with me until one random day he didn't look at me with contempt anymore. Then our relationship blossomed into something . . . more. Calling him my boyfriend wasn't enough to encapsulate everything he meant to me. And now he'd gone and done this—submitted the manuscript to his publisher and, without my knowledge, included me as a co-author even though he didn't have to.

When I took this job last summer, I thought I knew what I was getting into. I had *no* idea. By some miracle, it all worked out and I wouldn't trade any of it, even our rocky beginning.

Not all fairytales start with "Once upon a time," but they all end with the same thing—*they lived happily ever after.*

And so would we.

Fairytale Ending?

BY DANIELLE MERCHANT

One

You've heard the old saying, "Good things come to those that wait," or the one that goes, "The longer you wait, the better it will be." Patience, right? It all boils down to patience.

Let's use coffee as an example. You have your basic instant ground coffee; you dump a scoop of brown powder into a mug of, ideally, boiling hot water. Stir, and then there you go! You have yourself a mediocre cup of caffeinated brown liquid —all within sixty seconds or less. Or, perhaps a step up, you have the Keurig Machine; known for its convenience and perfectly portioned K-Cups. If you wait three to five minutes, you will get yourself slightly better than the instant stuff, a cup of coffee. Next, you have your good ole traditional pot of coffee, coffee. Now here, you have a few options. You could buy whole beans, grind them the night before, and really make yourself a good cup of joe, or you could go with less prep work and buy the already ground coffee beans. Either way, this coffee method-making process takes a little more time and effort. But in the end, you get a nice mug of steam—a step up from the previous two. Last, for my comparison's sake anyway, is the French press. Now, for those of you who have never used a French press, trust me, it takes a lot of time, measurement, and patience. So much time that I am not going to waste the paper space explaining it. But, for those of you who know or have had a cup of coffee from a French press, you people know it's worth the wait.

And *that* is what they all keep telling me, dear reader. Everyone from my best friend to my sponsor and even my Mom.

"It'll be worth the wait."
"It will happen in God's time."
"Good things come to those that wait."

Well, I am sick of hearing this, and more so, I am tired of waiting. So, I am taking matters into my own hands this Valentine's Day. My favorite holiday, the holiday of love, is three weeks away. I spent last year's holiday on the couch with my cat and a pint of Häagen-Dazs ice cream all night. This wouldn't be a bad way to spend an evening except that I had gotten dumped five hours prior to my sugar and Netflix binge. My intentions were not in the right place. I am over him now, though. That was a year ago, and I haven't talked to or seen him since that heartbreaking morning. If I am being honest, I am not over him. Like at all. But I would never tell him, or anyone for that matter, the truth.

Anyway! This year—I want—I deserve a trip to the city, a dozen red roses, and non-alcoholic champagne on the beach at midnight. I don't think my dream date is unattainable.

So, I will be busy orchestrating my love life for the next few days. Then once I find him and get him to fall head over heels with me, he will have two short weeks to plan out the perfect Valentine's Day.

"Hey, Siri," I call out to my latest version of the iPhone. "What are the top ten dating apps of the year?"

"Here is a list of the top ten dating apps. Would you like to see more?" The pre-programmed female voice answers my question. *Gosh, I love technology.*

"No, Siri," I reply. "Ten is plenty," I say out loud to myself. Ten, actually, is way too much. I'll try the top three and go from there.

I thumb my screen up on my phone to see the top suggestions for dating apps. Without hesitation, I download the first three listed.

Tinder
Bumble
Facebook Dating

Alright. Let's get to work.

Before I choose the best of the worst photos of me, let me paint a picture of what I look like physically. I am 5' 9 "; I have an athletic-to-thin frame and a figure comparable to a teenage boy. Flat everywhere. But what lacks in my body type I make up within my face. I have porcelain clear, lightly tanned skin with a few freckles sprinkled across my nose. I have naturally wavy honey-colored hair. The California sun does a good job highlighting my hair with her brilliant rays, and my hairstylist does an excellent job of covering the gray hairs that have sprouted in full force this past year. My eyes are as blue as the ocean I live near. Most would call me beautiful; some might call me rare.

So you get it, I'm not horrible looking. And also, I drive a reliable car, have all my teeth, and most of my bills are paid. If you're thinking what I am thinking, this perfect Valentine's Day date goal is not entirely unrealistic.

After I carefully select, then upload my profile pictures, I continue with the standard questions like height, what are you looking for, and do you drink. Then, I get to the "About Me" section. And I freeze. How do I describe myself in 100 characters or less?!

Okay, here goes.

I spend the next sixty minutes of my life typing, rewording, and retyping on the tiny little iPhone keyboard. But after that hour, not only do my thumbs hurt, but I have a Pulitzer Prize-worthy little paragraph on why you—perfect ten on social media but probably more like a seven in real life—you, a man, should swipe right on me.

Alright! I hit the create account button on the app, and just like that, I am putting myself out there. I am taking control of my love life. I always have and always will say, if you don't like something about you or your life, change it! Don't just sit there, enduring and complaining, do something about it! You are the artist of your own story! I'm sure you can feel my enthusiasm jumping off the page for being in support of having control of your life. Now, don't get me wrong. I am slightly spiritual, and I sort of believe that there is "a power greater than me." But in all honesty, I just agreed to that last one to get through my step work in AA. Those blue book thumpers, man, they are all about that higher power.

My point is, I am unhappy with my love life. I. Can. I Will. Change it.

Once I am satisfied with my Tinder profile, I hop down from the barstool I had been sitting on and close the curtains to my kitchen windows. I live in Petaluma, California. It's a lovely, beautiful town. And close enough to the city to be just far enough away. I have a one-bedroom apartment close to the central part of town. Just me and my cat. Butter and me. It's not the most fantastic apartment, but I have seen worse. It's like right below middle-class apartments, but barely above section 8 housing. Anyway, I don't plan on being here for long. I don't know where I'll end up, but it won't be in Northern California for the rest of my life. I want to get married, have a baby, own two homes, and publish my first novel within the next two years. I think I can do it.

Where was I? Right, so I plop down on the oversized

white reading chair that lives in the corner of my living room. When I say, "oversized," I mean it. It's probably the second-largest piece of furniture in my apartment. That's only true because I don't have much furniture to compare it to yet; I have only lived here for three months.

Before I can get situated in my chair, my phone vibrates and makes sounds like it is blowing up—Tinder alerts. Messages like, "You've been super liked" and "You have a new potential match" keep flashing across my screen. I start feverishly and recklessly swiping on guys' profiles. Some I match with, and upon closer examination, I am like, "Wait what?! Why did I even swipe right on him? He is 5' 6", and I am 5' 9". It would never work." I gotta slow down and pay more attention to the details on these men's pages.

I almost forgot. I'm sure all you readers are dying to know what my, a barely published writer's, dating profile says. Right? Well, I'm going to let you read it, but first, two things.

One, I wouldn't say I like to brag/talk/share about myself.

Two, I write fiction stories about other people and their lives. My life is boring.

Now that I have hopefully lowered your expectations of my dating profile, here goes!

Courtney
Hi! Thank you for checking out my profile. I'm not very good at writing and especially not so great at writing about myself! But here it goes! I am 29, a single white female. I live alone in a tiny home with my cat, Butter. She's my peanut. I work from home, I work out at home, and I love to cook. I like going out to dinner, but I am more of a homebody. I enjoy reading. Well, that's enough about me. I can't wait to hear from you!

And that, readers, is my first ever online dating profile. Thirty minutes and fifteen matches later, I am over it for tonight. I quickly download the other two dating services, but I don't have the energy to create one more profile, let alone two. So I'll do it in the morning. Exhausted, I peel myself from my reading chair and pour my tired body into my bed. Before I know it, I am sleeping, dreaming of sunshine and rainbows.

Two

T he sun wakes me before my alarm does. My alarm is set for eight every morning, but I tend to wake up when the sun does. This happens most mornings, and I am happy about it. On impulse, I reach for my phone to check my Tinder account.

Really, Cort? I think to myself. *This is how you're going to start your mornings now?* I hope my Prince Charming reveals himself sooner rather than later. This could get addictive and time-consuming. I have a few new matches, but I'm more excited about the three messages in my inbox.

I click on the first one. Blake. He is a 6′ 3", muscular, milk chocolate-colored man. He likes reading, working out, cooking, and banging.

Yes, for one of his likes, he listed banging. As though it is an extracurricular activity comparable to tennis. Knowing this and still swiping right, I should not be shocked when I read the message he wrote to me.

Blake: *hey, sexy. Your body is banging. I like it.*
Me: *Unmatch and delete.*

He didn't even capitalize the word "hey." The subsequent two messages aren't much better than the first. I don't reply and I unmatch myself from all three men.

I WALK over to the counter where the Keurig machine sits. I take out my favorite coffee mug, a blue and white ceramic cup with the word "Dream" and a giant black butterfly printed on it. Misty, my best friend, gave it to me one Christmas. As the coffee is brewing, I stare at the other two dating app icons on my phone. I am not too impressed with the first one. I cross my fingers that the next two are better.

The gurgling sound of the coffee machine signals that my cup of joe is ready. I take my mug of steamy goodness and plop my butt down on my favorite chair. Before my coffee cup even touches my lips, my phone rings. My guess is that it's one of two people; my Mom, who is back home in Wisconsin, or Misty, who lives on the other side of town. The nicer side of the city that screams, "I have made it!" I will have one of those homes one day. When I make it. Anyway, since I have already talked to my mom this morning, it has to be Misty!

"Hey!" I am right. It is Misty. She sounds chipper, probably from the three cups of VERY strong coffee she has every morning. Actually, that's just Misty. Always full of energy, no matter what time of the day.

Did I mention she is a retired drug dealer and that I am a sober alcoholic? That first part isn't true, but the second part is. I am, in fact, in recovery from alcohol. Misty is a stay-at-home mom and a part-time lawyer. That's how we met. She was my public defender almost five years ago. And man, a lot has happened in those five years. Misty has since then gotten married, had two beautiful little boys, and now is one of the best defense lawyers Sonoma County has ever seen. She makes like a million dollars an hour. A fair cry from her public defender days.

As for me, I am a barely published author (I have a few journal articles published in "Grapevine" and one very short story in an anthology of love stories). It's ironic I made the cut because I have many failed attempts at love. Apparently, I can write about love, just not live it. And in all honesty, there really haven't been that many attempts, just the one that I thought was love. Zach. That's it, he's the one. Now I spend my nights alone with my cat, eating "supposed-to-be-good-for-you ice cream," but it tastes like crap and watching reruns of *Friends*. At least I spend my time now better than five years ago when I spent my evenings drunk at a bar somewhere and making horrible—terrible—choices. Especially when it came to men.

Trust me; if you knew Misty and me each separately five years ago, you would agree with me when I say we both have come a long way in the past half-decade or so.

"I'm at your door. Let me in."

I put my cup of caffeine down and walk over to buzz my best friend in. I don't particularly like when she shows up unannounced, but it's better than her never showing up at all. So, I am happy that she is here. I open the door and let her in.

Twenty minutes later, we are both seated in the living room; I am back in my chair, and Misty is on the loveseat. She is reading my Tinder profile, scrolling through the pictures I had uploaded. She has this weird look on her face, one I've never seen before.

"You're selling yourself short here." She sits up straight. "If I can't talk you out of this, I, at least, can help you out with your profile," she says as she holds my phone up toward me and points with her index finger to the screen, which now displays a photo of me.

"What? I look hot in that photo," I say as I snatch the cell phone back from her.

"Cort. You need to appear like you got it all together and all you need is a man to share it with! You need pictures that make you look sophisticated, confident, educated." She is doing motions with her hands, which she does when she gets excited. "If you are looking for Mr. Right, your future husband, you gotta sell yourself! This ain't Wisconsin, Cort. You're in California, Sonoma County to be exact. Competition is high," she says. "I mean, look at me and Ryan. As soon as I got that promotion, he was all over me! Men want a partner, an equal. Not somebody who just lives off his money. Plus, you gotta be hot too. There's a fine line. It's exhausting." She finishes with a deep exhale.

"That sounds complicated." And personal, almost as if she is projecting herself onto me. I don't dare say this out loud, so instead I quickly change the subject back to me. "And I am not looking for my future husband, Misty. I want a hot man, preferably over 6'2", with a job and a car to fall in love with me before Valentine's Day so I can spend the holiday drunk on lust and not have to think about Zach breaking my heart a year ago. That jerk; I am still so mad at him. I mean, how could he? Okay. I am not over him."

I didn't mean to say that. Like any of it. I mean, I was thinking it in my head, but then somehow I put it in words, and it just fell out of my mouth.

"Shit." *That* I mean to say.

"I knew you weren't over him." My best friend nods; she understands. And she can read me like a book. "Okay. Here is the plan. The new plan." Misty stands up, something she does when she gets excited. "We are going to make you the hottest Tinder, Bumble, Facebook marketplace, whatever. The hottest dating app profile page that your phone is going to be blowing up with messages!" Next, her voice gets louder. "Screw finding Mr. Right. We are going to find you a ton of Mr. For The Night!" She is practically yelling now. "We have a lot of work to do," she whispers. "Come on." She grips my hand, and with my other free hand, I grab my phone from my chair. We are off to do make-up!

And then, we spend the next six or seven hours, basically the rest of the day and well into the night, taking pictures of me in my apartment, me down by the ocean, one of me kissing a frog, and another one of me "accidentally" bending over to pick up something someone dropped. Which they did, and I returned it to them. I just didn't know my butt was the subject of attention during my random activities of kindness.

It did turn out to be a good photo.

Anyway, at the end of that eight-hour job, I have a new plan with a new goal. To match, date, and break the hearts of as many men from social media dating sites as I can. Well, not actually break their hearts, but maybe toy with them a little. Just enough to get over what's-his- name, Zach, the love of my life. Yes, I will kiss as many frogs as it takes to get over my Zach!

Misty has left and gone home to her lovely children and adoring husband, and here I sit, potentially wasting the time that I should be using to write, searching for men just in order to be able to try and get over a different man. *What has my life come to?*

Alright, new profile pictures complete. They scream fun and sexy, but not crazy. Like a guy could think, she looks responsible and mature, but knows how to have a good time, too. You know that rap song, "freak in the sheets but lady in the streets" or something. It's like that. *Trust me.* Okay, up next is the bio. The "About Me" section isn't great, but it's not as bad as the first. Read it for yourself. What do you think?

Courtney, 29
I'm going to let my photos do the talking this time.

I hit the yellow "complete profile" button on the Bumble app. And just like that, I am up and running on two online dating platforms. It's nearly two in the morning, and I am exhausted. I get up from my chair and head to the bathroom. Twenty minutes later, I am under my plush white duvet comforter fast asleep.

Three

When I awake, it is bright out. I reach over and grab my phone from my nightstand. It's nearly noon. I am shocked and a little upset with myself for sleeping in this late; I must have slept through my alarm.

I have about a million texts, Instagram messages, and dating app announcements, but what stands out to me is a little bubble, a text from a number I recognize. A ten-digit phone number that will forever be engraved on my mind.

It's a text message from Zach. *What could he possibly have to say?* He broke my heart into a million little pieces when he left a year ago. Not once did he ever call to apologize, explain himself, or see how I was doing.

Well. Sorry, Zach, but I'm not going back. I am not reading your message; I will delete it, as I deleted you from my life 357 days ago.

Shit. I opened it.

"Hey. I know I should have reached out to you sooner, but I never knew what to say."

That's all it read. It was sent three hours ago. Okay, clearly he still doesn't know what to say, or it would have read more. I swipe the message left until a little red garbage can icon shows up, and then I trash it. Where it belongs.

Okay, let's see what these new boys have to say! I don't know whether it's the revamped profile or the dating app itself, but Bumble is producing the results I had hoped for!

Two hours later, I have three dates lined up over the next four days. I need new clothes. And to paint my toenails. I am going to be busy. Satisfied, I put down my phone, leap up from my bed, and I call Misty.

"Hey, sleeping beauty," she answers on the first ring.

"He texted me," I blurt and instantly regret doing so. *Why don't I think before I speak?* It's not like I don't tell Misty everything, but when it comes to Zach . . . well, she has always been "Team Zach" and thinks I overreacted. I take offense that she doesn't see my side. I mean, come on. He was the one who said we could date other people. And the one who left! Albeit, he apparently went across the country to take care of a sick, long-lost relative. But he didn't even call.

"Zach?" I swear she's psychic.

"Yeah," I say. "Why did you guess Zach?"

"He's back home. I figured he would text you at some point," she begins. "I think he got back two days ago. I ran into him at Target."

And she's just now telling me this?!

"I didn't tell you because I didn't want you to get all worked up." *See. Psychic.* "So. He texted you. This means you unblocked his number then, yeah?" she finishes.

"Yeah," I say. I have no defense or justification on this one.

"Well, did you respond?" she asks.

"No," I answer. "I deleted it. And didn't save his number." That last part doesn't matter much because I have it memorized.

"Okay," she pauses, likely trying to think of a way to

change the subject. "So! Any hits on Bumble?" Easy subject change, but well-played best friend, well-played.

We spend the next twenty or so minutes discussing my matches, the conversations with a few select potential suitors (somehow, I am still matching with guys under 6'), and the three dates I have lined up.

"So. I need to go shopping," I say in conclusion.

"Well, hop to it, girl. Your first date is tonight! Text me a picture of what you decide to wear!" I can tell Misty wants to be done with this conversation and probably has more adult-like things to attend to. For example, getting her attempted murder client to agree to a deal, so he doesn't get death row. Or bring her daughter to softball practice—either way, way more important things than my dating life.

When we hang up, I mentally catalog all the clothes in my closet and decide I do, indeed, need a trip to Ross. When you're trying to ball on a budget, you go to Ross. I look at my phone for the time again. T-4 hours and thirteen minutes until act . . . I mean, date one.

It's time for hair and makeup!

Four

Date 1

I 'll save you the sob story here. My date, Dave, showed up at the restaurant an hour late; he said he couldn't find parking, which doesn't make sense because, at the end of the date, he asked me for a ride home. I said no and got him an Uber. (He claimed he didn't have the app on his phone, which I think is a lie because I also paid for dinner. He claimed he lost his wallet on the way here.) So, an hour late, and I'm pretty sure he was drunk when he showed up. He, at the very least, was not sober. I felt like I was pulling teeth trying to get him to talk, and when he finally did, he started crying about his cat that had just run away. It wasn't like a tear in his left eye crying; he was full-fledged sobbing. Like the floodgates had opened and couldn't be closed.

When he got into his Uber ride, he said he would call me. And he did, four minutes later, and when I didn't pick up, he texted me when he got home, multiple times. He said he had a really good time, which I'm confused about if we were on the same date or not because I don't think hysterical crying in public is something I would classify as a good first date.

Anyway, tomorrow is date number two. I think it's going to go better than the first one. I mean, it has to. I silence my phone and crawl into bed. I am ready to put this day to bed (no pun intended) and start tomorrow's date with a set of new eyes! My baby blues are heavy with fatigue. I fall asleep quickly and sleep a dreamless slumber.

"I AM TELLING YOU, MISTY," I say into the phone the following day. I have my iPhone barely cradled between my ear and shoulder, trying to keep it in place while I Swiffer my floors and apply mascara to my long eyelashes with my other free hand. "Like, ugly cry. And then he said that I reminded him of his ex-girlfriend, whom the cat is named after." I put the tube of mascara down on my nightstand. "I mean, I feel bad for him and all. Remember when I thought I lost Butter, but she was hiding in my dresser sock drawer?" I remember that day like it was yesterday. I was a wreck.

"Well, you have another date tonight, right?" Misty says.

"Yeah, I do. In like," I hold the phone far away enough to see the time, "in like three hours. I need a nap," I say.

"Alright, get some rest, take a shower, make a pot of coffee, put on some heels, and get out there!"

I wonder why she is being so supportive of my mission to break innocent men's hearts in an attempt to repair mine.

"I'll start with the nap," I say. Misty knows I never wear heels.

"Good idea. Call me later!"

Date 2

Pictures lie. First, the guy was short, and second, he had hair in all of his profile pictures. What's worse is that he kept on trying to kiss me. He even stood on a step stool and asked,

"Will this help?" as he craned his neck with his hairless head up toward my face.

He stood there on his tippy toes, stretching up at me with his eyes closed and lips puckered. I felt so bad for the guy, and also, I did say I needed to kiss a few frogs before finding my prince, so I bent toward him, and when I leaned in for the kiss . . .

"Achoo!" Like, into my open mouth. It was awful and disgusting, and I didn't know what to do, so I ran away.

Date two was NOT better than date one.

———

"YOU ALWAYS SAY, third time's a charm, right?" Misty says. I'm on the phone with her the following day.

"Yes. And three is my lucky number, but Mist, I just don't know. I literally got spat in my open mouth." My body cringes, replaying the scene in my mind.

"Yeah, that's disgusting," she says. "Well, short of being kidnapped and tortured, how much worse could date three be?" *Great.* She probably just jinxed me.

"Fine." I give in, again; I'm not sure why Misty supports me going on these dates. "Hey," I begin. "Why are you supporting me? You hated my idea and dating apps in general from the get go. I thought, for sure, when I said I was ready to throw in the towel and surrender to the idea of being alone for the rest of my life, you would be there to catch it," I finish.

"Honestly, Cort. I'm waiting for you to wake up and realize that Zach didn't do anything wrong and that he is a good guy. You were lucky to find one prince in a lifetime. What makes you think you're going to find a second?"

And. There it is. Team Zach has spoken. I want to hang up on her immediately, but I did that once, and she gave me the silent treatment for a week. Apparently, it's rude.

So instead, I reply, "I don't think that's going to happen.

You seem to forget *he* left *me*. He said it was okay to see other people, and he didn't call. For a year."

"You blocked him. How do you know he didn't call?" *Why does she continue to defend him?* "Well, Cort. As much as I would love to continue to play Dr. Phil with you, I gotta pick the girls up from school. They have a half day today."

I am pleased to hear this, and that she is the one to end our conversation, so I don't have to hang up after all.

"Okay, well, I'll talk to you later," I say into the phone.

"Yep. Love you," she says before hanging up.

I want to chuck my phone across the room and put an end to any and all lines of communication with the opposite sex. Knowing that my first thought is usually wrong, and that I can't afford to replace a smashed phone, I set it gently down on the kitchen island and walk over to my writing desk. I fire up my laptop and get to work on my book. My publisher wants a love story. If I can't find love in real life, maybe I can fabricate it on paper.

I start feverishly typing away for the next four hours, and when I am finished, I have the beginning of an epic love story. The disappointing part of it is that it will never be mine.

When will it be time for my fairytale ending?

Five

Date 3

L ike I always say, third time is a charm! Ryan is his name. He looked even better than his profile pictures, which was a good start, especially compared to the last two dates, which I still don't know how shorty pulled off looking over 6' in all of his photos.

Ryan is 6'2" with dark, neatly trimmed hair. He has eyes that are bluer than mine. The first ten minutes of our date, I had trouble making eye contact with him and he probably thought I was nervous. Which, shockingly, I was not. Our conversation flowed with ease, topics ranging from gas prices to favorite holiday movies (we agreed on *National Lampoon's Christmas Vacation* as a top pick but *Elf* a close second) to trips we hope to take in the future and the biological difference between men and women. It was all going so well!

The kicker, I know you're waiting to hear what it is, the kicker is that Ryan downed four extra dirty martinis in a matter of an hour and a half. And he doesn't seem affected at all. This, my friends, would be called tolerance. Clearly, Ryan drank a lot and often. Most people would be stumbling out the door after two, but Ryan breezes through the restaurant's front door with grace. He walks me to my car, and like a perfect gentleman, he gives me a single peck on the cheek and asks if he can see me again.

Without thinking, I answer, "Yes, when?"

"How about tomorrow?" he asks.

I pause for a minute, pretending to be mentally cataloging my social calendar, but in all reality I know I am wide open.

"I think that should work. How about I text you when I get home?" I say.

"Please do." And he leans past me to open my car door, and I step into the driver's seat. He holds the door open a minute longer, looks at me, and says, "Courtney, I must say. You are even more beautiful in person. Your pictures don't do you justice. I am going to have to send Bumble a thank-you letter for finding you." He closes the door, and before walking away, he taps his pointer finger knuckle against the window. Then he walks off toward his own vehicle.

I sit, staring out of the car's front windshield. It was a good date, far better than the last two. I make a mental pros and cons list.

Cons
He's not Zach.
He drinks a lot.

Pros
He's tall.
He's handsome.
Dating him gets me off dating sites and closer to my Valentine's Day date.
He likes me.

Clearly, the pros outweigh the cons. I turn the key in the ignition and my little reliable Toyota Corolla revs to life.

Adjusting the rearview mirror, I catch a glimpse of myself in it; I am smiling. I drive out of the restaurant parking lot and hop on the 101, headed home. I resist the urge to call Misty, knowing that if I tell her the details of my date (like the number of drinks that were consumed on Ryan's end), she would immediately turn my smile upside down. Instead, I connect my iPhone to the car's Bluetooth, and Alicia Keys' song "Girl on Fire" comes on. I turn the volume to its max and sing along.

Six

" S o the date went well, then?" I'm on the phone with my mom the following afternoon, giving her the highlights from my date. "He sounds like a gentleman." I shared with her how he opened my door, slid out the chair to the table, kissed me goodnight on the cheek, and asked when he could see me again. I left out the excessive alcohol intake for now. Maybe he was nervous and doesn't always drink that much. I don't believe that to be true, but hey, a girl can dream.

"He was! And he's handsome. He must have an excellent job because he drives one of those battery-operated cars and mentioned something about having a membership to Fountain Grove Country Club." I'm talking fast; something I do when I'm excited but also when I'm lying. "And he dresses well! I am going to have to splurge on a new outfit."

I decide I'll inform my mom of his drinking habits if they are the same or similar again tonight.

"So, where is Romeo taking you tonight?" I love that my mom plays along with my hopeless romantic tendencies.

"To this Italian restaurant up in the hills. I forget the name of it, but it sounded fancy," I answer.

"I bet any restaurant in the mountains is fancy. You will have to send me pictures," she says.

"I will."

We spend a few more minutes on the phone, mainly talking about me, which happens often. She says she doesn't mind and that my life is much more interesting to talk about, especially since she is now retired.

"Alright, kiddo, have fun tonight. You deserve it. I love you."

"I love you more," I reply with our typical good farewell routine.

"Love you mostest; I'm the mom." She always wins this one.

I hang up and look at my phone for the time. I have four hours to find the perfect dress, paint my nails, apply a tanner, and I have to shave. I better hop to it.

RYAN ARRIVES at my apartment to pick me up precisely at 6 pm. I give myself one last glance in the mirror before answering the door. I almost don't recognize the reflection staring back at me. My hair, which I spent an hour straightening then curled with an inch thick curling iron, is lying flawlessly below my shoulders. My skin has a sun-kissed glow thanks to Neutrogena spray tan, and I spent more time on my eye shadow than I ever have to achieve that smoky effect the women have on those YouTube tutorials. But hair and makeup aside, it's the dress that makes me distinguished. I found that perfect black dress every girl dreams of owning. Of course, I can't afford to actually own it, so I am keeping the tags on and will return it after the date. I managed to hide them well enough using double-sided Scotch Tape. The little black ensemble cuts down to a V in the front, giving the illusion that I rock a C cup, which isn't true. It hits two inches above my knee caps to show off my slender toned legs and hugs what little curves I do have perfectly.

Feeling sexy and confident, I open the door to my apartment.

"Wow," Ryan says. He is holding a bouquet of lilies, my favorite flower. He extends his arm to hand them to me as he gives me a light peck on the cheek.

"Did you know," I start to say as I accept the flowers, "lilies are my favorite?"

"No. I didn't," Ryan says. "I just, well, roses are so cliché, and the flower shop was out of dandelions."

I smile and press the flowers gently to my nose. They smell amazing. "Thank you. Let me get these in water real quick, and then we can go."

Moments later, Ryan and I walk, hand in hand, down the stairs and out the front door of my apartment complex. When we get to the street, I notice he is driving a different car this time, a red convertible Lexus. He releases my hand to open the passenger side door.

"In case I forget to tell you at the end of our date—" He holds the door open as I get situated in the front seat. He looks like he stepped right off of the cover of GQ magazine. "I had a fabulous time tonight, Courtney."

My heart melts as he closes the door to the luxury sports car. I watch in awe of his appearance and gait as he walks around the front of the vehicle and gets into the driver's side.

We drive in shared silence to the restaurant, and for this, I am grateful. Had we been immersed in a deep conversation like the evening before, I would have missed the breathtaking scenery. The mountains appear to kiss the sky. I have driven through these hillsides a hundred times, simply to see the view and get to the other side of the mountain. Just passing through. Tonight is different, though. This time, there is a destination for my date and me among these trees. Tonight, I belong here.

When we arrive at the hillside restaurant, a valet meets us at the car to park the vehicle. He opens my door and offers a hand.

"Madam," he says as he gently and eloquently assists me out of the luxury car. It all feels like a scene I would write in one of my books, and I eat it up as though it's flourless chocolate cake.

The entrance to the restaurant is spellbinding. There are a handful of gold-plated water fountains, lush green trees that seem to not have been affected by this year's drought, and purple wisteria hanging from all around us. I feel like I stepped onto a page from the book, *The Enchanted Forest.*

Moments later, we are seated at our table. White linens cover the tops of the surface; symmetrically placed matching ceramic place settings are on each dinner table. Crystal glassware and more purple flowers are the finishing touches. Next to the dinner sets, more than I find necessary, is a silverware set. I wonder if there is a proper order of use for the three forks, two spoons, and a single knife I see in front of me.

To say the view is breathtaking is an understatement. The walls are floor-to-ceiling glass windows, and outside, the mountains as far as the eye can see. There is a small patio with four tables. Soft Italian-inspired music plays in the background, and from my position at our table, I can see a large wood-fired oven made of white-washed brick. It is the most beautiful restaurant I have ever set foot in.

Within seconds of Ryan and I sitting, we are greeted by a statuesque, 6'3" brown-haired beauty. She just might be the most beautiful creature I have ever seen. I know what you may be thinking, she is so tall! And she is, but her feminine face and features diminish any masculinity her potentially intimidating height may offer.

"Mr. Baker." I take it she and Ryan have met before. Until now, I didn't even know his last name. "It's a pleasure to see you again so soon," she says with a specific type of smile that makes me wonder if the two know each other from outside the restaurant.

To my surprise, I do not feel threatened by the thought of the stunning waitress and my date potentially having personal relations. In fact, I don't much care if they even have had sex on this exact table! I wonder if that means I don't care for my date. My thoughts are interrupted by Ryan ordering for us.

"Your crab cakes," he says. "I just can't get enough of them." He replies with that same type of smirk.

Minutes later, a bottle of expensive-looking wine appears for Ryan and a glass of San Pellegrino for me. Moments after that, the crab cakes appear. One bite in and I can see why Ryan, Mr. Baker, finds them irresistible.

So far, all is going well, except for the fact that Ryan is on his third glass of wine, and we haven't even ordered our main course. Also, he and the waitress seem to have some secret communication between their smiles back and forth, and it makes me feel a little uncomfortable. I am pretty sure when Ryan said the thing about the crab cakes, he was referencing some inside joke between the two of them. I shouldn't have suggested them as an appetizer when he asked me, "What looks good?"

When the crab cakes are finished (they were delicious), I excuse myself to the lady's room because the tag on the dress I'm wearing (and intend to return to Nordstrom tomorrow) is shifting. In order to save me any embarrassment from being caught red-handed, so to speak, I need to reapply the double-sided tape.

As I am walking back from the bathroom (tags now securely tapped on my skin), I look at Ryan sitting there. He is so handsome and generous with this date, the flowers, and his sweet compliments on my appearance. Despite all of that, though, when I gaze at him from across the room, I find myself wishing it is Zach I am returning to. I mean, Zach and I would never be at a restaurant like this, but, nonetheless, I find myself longing for my ex. Images and memories of Zach and I invade my mind. Him and I driving out to the beach with a pizza at midnight just to watch the sunset. Or that time when I thought I lost Butter, I called Zach, and he rushed over to my apartment to help me look for her. We scoured the perimeter of my apartment complex for almost an hour, just to come back inside to see her nuzzled up in my sock drawer. Tacos trucks, Yogurt Time, and coffee dates. Sweatpants and Netflix after an AA meeting on Friday nights. Those were our favorites.

My mind strolls down memory lane, and because of this, I am not watching where I am going. I collide with a waitress, our waitress, who is bringing a creamy white pasta dish to another table.

Bam! And just like that, I am covered in shrimp and Alfredo, and my plan to return this dress goes right out the window. Alongside it, my dignity.

Following my display of innate clumsiness, there is a commotion in the restaurant. Our graceful, model-like wait-ress apologized to me, even though I ran into her. Ryan rushes over to the scene of the crime, rescuing me from further humiliation, and before I know it, we are back in his sports car, headed down the 101 to my apartment.

When Ryan drops me off, he shockingly asks to see me again.

"Are you free tomorrow?" We're both seated in our respec-tive seats—he, the driver, me, the passenger.

"I am," is all I manage to say. I smell of fresh fish and heavy whipping cream. I am mortified and want to get inside my apartment and hide under my covers sooner than later.

"Great. I'll pick you up at noon. We will go golfing." He

leans into me, giving a small kiss; this time on my lips. I don't hate it, but in the same sentence . . . Zach.

As I make my way up the stairs to my apartment, I think, *Great. What am I going to wear this time? Also, why didn't I get a say in this? I hate golf.*

Seven

T he following day, Misty and I are sitting at Peet's Coffee; she is sipping a large caramel macchiato with a blueberry muffin next to her while I have a small house coffee. No cream, no sugar.

"You know, they say psychopaths drink their coffee black," Misty says to me while taking a large bite of her fruity pastry.

"Oh, yeah." I roll my eyes. "And who are 'they'?"

Sometimes I feel like Misty undermines me. I don't think she does it on purpose. I think it's just who she is. It used to bother me, boil my blood. I have gotten so used to it by now that it doesn't even phase me anymore.

"Professionals. Ya know, like psychologists who study human behavior. I watched some Netflix documentary about it." Misty is wicked smart. Obviously, she is book smart, she is a lawyer, but she also has common sense and is street smart. Despite that, the woman believes anything she watches on Netflix is true.

"Well, then, I am a sweet psychopath," I say as I reach for the sugar caddy that sits in the middle of the table. I grab a pink packet of artificial sweeteners and flick it in between my fingers. I tear the top part off, dump its contents into my coffee mug, and stir with a spoon.

"Right," is all Misty says. I think I won that one.

"So, give me all the juicy details!" Misty rubs her palms together, and I proceed to fill her in on my date with Ryan from the night before.

"So, Prince Charming is a player," she concludes. I told Misty about the flirting between our waitress and Ryan last night. "I mean, what do you expect? You met him online."

She's not wrong, I guess. I don't want to give her any more fuel for the fire, so I leave out the part about destroying my dress.

"You know, Cort. I am only supporting you in this dating scheme because you seem to think it will help," Misty's voice softens. She cares.

"Help what?" I already know what her answer will be.

"Help you get over Zach. My question to you, and you don't have to answer now is, why? What did he do that was so bad that you won't even take his phone calls?" Misty asks.

"How do you know I won't take his phone calls?" I answer with a question.

"Well, first, I know you. And second, I ran into him again the other day. He mentioned it. I just kinda played dumb." I doubt that the last part is true; Misty would never play dumb.

"I don't know, Mist." I lean my elbows on the table and cradle my head in my hands. When I look up, I am trying to hold back tears. "It's just, he left. And the way he left, and what he did, or more so, what he *didn't* do while he was gone. It's like he didn't . . . no, he never cared."

I desperately want to change the subject. Something I do well and often when I am stuck in an uncomfortable conversation.

"Where can I buy a golf outfit?" I ask. "Cheap."

Misty sighs. She is familiar with my tactic. "Sports Basement," she answers without hesitation.

"Alright, I'm going to run there; talk to you later?" I grab my white rimmed Gucci sunglasses, a birthday present from Misty, from the table and start to stand.

"Are you okay?" Misty asks me as I collect my Matt & Nat pouch hanging from the back of the chair.

"Yeah. I just, I'm a little anxious about this afternoon. Golfing. First, I hate it, and second, I am not good," I say. Before Misty can inject her opinion, I add, "But. I like Ryan. So I'll suck it up. I'm going to go find a killer golf outfit. Fake it until you make it, right?" I wink as I walk out of the cafe and toward my parked car. I can't help but think, if it were Zach, I wouldn't be stressing (again) about what to wear for a date I don't particularly want to be going on.

Ten minutes later, I pull into the parking lot of Sports Basement. Thirty minutes after that, I walk out $200 broker. Misty was right, though; I found the perfect golf outfit.

———

RYAN and I get to his country club at two in the afternoon. He spent the entire ride there telling me about the club amenities and the kind of members that belong (to an outsider, they might think he was bragging, but Ryan has this natural humility quality about him), and let me just say, they sound lovely. Still, they do not sound like my crowd. My kind of people hang out in AA rooms and community rec centers.

"You look fabulous," Ryan says as he unloads our golf clubs from the back of his Jeep, the third car I have seen him drive.

"Thank you." I accept his compliment with ease because I know I look great in my matching Nike outfit. I'm wearing a tight, slate gray skort with a white three quarter length tee. Both articles of clothing have the Nike swoosh logo printed on them, signifying their importance and worth. Unfortunately, the short/skirt combination is a little too tight, and I sat with a permanent wedgie the whole trip here, but I'm hoping that it will work itself out once I get moving around on the golf course.

Ryan hands me a golf bag, an extra set he said he had just lying around. I have it over one shoulder as we make our way into the country club. As we walk through the extravagant doors, I feel what I imagine Julia Roberts' character in *Pretty Woman* felt like in that department store—a fish out of water. Ryan must have sensed my awkwardness because he grabbed my hand, gave me a short but enduring kiss on my lips, and told me to wait while he checks us in and gets the golf cart.

I drop the heavy clubs to the floor and take a deep sigh of relief. I start doing four-square breathing, a calming technique I learned in rehab years ago. Then I mentally list what I am feeling. I feel out of place, uncomfortable (physically and emotionally), and I really just want this day to be over. Can't we just do what ordinary people do, Netflix and chill?! If I make it to the next round of dates with Ryan, I will suggest just that.

Ryan heads back toward me, and simultaneously, my skort creeps up my behind again. I perform a little shimmy at my hips to try and work it out, but it fails. It's stuck up there. Just when I think I will have to live with the awkward feeling, someone comes and pats Ryan on the back. He turns to the friendly stranger, and in that split second, I reach behind me to position the clothing article back in its appropriate position. As Ryan turns around, I do a small hair flick with my ponytail and give him my million-dollar smile, hoping he didn't see my little wedgie removal performance.

"Alright, hot stuff," he says with a pat on my butt. "Let's go hit some balls." He winks.

The sun is hot and bright. I feel as though my skin is literally baking under the sun's intense heat, and I quietly shame myself for not bringing along my sunscreen. I hate getting sunburn. Not only because of the damage it does to your skin, but I also believe it screams "irresponsible" when walking around looking like a lobster.

Ryan golfs like a pro. I wouldn't be surprised if he indeed is one. He looks the part in his Easter egg blue pressed golf slacks, white RLX polo shirt (I only know the brand name because of its logo embroidered on his left chest pocket), and matching light blue and white golf shoes.

I, on the other hand, didn't get the golf ball off the tee on the first shot. I picked it up and threw it a few yards away when Ryan was distracted, looking at something on his phone. The second hole, I hit the ball into the pond, which is natural talent because the small body of water is *behind* us. So now, here we are at the third hole. And my skort is creeping up into that uncomfortable position between my butt cheeks again, and Ryan is all eyes on me, so I cannot risk picking it out this time. I am going to have to grin and bear it.

Eight

"Wait, you what?!" I am on the phone with Misty the following morning.

"Don't make me repeat it." I just finished telling her about Ryan and my time on the golf course.

"You hit him . . . in the head . . . with a golf club." It's not even a question she's asking. She is just summarizing my mortifying date.

"It was an accident," I defend myself. "And I didn't *hit* him with my golf club. The stupid thing flung out of my hands and landed on top of his head. My hands were so sweaty from the heat, and my ridiculous skirt, short thingy kept riding up to where it didn't belong. It was a bad combination, and well, it just flung." I close my eyes and cradle my forehead in the palms of my hand.

"Well. That's the end of that, huh?" Misty says.

"No!" I practically yell into the phone. "When he dropped me off, he asked to see me again. Picture this, Mist." I stand up and start pacing in my tiny apartment. "He walks me to my door, ice pack to head, and he takes my face with his free hand, pulls it close to him, and gives me the most sensual kiss. But, then! He asks to see me again. I swear I feel like Kate Hudson's character in *How To Lose A Guy In 10 Days*. Like, he is on a bigger mission than I am to make this work." I stop to take a breath of air.

"What did you say?"

"Well, I agreed, of course! One, he is even hotter than Matthew McConaughey, and two, I don't have time to start over." I justify to myself. "But I suggested a night in, and when I did, he said he was going to propose the same thing. So he invited me to his house. He said he doesn't cook, but we can order takeout and 'Netflix and chill' were his exact words."

"Well, at least you won't have to operate any heavy machinery. You know, dinner place settings and golf clubs." Misty laughs at her joke.

"Right, good one. I thought, 'At least I don't have to buy a new outfit'."

"That too. Are you returning the golf outfit to Sports Basement?" she asks.

"I can't. It has some splashes of Ryan's blood on it." And after that piece of information, we say our goodbyes.

I set my phone down on the kitchen counter and stare out the window. My thoughts lead me to Zach, and unfortunately, I cannot just turn them off like a light switch. At the most random and unwelcome times, he floods my brain. I wonder what he is doing, where he is living, and if he thinks about me as much as I think about him. I don't really want to find out the answers to these questions for fear that they aren't the answers I want.

I shake my head, trying to rid the idea that Zach is better off without me. I hope and pray that he is as miserable as I am. And if he's not, well, I hope he catches a finger in the door or something.

The mess in my head is not going to aid in coming up with something to wear for tonight. I push Zach out and bring Ryan in as I mentally catalog every article of clothing I own in my head.

I arrive at Ryan's house in Fountain Grove, aka the "I've *really* made it" part of town, twenty minutes late. I'll blame traffic, but in all reality, I couldn't decide what to wear. So I left the house in a pair of black yoga pants, a white crop tank, and a knee-length powder blue sweater, but halfway to his house, I decided I didn't like my outfit, so I stopped at the Ross that was on the way.

"You look fabulous, as always, Courtney," Ryan says when he opens the large wooden door to his even more prominent home.

I am now wearing a DKNY form-fitting casual three-quarter sleeve cotton dress with a black and white stripe down each side, giving me a perfect hourglass figure effect.

"Thank you," I say as I kiss him back with an open mouth.

Ryan takes my hand and leads me into the kitchen. It is gorgeous, with gray and white marble countertops, white cabinets that border the perimeter, and a massive dark gray kitchen island. I'm in awe of the room and even more shocked that it never gets used.

"You have all of this," I wave my arm in a half-circle, "and you don't cook?" I set my purse down on the white and gray barstools.

"Yeah, well, maybe I'll have a lady friend to do the cooking for me one day." He winks and walks over to the fridge.

"A lady friend." I wonder if he means me?! Cooking to me is pulling back a plastic film on a microwave Lean Cuisine, but I could learn to cook if it meant I would be spending time in this kitchen.

Ryan opens the double-paned doors, that up until now, I thought were part of the cabinetry, and pulls out two bottles of wine. I notice one is Fre, an alcohol-removed wine I mentioned on our first date that I like. Next, Ryan reaches into one of the cabinets and pulls out two Reidel wine glasses.

I recognize them because my aunt in New York has the same set.

"Thank you," I say and take the glass of pink liquid with my hand.

"Cheers." Ryan holds up his glass, and we make a clinking sound as the stemware meets each other.

"I ordered sushi and pizza. I couldn't decide." Ryan shrugs. He is charming. If I could only get Zach off of my mind, I could get used to this lifestyle.

We make our way to the living room, which is even more impressive than the kitchen. I sit down on the sizable L-shape leather sectional. Ryan lights a few candles and puts on some mood music using his iPhone. I immediately feel my insides tie into a knot. I get a sense of the direction his evening is going.

The sushi and pizza combination are fantastic. We enjoy it while laughing about the events of our golf date. I am relieved that Ryan can joke about it now.

"Do you want more wine?" he asks as he pours the last of his bottle into his empty glass.

"No, I'm okay. Thank you, though."

Ryan walks over to me and, without saying a word, takes my hand and lifts me from the couch. He leads me to his bedroom, and the pit in my stomach grows.

I will save you the messy details here, but as soon as Ryan starts to lift my dress above my head, I get tangled up somewhere between the bedspread and my foot and face plant into his nightstand. I grab my forehead with my hand, and when I see blood, I start to stand, but stumble, and then just kinda roll off the bed to the floor. Bringing his expensive-looking lamp with me. I try to bounce back and stand on my own two feet, but I can't. I see stars.

Ryan peels me off the floor, tosses me my dress, and runs to the bathroom to get a damp towel.

"I guess we're even now?" he says as I press the cold

compress to my head wound. "You know, for hitting me in the head with the golf club," he clarifies, as if I had forgotten.

"It—the club flung. *I* didn't hit you," I say under my breath. "I think I'm going to go. I'm sorry," I say as I stand from the side of the bed and make my way to the kitchen to retrieve my bag.

"Are you sure you're okay to drive?" he asks.

"Yeah. Yes. I'll be fine." I beeline it to the front door.

"Text me when you get home, okay?" He kisses me on the good side of my forehead.

I pour my little body into my car and drive off. That couldn't have gone worse. Surely, he won't want to see me again.

Three Days Later

"You still haven't heard from him?" I'm on the phone with my mom.

"Nothing. I mean, I get it. But a simple text would be the adult thing to do. He's past thirty. Nobody just ghosts people when they are in their thirties."

My mom and I spend another few minutes on the phone. I know she is trying to cheer me up, but to be honest, I'm not all that disappointed. Sure, Valentine's Day is less than a week away, meaning my ideal beach date is unlikely to happen. It will be Butter, Ben and Jerry's, and me again this year. It could be worse. I could be drunk somewhere, or even worse, in jail. It wouldn't be the first holiday I spent in some form of institution.

I make a pot of coffee and sit down at my writing desk. I fire up my laptop and open my word document. Nothing. My mind is a blank slate. I need some inspiration. I put on music, which usually sparks something in me, but not today. I'm too stir-crazy even to attempt meditation, so last resort—the grocery store. I slip on my Puma slides and head out of the door on my way to Whole Foods.

I aimlessly stroll through the overpriced organic grocery store. My cart is empty as I approach the produce section. I walk over to the avocados, 2 for $5, and I grab six.

"Cort," I hear a familiar voice from behind me calling my name. I know who that voice belongs to even before I turn around. "Hey, I've been . . . "

I don't hear the rest of Zach's sentence because it's cut short by chucking three of the six avocados in my cart directly at his chest. And then I bolt from the store, leaving my cart in the aisle.

Once I'm in the safety of my car, I finally breathe. What could have possibly been the rest of Zach's sentence?

"I've been . . . an asshole?"

"I've been locked up all year, so I wasn't able to get a hold of you."

"I've been busy."

"I've been screwing random chicks I met on dating apps."

Seriously, what? As bad as I want the answer to that question, I don't, because there is nothing he can say that will take away the hurt and pain I have carried around with me for the past year.

I put the key into the ignition and turn it to the right. I screech out of the Whole Foods parking lot, almost hitting the curb as I do. My heart is in my throat, and my eyes start to cloud with tears.

By the time I get home, I look like a raccoon from crying. I run up the stairs to my apartment, fling the front door open, and swoop Butter up on my way to my bed, where I vow to myself that I'm not coming out until next Valentine's Day.

Nine

Waking up the following morning, I reach for my phone and have two missed calls from Mom, text messages from Misty, and a Facebook friend request from . . . Zach! I text Mom that I'll call her later, and then I say to my phone, "Hey, Siri. Call BFF on speaker."

"Calling BFF on speaker," the Australian version of Siri answers me.

"Hey," Misty answers on the first ring. "Where were you all night?" she asks.

"Hiding under my duvet blanket," I answer.

"What? Is this about Ryan?" she asks.

"What? No. Zach," I answer.

"What now?"

I tell her about the encounter at Whole Foods, how I threw avocados at him, and then ran from the store.

"Cort, I'm sorry, this will sound harsh, but what the hell is wrong with you?" She is right. That does sound harsh.

"I don't know. And I got a friend request from him this morning. It's like, I think about him all the time, but yet every encounter I have with him, I destroy it. Without even thinking, I just react. I love him, but I hate him. I'm still so angry."

"Why don't you be an adult about it and talk to him?" Finally, the voice of reason speaks.

"I don't know. Maybe I want to hurt him as he hurt me."

"Well, an avocado to the chest . . . I think you proved your point."

"I'm going to workout," I say, hopefully ending the conversation.

"Good for you. That's something I haven't heard you say in a while." Which is true. I've been so busy orchestrating and then sabotaging my love life that I have put my own needs aside. "Call me later. I'll think of something fun for us to do."

"Okay," I say, then hang up.

I put my phone on Do Not Disturb. Opening my Pandora app, I play my "Girl Power" playlist, and dance around the room like no one is watching.

"You want to do what?" I ask Misty later that evening.

"Escape Room," she says again. I heard her the first time. I just think it's odd. "Yeah, it'll be like five or six of us. It's in Windsor. I'll drive us." It sounds like she has it all planned out.

"When?" It also sounds like another activity I don't want to be doing. At least this time I won't need to buy a new outfit. I can just go as I am.

"Tomorrow at 11 am."

"What?! How did you plan that and get people to commit so quickly?" There's no getting out of it; no time to plan my escape route from the Escape Room, no pun intended.

"They had an opening, and I know many people," she says. "It's like it was meant to be." Now she is just mocking me.

"Well, do I know anyone that will be there?" I already hate this, but I also know I need a distraction from myself.

"Depending on who actually shows up, yeah, you should know one or two. I gotta run, the kids. I'll pick you up at 10:30 am tomorrow." And she hangs up.

I walk over to the fridge, open the freezer door, and pull out a pint of Halo Top ice cream. *Escape Room*, I think. *Isn't there a Netflix movie about that?*

I plop down, spoon in hand, and search for the movie I am thinking of. Indeed, there is. I hit play and settled in —*Escape Room.*

Ten

Misty arrives at my apartment at 10:15 am, early as usual. I don't know why she does half of the things she does. This used to drive me crazy as well, but I have become accustomed to knowing that in Misty's world, 10:30 is really 10:15, and my gosh, I had better be ready! She hates to wait.

"I thought we would stop at Peet's for coffee. My treat," she says when I get into her car. "You look cute," she adds.

For the first time in a week, I feel like myself, dressed in my own clothing.

"Thanks," I say as I situate myself in the front seat. "So, how many people are going?" I ask.

"I'm not sure. We will see when we get there. You should know a couple of people, though."

WE ARRIVE at our destination on time. Misty leads the way into the building and to the front desk to check us in. The young woman behind the counter can't be more than seventeen, likely her first job.

"Welcome to the Escape Room! Do you have a reservation?" she asks us with a huge, fake grin on her face. I always appreciate the forced kindness from people who don't particularly like their jobs.

"Yes." Misty steps forward. "It's under Huber," Misty says her last name particularly slowly.

"Oh, yes! Okay, well, if your friend wants to get to our waiting room where the other participants are." She extends an arm out to her left, pointing to a massive steel and wooden door. "I'll finish checking you in." She nods her head.

"Perfect," Misty says to the clerk. "I'll meet you in there, Cort."

Great, we're separating already. Aren't you supposed to stay together and work as a team on these things? I don't argue, though. Instead, I walk in the direction the young lady pointed to, open the door, and step in.

Once inside, the door shuts, and I'm almost sure I hear a click sound behind me, locking me inside.

What the heck? How will Misty get in?

The sound of a door clicking used to give me PTSD from my time in jail, I have overcome that, thankfully.

The room is set up like a library. Books sit on shelves from the floor to the ceiling. There is a beautiful fireplace in the corner and a vintage-looking deep plum purple couch in the middle. A man is sitting with his back to me on the couch, and when I take a closer look, I'd recognize the back of that head anywhere.

It belongs to Zach.

"What—" I struggle to form the proper words for how I feel. "What," I say louder, and Zach's head turns around, "are you doing here?"

Zach starts to stand slowly, with his arm half raised and his hand held out toward me like a stop sign. As though he is cautioning me not to panic. I immediately turn toward the door I just walked through.

"Cort, wait." Zach is standing fully erect and walking to me.

The door is locked. *Shit. Misty.* She orchestrated this whole thing, and I couldn't be more mad at her. What in the world was she thinking? When I get out of here, I am going to . . .

"Courtney, please. Listen. It was my idea." So yeah, Zach is also pretty much a mind reader.

"Your idea, Zach. Your idea is to lure me to an Escape Room, pretty much locked me in, and then what? What's your plan here?" I am mad, but also . . . Zach.

"I don't know. I had to get your attention somehow." He's standing an arm's length away, and it's taking all of my inner strength not to reach out and grab for him. To kiss his familiar lips and run my hands through his shaggy brown hair.

"Ouch!" I punched him in his upper arm. "I know you think I deserve that, and the avocados you threw at me, but Cort, hear me out. Please."

"One hour starts now," a loud female voice comes through some hidden speakers overhead.

"Well, shall we?" Zach smiles at me.

My heart flutters, then plummets. I am forced—locked in —with him for sixty minutes. What will I do now?

"I mean. I think there is a prize at the end of this thing if we make it through," Zach adds, knowing I love contests with prizes at the end. "I remember Misty saying something about a gift card to a local restaurant or a T-shirt."

The first room is a piece of cake to get out of. There is a key easily visible on top of the fireplace. We open the small door on the opposite side of the room and crawl through.

"Why didn't you call, Zach?" We are barely five minutes into this thing, and I ask him the question I've wanted the answer to for over a year now.

"I did. But by the time I did, you had already blocked me on every communication platform possible." He's not wrong.

Day three, to be exact. "And then my uncle died. And my aunt and her kids were a mess. I never knew them well, but when I got out there, I felt an instant bond with them all. They have two little boys. When my uncle, Tim, died, they fell apart. I felt like my responsibility was to help them put the pieces back together."

I feel guilty. Worse than guilty. I was not only a bad partner to Zach, but a bad friend. While he was going through a horrible family loss, I've been sitting here hating him, seething with anger and jealousy. I should have taken the time to care. Open my eyes to what he was going through in his life, and to know that it had nothing to do with us.

How could I have been so foolish, so selfish, and so childish?

"I figured you and I would go back to you and I when I sorted it all out, but, I guess you had different plans. Misty said you were dating and angry with me. I couldn't leave my family; I couldn't fix us."

"You told me that you were going to see other people."

"No, I didn't," Zach's voice inflates. He is getting frustrated. "You asked if it meant we were going to date other people, and I told you to do what you had to do. I didn't want you to wait for me if you didn't want to."

Man, I misinterpreted that one.

"Come on, let's get through this game." Zach smiles.

Zach starts climbing furniture, taking pictures off the walls, and running his hands over the ceiling.

"It's not going to be in the ceilings," I say. "It's going to be noticeable. Look under a chair or something." As I am giving instructions, I see a key taped to the side of the coffee table.

"Have you done this before? Why are you so good?"

"I YouTubed tips and tricks last night." I shrug my shoulders

"You always do come prepared."

"Too prepared, you used to tell me. I tried to plan too much."

"Yeah. But that was always part of your charm, why I liked you. One of the reasons you were perfect for me was that you filled in my gaps, and I have a lot of them. Being a planner, as annoying as it was sometimes, I loved you for it." Zach looks at me with his puppy dog brown eyes.

When I look at him, it's like looking into his soul. And what I see is pure, honest, and good. How could I have been so selfish? He was only taking care of his family. At that moment, I realize it wasn't Zach who left us. It was me who left him.

"Courtney, don't think there hasn't been a day that has gone by that I haven't thought about you. I only knew that while I was away, I couldn't give you the amount of attention and time you not only deserve, but that you need."

Am I really that needy?

"Am I really that needy?" I then say out loud.

"Yes. You are. But that is also something I adore about you. And something I want to give to you when the timing is right," he says.

I'm about to ask if the timing is right now, but before I can spit the words out of my mouth, that voice over the intercom interrupts me.

"You have thirty-five minutes remaining."

"Let's beat that clock, Zach." I smile.

"Let's do it, Cort."

We find the next key in a puzzle box. It unlocks a padlock; this time there is a riddle, it reads:

A princess is stuck in a castle tower with a locked metal door. There are no windows and nothing in the room besides a piano. What does she do to escape?

Zach and I stare at each other with blank eyes. No clue. I

204

look around the room we are in, and I spot a mock baby grand piano.

"I got it!" I yell. "We play the piano until we find the right key!" I rush over to the large instrument and sit down on the stool.

"How in the world did you figure that out?" Zach asks, then follows my lead.

"Come on. I write fiction stories, for crying out loud." I start hitting every key until something happens. I'm about midway down the keyboard when a door flings open.

"You did it!" Zach looks at me. "Nice work, let's go." He grabs my hand and pulls me up to stand. Our hands fit together like a glove, like they were never apart, and together we rush through the open passageway and into the next room.

This room is different from the other two. Whereas the previous ones had a historical feel, this one is a much more modern feel with computers and tablets and bright lights overhead.

"I heard you were dating a guy?" Zach says, catching me off guard. "Misty told me."

Of course she did.

"Yeah, that was a waste of time." *And money,* I think.

"What happened?" he asks.

"He was the wrong guy," I answer. "I was just trying to get over you."

"By getting under someone else?" Zach says with a wink, but I can tell he is genuinely hurt. His deep voice cracks and his beautiful brown eyes bulge. I think he even clutches his fist a little. I would be lying if I said I was not pleased by this display of action.

"That didn't happen." At the time, I was disappointed with myself, but I am thankful for it now.

"You can't force things that aren't meant to be, I learned. The Universe will always intervene," I say.

Zach isn't nearly as spiritual as I am, but I think he gets it.

"Well, I'll thank my lucky stars, I guess." *Gawd, I love this man.* Like my mom plays into my hopeless romantic tactics, Zach goes along with my "The Universe has my back" beliefs. I am grateful for them both.

Zach and I make it out of the Escape Room in record time. Misty and the young worker are waiting on the other side of the door. I'm not even mad anymore. I run up to Misty and give her a tight hug.

"So, what's the prize?" Zach asks.

"Well, a T-shirt," the teenager says. "And, typically a gift card to Mack's Restaurant, but they stopped doing that, so you get a 2 for 1 at Yogurt Time," she says with a tone of disappointment.

"Our favorite." Zach walks over to me and takes me into his arms. He swings me in a circle, and I bury my head between his neck and shoulder. It feels like home.

Epilogue

One Year Later

We came a long way in one year. I'm talking about Zach and me. After escaping the Escape Room, it was like we picked up right where we left off, except better. I owned my part for not having faith in us and trying to force something to happen in my time, not in God's time. And the selfish, childish part. So, remember that perfect Valentine's Day date I had all planned out in my head? Well, it happened. Not that year; Zach and I had some work to do first, but one calendar year later, it happened better than I could have imagined.

"You are breathtaking," Zach says when I open my front door. He kisses me passionately and then hands me a dozen red roses. I know I said I like tulips, but what girl, deep down, doesn't want a bouquet of roses on Valentine's Day?

"Thank you," I say. I'm wearing a pair of my favorite boyfriend-cut jeans from The Buckle and a white crop tank, showing off my abs and my dedication to health and fitness. I layer the shirt with my favorite flannel and a vest for added warmth if needed.

"Are you ready?" he asks.

"I am." We head out the door to the car and drive to our destination—the beach. When we arrive, two big horses are waiting for us alongside their hostler. We get saddled in and ride off into the sunset.

So, readers. I guess it all goes back to what I was saying in the beginning. With a bit of patience, I got my fairytale ending.

Oh, and that book I was working on? My publisher loved it. It comes out at the end of summer. I think it's going to be a hit.

All A-Boat You

BY CHELSEA LAUREN

One

All I wanted for my 30th birthday was a boat, the sunshine, and my two best friends. It shouldn't have been that difficult. I live ten minutes from the river. Rich people flood the marinas this time of the year, all bringing their own boats to rent out while they jack up the prices in my small town. I am willing to spend the money. I just can't figure out the damn website to rent a freaking boat.

I slam my laptop shut and shove it into my work bag. Recently, it feels like everything is moving so fast, and I'm just in the backseat. I try to take control. Try to be positive and live my life to the best of my ability, but something keeps tearing me down.

I put in the work. I go to therapy; I work out at 5 am; I have a kick-ass job, figured out how to style my surprisingly gorgeous locks, and signed up for countless dating apps. So why is it I can't find a guy to settle down with, afford my own apartment, or book a damn boat reservation?

My phone buzzes; a calendar reminder of my Thursday night dinner with one of my best friends. Just another reminder of how the internet wasn't working in my favor; it was infuriating booking her bridal shower. Oh, did I mention my two best friends are getting married? Not together, but a year apart. Always a maid of honor, but when will I be the bride?

I'm GREETED by the smell of onions as I open Kinsley's door. Her St. Berdoodle comes bounding down the stairs, panting as she jumps up on me for a hug. The excitement from Willow, Kinsley's pup, helps wash away any lingering frustration. In just a few moments, I can destress, vent, and eat some delicious food. Willow and I chaotically make our way upstairs to where Kinsley's in sweats, scooping baked spaghetti squash into a glass bowl. Taylor Swift is blasting in the background. Some mellow song about trying.

I am, Universe.

"Hey!" she greets, leaning over to her phone and tapping the song off with her clean pinky finger. "I hope you don't mind meatloaf and spaghetti squash again. It's becoming a staple."

"Not at all." I laugh. "I loved the meatloaf last week." I put my belongings down and sit on the floor, petting her pup, who is energetically hopping in front of me, unsure of if she wants ear scratches or butt rubs. "Are you free for my birthday?" I ask. I feel like every weekend has been swamped lately between our own personal lives and her wedding planning.

"Of course. It's your 30th. Boat trip, right?" Kinsley glances at her wall calendar as if she could read that my birthday is on the schedule, even though it's currently May and not June.

"I'm trying!" I exclaim, pushing myself up from the floor to grab us both plates and silverware. "I cannot get anything booked. But we'll see."

"Have you been to any place or just online?" She dishes food onto both of our plates, and my stomach rumbles. I *did* manage to find time to eat at work today. Except, it was only a half of a protein bar.

"Nah, I'm going to try and go this weekend. So many places say they aren't quite open yet, which is dumb because it'll be the season before we know it. Wouldn't they want things booked out?"

"You'd think," Kinsley offers. She pours us both glasses of water before handing me one and my filled plate. "Hopefully, you'll have better luck in person. Maybe we need to travel north?"

Two hours north of us, there is a massive lake, but it's also a tourist destination. I'd rather remain close to home if I can. Less expensive and fewer people. I deal with too many people on a daily basis. It isn't too much to ask to have some controlled peace on my birthday.

Willow sits up straight, her paw on my lap. "Or maybe," I start, petting her on the snout as her curly head tilts. "You and I will just cuddle all day." The pup pants at my words, eyes wide.

Two

Of course, I am running behind because a crisis happened at work. And I didn't have time to eat my lunch. I stupidly brought something that needed to be microwaved because I told myself today I'd actually stop and breathe during lunch, but that didn't happen. Instead, I'm hightailing my grumbling stomach down to the water. There's a sailboat rental place I've wanted to check out. At this rate, it almost feels unnecessary. Like the world is telling me, I shouldn't rent a boat with the obstacles it set up for me this week. But I am treating myself, damnit.

It's already past five and Google Maps tells me my location closed five minutes ago, but maybe it's possible that someone is still around. I'm not usually the type to even go into a place thirty minutes before closing, but today, I have to try. I navigate my car between the narrow streets and pedestrians casually walking to their waterfront dinner reservations and find a parking space in the last spot of municipal parking.

Finally, someone is on my side.

I dash out of my front seat, grab my backpack with my wallet in it, and jog toward the tiny booth that says "Rowan Sailing." It's right near the edge of the Riverwalk. If someone were to drive into the booth, it'd tip backward into the water. A group of women, maybe in their mid-thirties, giggle as they stumble down the walk. They've got sun-kissed skin and bikini straps coming out of their t-shirts. One is carrying an opened bottle of wine as if our state has changed the open container laws.

No one is in the booth, though. Instead, a stupid sign is on it saying they are closed. *Of course*! I scream in my head; wishing I could let out a screech right here and now, like the toddler who threw a tantrum at work today. Likely I'd feel better. I just want one thing to go right. I know it means that I'm at my wits' end and I need rest. That I've overworked myself, and while I've maintained my self-care schedule, I may have self-cared a little too far to not allow my body and mind to rest at the same time.

I contemplate kicking the booth. Maybe some physical pain would relieve my tension. But I'm wearing my new black ballet flats and I don't need to scuff them. *Or* cause a toe injury for tomorrow's gym class.

"Excuse me, you look lost. Can I help you with anything?" a deep, husky voice sounds off to the left.

I glance over, and a tanned Greek God near my age offers me a smile. My face warms; subconsciously gazing at him. He's wearing red swim trunks, Adidas slides, a gray t-shirt with wet specks over it, and polarized black sunglasses resting on his head, pressing down his brown waves.

Focus, Evie. Don't be so shameless.

I blink to refocus, shaking my head. "No, uh, it looks like what I needed is closed." I nod toward the boating booth. "Thank you." I turn to head back to my car. I'm taking this as my sign to give up. I've tried. I put in the time. Nothing is coming.

"Wait!" His voice is a slightly higher pitch as he yells out. Clearing his throat, he starts again, "I'm Everett Rowan. Are you looking to rent a boat?"

My shoulders cave in as a level of stress dissipates. His words are music to my ears. This place was my number one choice because they offered sailboats versus just a pontoon, and they had a wine and cheese option.

Yes, I could just bring wine and cheese on any boat, but it beats having to be responsible. I'm over *responsible.*

I swivel back around. He isn't standing behind me anymore or waiting for a response. Instead, he's unlocking the side door of the sailboat booth before stepping into it. It reminds me of an outhouse with the size of his operations. But I suppose if most of your day is on a boat, there isn't need for any fancy structure.

"C'mon over, let's talk about what you're looking for. Unless—" he pauses, offering me a close-lipped smile, "maybe you aren't looking for me."

I watch him for a moment as he lifts a laptop onto the short counter and flips it open. His eyes squint just slightly, looking at the bright screen in the dark cubby. He's handsome. Honestly, way too attractive for me to get on a boat, be myself, and have a glass of wine or two. I might make a fool of myself and that's the last thing I need to ring in 30 with.

"Is something wrong?" he asks, looking over at me, brows slightly furrowed.

"N-no, uh, I am looking for you. Sorry, I just didn't realize . . . I thought it was an older gentleman who ran this business."

He beams with a nod, and I force myself to walk the few steps to his booth. His eyes are an emerald green; his skin crinkles on the edges as his smile grows.

"You must be talking about my grandfather. He retired last season. Pushed it as long as he could, loved being on the water—still does—but it was too much for him to manage. So now I am taking over the operations. Making some changes. Have to update the website story, but I've been swamped with backlog emails that I haven't had much time."

He's got an answer and reason for not returning my emails. Though, I'm not sure if that settles my brain or not.

"I totally respect if you had a different impression and don't want to move forward. But I have to say I've got some pretty sweet packages—even ones not listed on the website if you'd like to check out the selection?"

He pulls two laminated pieces of paper down from the wall and rests them on the counter. I don't enjoy being bombarded with new information, particularly because my day job requires it. I like to be able to process information on my own time, in my own safety. But now, I'm perusing different packages, past this guy's work hours, and I can't exactly just say "fuck it" and walk away.

I hear my best friend Nora's voice. *"Make your move, girl! Buy a package, and ask about his,"* she'd say with a wink.

I clear my throat, shifting on my feet. There are about four new packages on this sheet of paper but all the words mesh together as I try to decipher what I want for my birthday, what this is saying, and Kinsley and Nora trying to tell me to get more than just a boat.

The guy is shuffling in his small rectangular box, and I don't have the nerve to look up and see if he's working or if he's impatient with my silence.

"Not to be forward," he begins, and his voice sends shivers down my spine. "I'm starving, and I promised to treat myself to my favorite dessert up the road at the end of my day. And well, since I'm technically closed . . . my stomach is—"

"Oh!" I exclaim, stepping away from the booth. "Of course. I'll leave. Thank you for your time."

I shuffle back, stumbling over the uneven sidewalk. I can figure out another place. Another time. Maybe never. As I turn, I hear the slam of his door.

"I think you misunderstood." His voice raises just slightly. "I'm not great at this. But what I was trying to ask is if you'd like to grab some tea and dessert? I could, uh, talk to you more about the packages?"

I can't turn to look at him as my nerve endings are on fire, flooding my insides with embarrassment. *Patience, Evie. All you needed was patience.*

"I'm not trying to rush you," he continues. "I just kind of get hangry and would not like to take it out on you."

My stomach gurgles silently at his words. Tea and dessert do sound quite perfect. Whoever believes dessert doesn't come before dinner has a miserable life.

He isn't asking you out, Evie. He just wants to eat while you make up your mind.

I spin back around, plastering a smile on my face. "Sure, that sounds great."

His face brightens as he grins. "Perfect! One moment; let me lock up."

Three

I can barely hide my excitement about the cafe he chooses. Just up the block from his booth, there's a cafe with Paris-esque outdoor dining, where you can gaze out to the river and people watch pedestrians strolling on the River-walk. This cafe is raved about for its delicious cakes and sweet treats, more particularly, gluten-free desserts. Kinsley keeps mentioning we should go, but between our schedules and her budget, it's fallen through the cracks.

Our walk to the cafe was silent. He had given me the laminated papers to look over while we walked, but my clumsy body didn't have that ability. When we arrived at the cafe, he opened the door for me, and now I'm gazing at the glass-covered drool-worthy desserts.

"I'm not sure if you've been here before, but they have the most incredible turtle chocolate cake," he says. I have to somehow ask for his name again because I definitely was only half-listening when I thought he couldn't help me.

"I'm gluten-free," I manage to get out. My brain is trying to scramble between looking at the menu behind the barista for a tea I might enjoy and figuring out what desserts are gluten-free. All while trying not to embarrass myself with this guy who, for some reason, wants to hang out.

My ears ache as a group of friends enter in line behind us. It isn't terribly loud in here, but this isn't how I anticipated my evening being.

"It is gluten-free! But another incredible gluten-free item is the lemon tart. I have to be in the mood for lemon, so I only get it every-so-often, but the turtle chocolate cake?" He glances over at me with raised brows. "That is my absolute weakness. I get it with a London Fog and I'm the happiest man alive."

"They have London Fog?" My voice squeaks through my excitement and nerves. I know what I like with drinks and I try to stick to it.

His eyes catch mine, and I keep from looking away. The intensity in them has me catching my breath as his eyes narrow just slightly. "What type of milk?"

"Almond," I whisper.

"Grab a seat outside for us, and I'll grab the best for us." His head nods toward the door before we move up in line.

This now feels like a date.

I do as he asks because the last thing I really want to do is make any decisions. I choose for everyone every single day.

Thankfully, it's much less crowded outside. The sound of the water crashing up against the docks calms my nervous system. I choose the closest seat to the water, off to the right of the cafe. Placing the laminated papers on the table, I immediately grab my phone out of my small backpack I use as a purse. I open up my group chat with Kinsley and Nora.

Me:
Uh, I'm at Riverfront Cafe with a guy from the sailboat place.

Nora:
WHAT?! GET IT GURL!

Kinsley:
How did that happen?? Wait, so is sailing definitely happening?

Me:
I don't know haha. I was looking at the package options and he said he wanted dessert and asked me to come with. He's ordering for us now.

Nora:
Is he cute??
Oh my god, do you wanna look at his package?
What does he look like? What's his name? What's the name of the sailing company?

Kinsley:
Rowan Sailing, Nora. He's definitely after more than just your business! You have to let us know how it goes!!

I HEAR the cafe door open and I type quickly on my phone, *I gotta go. He's back.* I shove my phone into my backpack and strap it on the chair.

The Greek God is carrying two mugs filled to the brim. A barista walks behind him with three desserts. *Three* desserts.

Holy hell, is he trying to share?

He places one mug in front of me and then steps out of the way for the barista to put down what looks like the turtle chocolate cake, the lemon tart, and a cheesecake of sorts. He beams at me once he takes a seat across from me. A little kid at heart, treating himself to dessert before dinner. Butterflies erupt in my stomach as his foot gently taps mine as he adjusts in his seat.

"So, I realized that I never asked your name. I'm sorry for being so impolite. I really just had this chocolate cake on my brain and couldn't focus." When he's done rambling, he reaches his hand across the table for a shake. "I'm Everett. It's nice to meet you."

I place my hand in his, and his grip strengthens. Goosebumps erupt on my skin with the heat radiating off his hand. "I'm Evie. Nice to meet you too."

His hand doesn't release immediately. Instead, he gazes at me. His grin reaching his ears, eyes crinkling at full force. "You have a beautiful name," he says softly before letting go. Everett then hands me a fork. "I hope you're hungry because you will not regret this."

Before I can even process where to start, or really what the hell I'm doing here, he splits each dessert into two. He then takes one of the plates and disperses the halves onto it before pushing the plate toward me.

All I can do is stare at him. This guy who interrupted a business transaction for a slice of cake just gave me half of said cake.

He likeeeeesss you! I hear Nora's voice in my head.

"This is my favorite way to start my weekend. My weekends do involve working now—"

My heart sinks at the thought of him working weekends. I can't pursue him. We'd never see each other. I mean, what does he even do throughout the week? Most packages I had seen around the area were Thursday to Sunday.

"What did you do before this?" I ask, sliding the tea closer to me. I lift the drink carefully and take a sip. The warm liquid tries to block out the negativity seeping in. If I want to find someone and be with them, I have to be open to any and all possibilities—with standards, of course.

"I was a mechanic at my friend's shop. I was the only one who could work on boats there. I still do that every-so-often, but now, instead of doing other jobs for them, it's only when a serious issue comes up for a boat. I'm trying to make this full-time spring through fall."

I nod. I have zero idea of how to fix anything on my car, even change my tire. Nonetheless how a boat operates.

I take another sip of the London Fog and sit back in my seat, gazing out at the water. There are a few boats coming in, but some are heading out, likely to catch the sunset in an hour or so.

"So you're looking for a boat rental?" Everett asks, sitting up before he digs into his chocolate cake. He all but lets out a moan as the cake enters his mouth.

I swallow, reaching for a small bite of my own. When I close my mouth and the cake melts onto my tongue, I know I've fallen in love. My eyes close involuntarily as I taste the chocolate, caramel, and pecan pieces all mix into one.

A soft chuckle escapes Everett's lips. My cheeks are definitely red when I open my eyes, but I can't even be embarrassed. This boy has spoken to my soul about what I needed to close out this stressful week.

"Incredible, right?" His eyes peer up at me and he dips his fork into the lemon tart.

"Unbelievable." I'm more hesitant to try the lemon tart, as that's my favorite. I don't want this moment to be ruined. But as soon as I see his lips pucker just slightly, and a moan escapes his lips this time, I dig in. It's tangy and sweet, melting in my mouth, complimenting the chocolate. "Wow," I breathe out. This boy can have my heart.

His left foot shifts under the table again, touching mine, but I'm nearly certain it isn't by mistake. Everett's smile is genuine, and held just for me—in this moment.

"Thank you for introducing me to this place. My friends and I keep mentioning to check it out but our schedules always clash," I offer, taking another bite of the lemon tart. I need to regulate some sort of normal conversation as he's carried us this whole time.

"I get that. Recently, I've just started to take myself out to places I want to try or experience because it seems everyone's married, has kids, or is just busy with their partner."

"Oh, thank god," I breathe out before quickly covering my mouth. My pits sweat at the realization of what I said. "I'm sorry!" I laugh softly as he chuckles. "I meant thank god in the sense that someone understands my position. Not thank god that you're single."

"No?" His brow quirks, and I'm 100% a ripened tomato. "You're not thankful that two single people met just in time for the sunset on a Friday night? That instead of being home alone, you're actually in the company of someone else who was about to be alone on a Friday night?"

"Well," I perk up. *I mean, yes, this is ideal.* "I do enjoy my Friday nights in peace. My day job is stressful, so it's nice to be able to go home and decompress."

"Though, the end goal is to have someone to decompress with . . . right?"

Peaceful solidarity with a partner sounds incredible.

"You're right." I laugh. "I do need to take myself out more. It's better with company, but I shouldn't miss out on experiences just because I don't have a partner."

"Exactly. We only have one life, right? Just because the Universe is taking a little too long to find us someone, we shouldn't miss out on things couples do."

I lift the mug mainly to shield my face from the wide smile erupting.

"I'm going to ask a question now, and I don't want you to run, okay?" he says.

I laugh out loud, covering my mouth. I've walked away from him twice already, and he still wants to talk to me?

"Might be presumptuous, but would you like to watch the sunset out on my boat? I haven't really enjoyed it yet. The season started in full swing, and I only had the opportunity to make sure everything was operating properly before it was filled with guests."

I glance around the area, trying to figure out who is setting me up. There's no way Kinsley or Nora would play this sort of joke on me. They know my heart is too fragile to mess with in this way. But my life isn't a Hallmark film. I've tried that—they don't exist.

"You don't know me?" I question, because maybe he does? Maybe he knows more about me than I can understand? When I started getting overwhelmed in the cafe, he suggested I walk outside, but that could easily be because he wanted to surprise me.

"I know your name is Evie; you're interested in a sailboat ride, you're the single one of your friends, and you've got a pretty infectious laugh as well as great taste in cake. Honestly, that's more than I know of most of the guests that come onto the boat . . . that is, until they are stumbling off at the end of the ride." He chuckles, and I think back to the girls he had just let off before I met him. I can only imagine the stories he hears when people forget he exists.

Though, I'm not sure how anyone can forget he exists.

I take another sip of my tea, and then I try a piece of the cheesecake. Nice and simple plain cheesecake to not overwhelm the rest of the desserts.

"Sure," I hear myself say after I swallow my bite. To hell with it. He's got a business that operates right in this location. If he tries any funny business, his business can be ripped away from him. He has far more to lose than me.

At my words, he jumps up from his seat and motions with one finger before he rushes inside. He's an odd one; confident within his body, so sure of himself. I always said I wanted to meet someone in person, particularly after some awful online dating experiences. But it can't be this simple, right?

The Riverwalk is getting more crowded as dinner reservations are starting in the area. A few more people are carrying coolers onto boats. I always wanted that life. The one where I hang up my work stress and hop on a boat for a Friday night ride. And here I am, it's staring me right in the face.

Suddenly, Everett is in front of me with two cardboard containers. "I was thinking we could bring the cake on the boat? I'd love to bring you to the best spot for the sunset, but we have to leave in the next few minutes."

And before I know it, I'm downing my tea, carrying my cake, and we are dashing down the Riverwalk back toward his booth.

Four

Watching Everett get his sailboat set to sail is something I can do more of. Admiring the way his gray t-shirt rises on his torso and how his biceps flex with each pull of ropes. He is in his element as I sit on a bench seat, shoes kicked off, feet straight in front of me. The silence is lovely. Being able to decompress *with* someone is a nice surprise. I can with Kinsley and Nora, but this is different. With my friends, we always have things to say, to catch up on, new topics to talk about because there is never enough time in a day. And while I hope to have that experience with a partner, at some point you just have to be with your partner. And this . . . this I think might be what it feels like.

Everett's sunglasses are on his face now as he steers us toward the open water. We pass a few boats stopped in various places. Each one cheering a "hello" in the distance. Once we sail into the middle of the river, he cuts the motor and we gently float. It isn't terribly windy, so we're able to hover. Our view is of the main bridge that connects two counties. One of the most blinding drives when you hit it at sunset, but here, out on the water, the sun glistens off the bridge.

"Would you like some champagne?" His voice causes my

body to jump, and I turn toward him. "It's a bit sweeter than the average champagne, but as you can tell, I have a sweet tooth."

"Perfect." I grin. "I prefer sweet, too."

"I'll go grab some." Everett heads down the few steps that lead to the cabin door. He ducks through the doorway and disappears.

The boat isn't as large as I expected. It'd be a tight squeeze for Nora, Kinsley, and their fiancés for my birthday trip, but definitely doable. With two bench seats, the captain's chair, and at least two locations in the front to lay out in the sun, we wouldn't need much more.

Everett reappears with a bottle, two champagne glasses, and his sunglasses on his head. I'm nearly pinching myself that this dream of mine is becoming a reality in the most bizarre way. It feels impossible that an hour ago I was driving down here raging about work and a sailing company, and now I'm on the freaking boat!

Everett rests the glasses next to the steering wheel, and with ease, his fingers rip the wrapping off the bottle and he's twisting the cork all in one go. Note to self: never try to open a bottle of champagne in front of him. Or likely any bottle of alcohol. It's his day job, not mine. He pours two even glasses and then hands me one.

"To new beginnings," he says, tilting his glass to mine.

I squint up at him, shielding my eyes from the sun with my free hand. *New beginnings. Are we beginning?*

You've got this, Kinsley's voice tells me.

I clink my glass against Everett's. "To new beginnings."

We each take a sip of the champagne, and my goodness, this guy has the key to my heart. I've never cared for champagne unless it's in a mimosa, but this? I could down all this in one go if I wanted. I'm not even that much of a drinker.

"May I sit next to you?" he asks, and I move down a little

so he can be closer to the champagne bottle. I can feel the heat radiating off of him with our proximity.

It's been a while since I've wanted to pursue something as most guys suck. Online dating has gotten me a free meal, one sloppy kiss, and my friends questioning who the creep I'm dating is. A part of me wants to savor this. Not give them any information until I know it's something because I can't get my hopes up again and have them crushed. I feel too old for this.

"This is really stunning, thank you," I say softly as I look over toward the water. My nervous system has regulated, even though I'm sitting next to him. My body has deemed him safe, and thank goodness, so I'm not found at the bottom of the river.

"Thank you for joining me. This is a much better turn of events." His eyes focus on me, and I debate in my head if I want to jump into this intimate moment. The sun is setting and I know there will be a golden hue casting on him with his green eyes and tanned skin. I want to know he's someone I can have without going through the process of getting him.

I glance over, and his eyes soften.

"Can I tell you something that might make you not want to continue this conversation?" His words have my blood running cold. This is the moment I'm either going to die or he's going to make me wish I didn't get on this boat.

I take a sip of champagne, swallowing audibly. "Yes."

His eyes dart between mine, squinting just slightly. "I've never been in a serious relationship before. Most people seem to run at that, but I haven't found the right girl. And I'm only telling you this because I feel something between us that makes me want to get to know you better. But if you aren't okay with that, then this doesn't have to be anything more than champagne and the sunset, and we will go our separate ways."

I let out a breath as he finishes. *That* is bad? *That* keeps people from dating him? I mean, I get it. It's one of the reasons I'm in this position here. I take another sip of my champagne. It's now or never.

"Let me one up you," I whisper, and his brows raise with a smirk. "Not only have I not been in a serious relationship, but I'm also a virgin. Too work-focused, and suddenly, I'm nearly thirty with no experience."

Everett's free hand reaches over and rests on top of mine, that's gripping my thigh. "Thank you for sharing that. I imagine you've experienced some jerks if you've gotten to the point of telling others?"

I laugh, but I blink away a few tears. It's what I dread most about dating. I can't do anything about my experience. I'm not even ashamed of it. I wouldn't be where I am in my career today if I had dated around like my other friends. But now I don't want just a career. I want more.

"I'm not a virgin," he says slowly, "but I don't have much experience. I didn't necessarily want to lose my virginity when I did. I don't regret it per se, but it has made me feel inferior at times."

"Gosh!" I exclaim and let out a loud sigh as I sink into the cushion. I feel so much lighter expressing that. Even if this goes no further than this moment, there is a guy out there that isn't intimidated or disgusted or confused by me being a virgin, as if it somehow makes me less than. Undesirable. Or on the contrary, oversexualizing me as they count up their virgins they've "deflowered."

"Do you want more champagne? That seems like enough vulnerability for the moment." He chuckles as he takes a few more sips of his. The moment his hand leaves mine, an emptiness consumes me. Our hands weren't even interlocked, but they connected.

"Yes, please."

After he pours us both another glass and the bottle is back on the table, I take the opportunity to grab his free hand in mine, this time interlacing our fingers.

Together, we slouch just slightly toward one another, and stare out at the sunset.

My phone blaring causes both of us to jump. The world is dim around us, the sunset long gone. We had somehow started in our own spot, and I found myself wrapped in his arms as the golden oranges and yellows created magic in the sky.

I stand up, trying to find my backpack that got kicked off the seat earlier. Pulling out my phone, I see a Facebook Messenger video chat from Nora and Kinsley. *Fuck a duck; it's nearly been three hours since I messaged them.*

"Sorry, I have to take this." I step away from where Everett and I were sitting and click open the video, turning the volume down as low as possible.

"Thank god you're alive!" Nora yells through the phone. Apparently, my phone isn't too quiet because Everett laughs as he stands up and heads to the captain's seat.

"I'm alive," I confirm, trying to give them eyes to shut the hell up.

"Where are you?" Kinsley chimes in. "Oh my god, you're on the river!"

"On his boat?!" Nora screams.

"Did you watch the sunset?" Kinsley asks.

"Can we meet him? Where is he? Hey guy with the boat, come here!"

"Nora!" I hush. I'm grateful I can only make out the shape of his face, so there is no way he can see the blush and beads of sweat forming.

He must mistake my glance as a welcoming for him to come over and greet my friends because, all of a sudden, he's closing the distance, and my heart rate accelerates. They haven't met any of my terrible dates because they've all been, well, terrible. I barely know this guy.

But that isn't true. I know my body fits against his easily, and that our breathing syncs when in each other's arms, and that his fingertips make me shiver. I know that I don't want this night to end and the thought of traveling back to the Riverwalk . . . to have to separate in our own cars . . . that feels nearly impossible at this moment.

"Hello!" Everett greets, and I blink, realizing he's right next to me. Our faces can barely be made out through the tiny screen, but Kinsley and Nora are both well lit in their homes.

"Why hello, I'm Nora!"

"And I'm Kinsley!"

"I'm Everett. You must be Evie's best friends?"

"Ride or die. Hurt her, and I hurt you. Got it?"

"Nora!" I exclaim, only letting out a laugh to break the tension I feel within me.

"If anyone hurts Evie, I'll join you in hurting them," Everett says casually, as if it's the easiest thing he's ever promised. He has no idea who he is speaking with.

"Good answer," Kinsley responds.

"Where are you from?" Nora asks.

"Raven, about thirty-ish minutes from here."

Raven is an incredibly small town in the mountains. I wonder if he still lives there and commutes.

"How long have you operated this sailing business?"

"Less than a year. Took it over from my grandfather. Was a mechanic before then, and well, still am."

"Do you know how to operate a sailboat?"

"Nora, let the guy breathe!" Kinsley says.

"Yes, I know how to operate a sailboat. Was born and raised on one. Took my first steps on one too."

What a freaking life!

"What are your intentions with Evie?" Nora asks, and I all but crumble from embarrassment.

"If she's interested, I'd love to take her to dinner tonight, and then we'll go from there."

"That's our cue, Nora!" Kinsley says. "Have fun, and you must notify us the moment you walk through the door. He still cannot be trusted until he returns you home safely."

"Or if you're spending the night, you know, just let us know," Nora adds with an exaggerated wink.

My knees nearly buckle. I hate my friends.

"Okay, bye!" I say and turn off the camera. "I'm so sorry," I rush out. "They're protective when they know I'm on a date, and it has been a while since I messaged them—"

"Are we on a date?" Everett whispers, coming to stand in front of me. "When did it start?"

My stomach drops. I've said the wrong thing and messed it up again. "Oh um, I uh, I texted them at the cafe."

A smile graces his face, and his eyes light up. I control my breathing as I exhale. My poor body needs to rest.

"Cool, that's when I thought it might be a date, too." His hands reach forward and his fingertips graze my neck before they rest on my cheekbones. "What do you think, Evie? Would you like to continue this date with a proper meal? Maybe tacos up the block from the cafe?"

I inhale, and I can feel his breath on my lips. His head tilts toward me, and all I can do is whisper a "yes" before his lips crash into mine.

Everett cups my cheeks, steadying my stumbling form, righting me. His lips are soft and plump, and not terribly moist like the last guy's. My body tingles in places I never knew possible, and I take a step forward, wrapping my arms around his neck. Needing to be closer, needing to grasp his aura.

And when his lips break from mine, his head rests against my forehead. He's breathing heavily, tangling his fingertips into my frizzing bun.

"How is this possible?" he breathes.

"The feeling of emptiness when we separate?" I question, feeling the gap grow larger than when he let go of my hand.

"It feels like you may be who I've been searching for."

I take a step back, allowing the hollow weight to consume me. I need to pause. Take a moment. *This is insane. Is this how it is? When you're not looking? When you've given up hope? Is this what everyone's been talking about?*

"Let's go get tacos," I say.

Five

I wouldn't call myself a calm and collected person. I'm highly sensitive, an empath, and I work in a terribly stressful career. However, I'm great at faking my calmness when in director mode. If I'm the boss, I'm level-headed, even-toned, and clear about my intentions. When I'm off the clock? I sometimes wonder how someone allows me to be in charge of other adults in a field of chaos.

Cue to me laying on the floor, spread bald eagle, in my one-bedroom apartment. Kinsley and Nora are sitting at my feet, both drinking their coffees, while my caffeine turns cold. Honestly, the last thing my anxiety needs is caffeine. *Especially not a London Fog as a reminder of him, which reminds me of his hold, and his fingertips, oh, and how his lips tasted.*

"Fuck a duck!" I groan. Their silence is infuriating.

"I honestly don't know what we're stressing about," Kinsley says hesitantly. I glance over at her as she takes a sip from her cardboard cup.

"It seems like it went well?" Nora's confident voice is even hesitant.

It did go well.

"I told him I was a virgin!" I exasperate, throwing my hands up. "He's going to run. They all do."

"I'm confused," Kinsley says. "That happened before dinner, right? Evie, he asked you to *dinner*. He chose to continue the date. I understand that you said this on a boat where he was trapped, but he didn't have to ask you out. You two could have gotten into your separate cars to never see each other again."

"She's right," Nora butts in. "And the looks he gave you while we were on video last night? Girl, he's into you."

It can't be that simple, though, can it? Because it hasn't been in the past. I always go on a date or two and then get ghosted, or they get frightened to be with a virgin as if it's the scariest thing in the world. As if I'll break because they are the first to experience it with me.

My virginity is starting to feel like trying to get a job where you need seven years of experience for an entry-level position.

"Did you exchange numbers?" Nora asks. Suddenly, her phone is out, and she is tapping away. She isn't ignoring me; she's doing something way worse.

"Lemme see his social when you pull it up," Kinsley says, crawling over to Nora, hovering over her phone.

"You guys are the worst. And yes. We exchanged numbers, and he wished me a goodnight when he got home."

"He what?!" Nora exclaims.

"You didn't tell us that!" Kinsley shouts. "And you're on the floor panicking?"

"Get your butt up!" Nora motions with her hand. "No more moping. This boy is into you."

I laugh and roll my eyes as I push myself up, crossing my legs. I know they are right, but sometimes working to the next level is damn near impossible. "But what is the next move? How can we be sure?"

Nora hands her phone over to Kinsley, and she starts scrolling. "Gosh, he's handsome," Kinsley says.

"He is *fineeee*," Nora drawls.

I hate them. I already found his social media; thanks to Nora training me well. I spent most of the night looking through his Instagram, reading his captions and analyzing his photos. We have a few mutual friends on Facebook, but no one that I am close with.

My phone dings from the kitchen counter, and I freeze. *It can't be, can it?* The three of us make eyes before Kinsley darts up and across the room.

"Evie!" she yells. "This man is asking you out. Tonight."

I swivel toward her, and she tosses me my phone, which falls a couple of feet from me. I type in my passcode and immediately see his message:

Hey Evie, I hope you don't find this too forward. Though, I suspect you already know I am. But would you like to attend one of the sunset cruises tonight? I'd love to take you out for dinner, but I work during the normal time. I have a group tonight that are usuals, so it wouldn't be weird to add you along. And they aren't my friends; don't worry. I wouldn't put that pressure on us yet. I just know I want to see you again. And . . . you'd get a sneak peek into the packages I offer?

"Let me read!" Nora yells, reaching for the phone. "What has you blushing so hard?"

"He wrote a paragraph."

I jump, startled to find Kinsley reading over my shoulder. I shield my phone from her as if she didn't just read the entire thing. Suddenly, I feel protective. He is aware enough that adding friends into the equation could complicate things, which might mean he hasn't told his friends. Meaning, I've already overstepped that boundary.

My friends are different, though, right? We discuss and dissect everything. It's feminine nature.

"Are you really going to hold out on me?"

I glance over at Nora before letting out a sigh and sliding the phone across the carpet. I push off the ground and head to the kitchen, finally taking a sip of my lukewarm London Fog. Just the taste of it brings me back to the cafe. I was comfortable and happy. I felt good in my skin. The look in his eyes? I did see it; I recognized it was just for me.

"You have to go. I mean, another sunset cruise, two nights in a row? This is the life you've wanted. At least experience it while it lasts," Kinsley says, falling back onto my couch.

I do want to go, and I'm curious about the packages. I still want to book a ride for my birthday. But other people would be involved, and I don't know how—

"Done," Nora exclaims. "Meet him at five-thirty on the dock."

My cup almost falls out of my hand. *Fuck.* I rush back to the living room, grabbing my phone. Nora had responded for me.

That sounds perfect! What time should I meet you?

He sent over a wide-smile emoji.

5:30 would be great.

"Why did you do that?" My voice wavers. I think I'm excited, but I didn't have a moment to process. "What if he thought I responded too soon?"

"No one has time for games," Kinsley says. "We are too old for that."

"But—"

"Relaxxxx," Nora draws out. "Let's get you ready."

Six

How do you get ready for a casual-not-so-casual, not-really-a-date date? Beats me. I barely know how to get ready for a stereotypical dining date. Much to my argument, I ended up in a sundress with bike shorts underneath. Nora said it was casual and sexy, and "Heyyyyy, if he sees your shorts, he may see more."

I do look hot. My tight brown curls were twisted tight into a bun at the base of my neck and I only put on the slightest amount of makeup, just making sure to even my skin tone. I feel comfortable too. Comfort is the most important. I just have to hope the wind cooperates.

I pack a few of my favorite cardboard boxed wines. I'm not paying for this boat ride; therefore, I shouldn't enjoy the amenities. At least, I didn't think so. But another casual night, watching the sunset on the river with some liquid courage? Paradise.

What I didn't anticipate was the group of people hanging around Everett's booth. For some reason, after yesterday, it almost felt like a sacred space between the two of us. Obviously, I knew that people would be on this boat, but it is a cluster of obnoxious friends—couples, it seemed, no less.

Maybe that's what spurred the invite. After meeting me, maybe he no longer wanted to be alone?

Warmth spreads through my body at the thought, and I manage to take a few steps forward. Everett comes out of the booth, mouth open to talk to the group, but he catches my eye and a smile takes over.

My steps carry me faster, and soon, I'm a part of the cluster. Seven sets of eyes all gaze over me. It's the intensity of Everett's that has me praying my cheeks maintain their pale ivory tone versus a crimson.

"Guys, I have invited Evie here to join tonight's boat ride. She won't be interfering with the group, as she's a friend of mine, but she wanted to check it out, and I figured you were the best crew to upsell me." His speech ends in a wink toward the crowd, and my knees buckle.

"Absolutely! Evie, you have no idea what you're in for," a woman in a stunning mustard yellow romper says. Her brown eyes sparkle, highlighted by pink hues of eyeshadow.

This is weird. A very weird situation. I could be spending the night doing my own thing. Picking up a book to read or binge-watching a new show . . . maybe it is possible Nora or Kinsley are even free. Why am I choosing to go on a boat with strangers?

The rest of the crew greets me, all with friendly smiles and loud laughter. It seems like they may have already started drinking.

"Alright, go on ahead and get on the boat. We'll be right behind you," Everett says. They barely wait for him to finish speaking before they take off. "Hey," his voice lowers as he looks at me. "Thank you for coming. I know this is a strange request."

He closes the distance between us, and my breathing halts as I anticipate his next move. Are we there yet? We just greet each other with a kiss now after the first date? His lips gently touch my cheek before he pulls away.

The feeling of loss I had the night before? Nothing like the emptiness that just squeezed my heart dry. I've never felt this way before. Like I might not be able to take another step without the clarity of his lips.

Everett locks his booth up before reaching out his hand. Our fingers interlace seamlessly, and before he has a chance to head toward the boat, I yank our hands back.

"Yes?" A smirk crosses his face; his eyes dancing to read mine.

All feelings consume me, blocking out any logical thoughts. I lean forward, crashing—and I mean, crashing—my lips into his. His hand squeezes mine, pushing me back just slightly to steady our wavering bodies. I almost pull back, but his teeth nip at my bottom lip, solidifying our kiss. His free hand palms the base of my neck, and we both inhale, in-sync, as our lips sink deeper into each other.

I see you, Mom. Thank you, I think. My mother came through a medium a few months back, saying I'd find love when I was thirty. It seemed like a big task. After countless dates, never amounting to more than one, I didn't think it was possible.

"Love birds, let's go!" someone yells, followed by a group cackling.

It's the way I can feel his lips turn up into a smile against my own. And the hesitation in his fingertips that trail from my neck down my spine, all the way to my free fingertips. And when we part, his eyes tell me everything I need to know: we are falling.

EVERETT DOESN'T HAVE to sell me on a boat ride. I already knew that I wanted his services before I met him. And now that I know he's the captain? I'm sold tenfold. But I have to admit, this sunset service, with a charcuterie board, crab cakes, and red and white wine, from a local winery thirty minutes away, seemed like the best way to celebrate a birthday. Everett sailed up and down a short path on the river before he anchored near where the two of us watched last night.

While he steered, the group commandeered me as their own friend. They are in their mid-30s. They do this boat ride every two to three weeks over the summer. This is their first one of the season, but they had started the tradition nearly ten years ago. It is a pricey hobby, for sure, but they all have pretty demanding jobs—not unlike my own—but their salaries are twice mine.

I find myself tipsy on my wine and well-fed with cheese. Everett even has a stash of gluten-free crackers in the cabin that I am able to steal.

The best parts of the evening are watching Everett in action. His focus and concentration on maintaining the masts, how he squints his eyes despite having sunglasses and his hand shielding the sun, and his genuine laughter he provides to the conversation. He mentions that while his grandfather was in charge up until this year, he often took the weekend trips to give his grandfather a break—which is how he became so well-acquainted with this crew. They are already booked out for the entire summer and have tentative dates next year.

A part of me hopes that I might be able to join them again, but as Everett's partner instead of friend.

As the sunset starts, Everett sits down, ready to relax. His arm easily wraps around my shoulder, and I lean back as if we have done this hundreds of times. In his free hand is a glass of red wine that he sips casually. The conversations simmer as each couple pairs off and takes in the moment. Just listening to the birds swooping through the air back to their nests and the lapping of the river against the boat. I can feel Everett's heart-beat against my back, almost in-sync with mine. Thankfully, it hasn't been very windy and my dress is cooperating, but another sip of wine in and I think my guards will start to lower.

244

"You look beautiful," he whispers, his lips grazing my ear. His hot breath causes shivers to erupt through my body. "I would love to have dinner with you afterward if you'd like?"

"Yes," I breathe, sinking deeper into his embrace. I want to get him back to my place. Have peace and silence with him in privacy. Not to necessarily go further than we have already, but to help me recharge from this social energy that seeps into my bloodstream.

"What do you think about this for your birthday? I haven't even asked you when your birthday is." The handsome man still whispers, as if he isn't slowly undoing me with each word.

"June 12th, and yes, this seems perfect. My only request is—"

"Sweeter wine?"

My head swivels around immediately. "Exactly," I giggle. "That would be great. Or I could bring some."

"Nonsense. My packages are customizable. Even if they weren't, I'd make sure I had what you wanted. Let's get you booked in before we head off to dinner?"

I nod and shift my body so I can rest my head on his shoulder to admire the oranges, pinks, and yellows of the sky.

My cardboard boxed wines have me inviting Everett to my apartment. The first and only date who has ever stepped over the threshold. My tipsy heart hopes he's the last date to do so. Instead of eating out, we decided to get takeaway from the taco place up the street from the river and bring it back to my apartment. But now that the tacos have settled and soaked up some of the alcohol, I can't help but question if I made a mistake. Surely an invite back to someone's house means that anything is game, right?

"So tell me more about yourself. Tell me about your

friends and what you love to do for fun," Everett says, sinking back into the couch.

We had covered all basics already, but just a brief synopsis of both of our lives. We seem to interject each other's conversations, going back and forth, and then get distracted from the original conversation. But now, the two of us are sitting on my three-cushioned couch; Everett is cross-legged; I have my feet pulled up to my chest.

There is so much I could unload on this guy. Despite the feelings I've been having, I definitely only want to give him the cliff note version of my life because I don't have the energy to truly unload my baggage. I often let the guy do that first to see how vulnerable they could be. But maybe today is different.

"My friends and I can be wild. We feel chaotic. We always overbook ourselves, and have had to schedule time in order to see each other, or weeks go by and we wonder why we feel so crappy to only realize we haven't all been in the same room."

"I know that feeling well. My best friend Nate and I are similar. He's been in my life for years, ride or die, but the hecticness of adulthood takes its toll for sure."

"Exactly!" I exclaim, throwing my arms up and slapping my hands down on my knees. "And Kinsley is getting married at the end of the summer, so if days aren't slammed with work, they are slammed with other obligations and all her wedding stuff. I love it, but I also can't wait to breathe for a second."

"Maid of honor?" he questions, and I nod with a smile. "I can only imagine. I was Nate's best man a few years ago, and I felt like that was hard. The maid of honor and/or bridesmaids have the hardest jobs. There seems like so much more a bride needs to do."

"1000%." I laugh, leaning my head against the back of the couch. "I love it, and I love her, but the best man does get off quite easily. Nora helps, though, which is fantastic because I couldn't do half of this without her."

"So, does this mean that I got lucky this weekend by getting time with you, but that there might not be time in the future?"

Drinking two cardboard boxes of wine starts to hit my exhaustion. I'm comfortable and relaxed in Everett's presence, and I feel myself growing tired. I offer him a smile, but I don't lift my head from the couch cushion.

"I think I can make time for you."

"You think?" His smile is sly as he rests his head on the cushion next to him.

"I'd like to," I whisper. "If you'd like to?"

"Evie, I haven't felt this connection with anyone. I'd very much like to. I don't even want to say goodbye."

A soft smile graces my lips. My eyes travel from his eyes down his face and back up again. I have two options. Tell the boy he needs to go or ask for what I'd like, for him to come to bed with me and just cuddle.

"I'm not ready to have sex," I blurt.

Or there is a third option, apparently.

Everett lifts his head quickly off the couch. "Did I? Oh no, no, I'm not suggesting anything you're not comfortable with. I just know it's getting late, and we are both getting tired, which means a goodnight is closer than a hello."

"Would I be a tease to ask you if you'd like to stay the night? But just, like, maybe, uh, not naked?" My face is definitely crimson now after stumbling over my words. *Who the hell talks like that?*

When I lift my cowardly eyes, his cheeks are pink, but his eyes are so fucking hopeful it makes me want to immediately fall into them.

"It would not be a tease. You're saying you want me to stay the night? In your bed? Evie, I'd do that in a heartbeat. Sex or anything sex-related is entirely off the table until you tell me you're ready. But if you're giving me the opportunity to cuddle you? What are we waiting for?" He looks like he's about to bounce off the couch and find my room.

My laugh is breathy, and a weight lifts from my shoulders. I knew it had been there, but I didn't realize how detrimental it was. I was relaxed in his presence, but with that cleared up, my exhaustion seeps in faster.

"Yes, I am," I whisper.

He stands in an instant, holding his hand out for me. "Well then, I'd love to continue talking to you, but I'd love to do it horizontally."

I've never laid next to a date in bed. Not once. Only dreamed about how lovely it would feel with someone's arms wrapped around me. My body nestles back up against his. The warmth he radiates almost makes the blanket obsolete, but that's like an added security blanket. His arms wrap around my midriff, like a goddamn bear hug, and his chin rests on my shoulders. I can hear and feel his breath against my skin. I've never set a time limit on when I'd have sex with someone, as I never made it far enough to make that decision. And now I'm not sure how long I might be able to hold out. His touch has me questioning how he'd feel in other locations. My defenses are shrinking. My being becomes one with his.

My brain is practically mush while horizontal. I don't remember the last time I've felt this relaxed. But instead of asking me questions I don't have the brainpower to answer, he tells me about his family and his life. He is an only child as well, but instead of my one-parent household, he grew up with both. He lost an uncle, which is the closest to death he's ever been. He might not be able to completely understand the loss of a parent when I get the courage to mention it, but he seemed close with his uncle.

I don't remember the last thing he says before my eyes drift closed, but I do know that I haven't felt that at peace in a long while.

Seven

And just like that, time swooped in and created chaos. A month out from my birthday, weekends are packed, and nights sometimes provide sanity. Though, only sanity on the nights that include Everett cooking dinner and me stumbling back into my apartment shattered after a long day of work.

During the week, his sunset cruises are few and far between, that is, until the summer properly hits, he says. Instead, he has more daytime trips with retirees. Therefore, I quickly learned that he loves spending time in the kitchen, even more so when he learned I had PCOS, and made it his mission to learn new recipes that help my PCOS instead of counteracting it.

Right then and there, I was nearly ready to marry him.

Kinsley and Nora know of Everett, and know we are spending time together, yet they don't know how *much* time we are spending together. Honestly, most days it still confuses me that I have someone wanting to spend time with me, someone checking in on me, someone I *have* to talk to. I've had no issue with him spending the night since our second date. That I love. I love falling asleep in his arms and kissing him goodbye in the morning as I rush off to the gym. And coming back to breakfast made all before I, again, race off to work? I have to pinch myself constantly.

What is hard is the transition from zero to one hundred of someone being around. I'm not alone anymore. I have someone who cares about my whereabouts, who cares about my day, who relies on knowing my schedule. I have someone who checks in on me. No longer can I overwork at the office without Everett asking my ETA for dinner, or even wondering if dinner needs to be delivered to me.

I had worked so hard to get to a self-reliant place. Where I didn't need anyone. And now trying to balance my own time with the time of someone else's? While lovely is also a challenge. I don't want to sacrifice any of my old routines. Thankfully, after the first few dates, we have chosen to stay in each night and only go out on the weekends. Don't get me wrong, I'm not necessarily a homebody, but this month everything is on the line at work, so naturally, that's when the Universe presented me with Everett.

Despite Everett telling me it's more than okay that I'm not around as much as I hope to be one day, I can't help the guilt that festers inside me. It's all a countdown, though. It was before Everett came into my life, and still is. The weekend of my birthday, two weeks' time, is when things start to settle a little.

Tonight is the night before Kinsley's bridal shower. A secret I've managed to somewhat keep over the past two years. I'm grateful the bridal shower is just for the women versus being co-ed because I'm not ready to introduce Everett yet. My fingers are crossed for his appearance at the wedding, though.

It's rare that I've been able to keep the intensity of my blooming relationship a secret. But since I've been mastering the art of secrecy for wedding planning, hiding Everett in my own little bubble has been easier than anticipated. It also helps that

Kinsley is less than ninety days out from her wedding, so her time is well-consumed, and I've been rest assured, as the maid of honor, that my assistance, at the moment, hasn't been needed aside from the shower. And Nora is in desperate need of a new job, but until then, she's holding her head above water, remembering that she needs to survive long enough in order to pay for her wedding.

I don't mind the privacy, though. There have been so many what ifs and anticipations of who might be my partner. All of them have led to sadness. So when Everett and I got off the sunset cruise that first Saturday, I made the decision to become a little more private. I wanted to see where we could end up before my friends became too invested.

Thankfully, I suck at answering text messages, anyway. So if they happen to question me about him, I can either change the subject or be blasé. Though, I have found myself quite attached to searching for Everett's name with each notification.

Just as fast as my schedule changed with Everett in my life, I immediately got used to his presence every evening; Fridays are always jarring to walk into an empty apartment. I had quickly given him a key—fourth day to be exact. The first day, he showed off his cooking skills. It felt unlike me that first week we started dating, but there was zero apprehension or doubt that it was the right decision.

On Friday's, he has a sunset cruise, so instead, I'll be preparing us a meal tonight—that is, after panicking that everything I put in place for Kinsley's shower is on point. Everyone knows where to be, at what time, including her—well, she knows she has to be ready at her home by ten thirty in the morning.

As I'm organizing decorations into bags and placing them by the door, the door suddenly swings open and the savory smell of tacos consumes me.

Fuck a duck. I glance at the clock in the kitchen before

finally making eye contact with him. It's nearly an hour after the sunset cruise ended.

"You weren't answering your phone, and I know this morning you were stressed, so I figured tacos might be the best bet?" He offers me a heart-warming smile that has my stomach fluttering.

I stand up straight; I'll finish quadruple checking everything later. "You didn't think I'd come through with making dinner?" I ask. I'm honestly not sure if I'm busting his chops or not.

His face drops for a moment at the thought. "Oh, I'm sorry, Evie. Did you cook?"

My silence has his eyebrow cocking. He lets out a soft chuckle, and I sigh. I did truly have the best intentions. I don't deserve him.

"Well no, but—"

"Apparently, I know you quite well." He winks and side steps around me. He leans in for a kiss and then heads to the kitchen. "Take a break for some dinner, and then whatever else needs to happen, I can help you with."

I step away from the chaos of bags. I likely overbought. We may not even use half the stuff or need it. There are even gifts packed away; some for the guests, and then others for Kinsley, if her guests fail to follow instructions, which some seem quite good at.

I should be done. But after a full stomach, I'll do one final sweep and then I'll be able to sleep well.

Tacos are dished on plates when I make it to him and he pours passionfruit seltzer into wine glasses. He carries the plates, and I grab the glasses as we make our way to the couch. I have a small dining table, but it's overrated because then I can't lean back into his arms after I'm stuffed from dinner. Though, for how stressed I'm feeling, I shouldn't give myself the option to relax.

"What did I do to deserve you?" I semi-whisper under my

breath. It's a thought of mine, but I think I also want him to hear me.

"I've been asking myself the same thing." His voice is confident as he sits on the couch and hands me my plate when I'm ready.

I'm not quite sure what I've given him in return for all he's done for me.

We start eating, and I can't help thinking that our little bubble will have to pop soon. Sooner or later, Nora and Kinsley are going to grow impatient on the lack of Everett news and start asking me questions. Nora won't be swamped at work in a few weeks, and while Kinsley will probably continue drowning in owning her own business and trying to plan a wedding on a strict budget, she'll need a distraction.

"What's on your mind?" he asks, leaning over to take a sip of the seltzer.

I'd love an actual hard seltzer, but if tomorrow is anything like I hope it is, I do not need the extra booze.

"My friends are going to want to meet you soon. That is, when life is less distracting for them." These tacos are exactly what I need right now. Since meeting him, our taco consumption has increased, but I'm definitely not complaining.

Everett's fingertips reach out, resting on my knee as he holds his plate in his free hand. My dress has fallen an inch above my knee, and the direct contact of skin-to-skin has me shivering.

"You say it like it's a bad thing?" His eyes gaze at mine with a slight squeeze to my leg.

"No, absolutely not. My friends are just . . . they'll interrogate you." I awkwardly laugh. There isn't a way to make it any less intense. They can be the definition of intense.

"You act as if I didn't interact with them the first day I met you." He chuckles, bringing his hand back to his plate to finish his tacos. "I asked you out again; they didn't scare me away."

My face warms at the memory. Just one month ago. It feels like the shortest and longest period of time. "Honestly, I wasn't so sure we'd ever speak again, and now—"

"And now," he interrupts, and I eat the last bite of my taco, placing the plate on the coffee table. "I'd love for you to be my girlfriend."

I nearly choke as I swallow my bite without fully chewing. Before I met Everett, I couldn't imagine spending every free moment with someone, letting them sleep over, *in my bed*, all before being "official." Whatever "official" even means at our age.

But Kinsley had warned me of this. The rush of my time with Everett is similar to her and her fiancé's. They met one night, and by day three, she was sleeping over his house every night. But I barely even know what "girlfriend" means. Would my responsibilities change? Up until this moment, it was as seriously casual as my heart could make it. I still have my walls up to an extent, so if he ever wants to run, he can. But if I really think about it, I suppose him having a key and sleeping over every night is anything but casual.

"My mom is dead," I exclaim.

It's his turn to start choking on my words, so much so he's leaning over the couch, head hovering between his knees.

Jesus Christ, Evie. Way to be subtle.

"I'm sorry, I—" I move over toward him, running my hand up and down his spine. "I just realized that you didn't know, and I don't know when to bring up that conversation because I never wanted to bring down the mood. But I can't be your girlfriend without you knowing that."

My face is the temperature of lava, for sure. If he hasn't left me yet, it's only a matter of time. It's always a ticking love bomb, right?

Everett sits up, but I don't remove my hand from his back. He runs his hair through his perfect locks. His smile is somber;

but I don't know if he's representing pity or wants to retract his question.

His hand grasps mine, letting our interlaced fingers fall into his lap. "Evie, whether your mom has passed does not change the fact that I'd love for you to be my girlfriend."

I know that, deep down, obviously. I wouldn't have fallen for him if it did matter.

The tacos solidify in my stomach as I inhale. *Fuck a duck.* I've fallen.

"You only speak of your dad, anyway. I figured eventually you would open up about where your mom was. I just didn't want to push until you were ready." His words are gentle as he caresses the top of my hand.

Tears brim my eyes as I nod, giving his hand a squeeze. I think she brought him into my life. The idea heals a small portion of my heart, but the jump is so fucking terrifying. I'm already in the deep end.

I've never been a girlfriend. I've never allowed my walls down enough to truly and irreparably be hurt. I've been hurt by dates and a catfishing situation, but the vulnerability that comes within a relationship? The potential future pressure? No matter where we go from here, my heart is attached to every single moment.

Is it better or worse that my plus one to a wedding would actually be a boyfriend instead of just a date?

"Evie, if you're scared, just know that this is all new for me, too. We can experience this together. Figure out what works for you and me, not everyone else. But if I have incorrectly assessed the situation, please tell me soon because I don't like having my heart on the line with silence on the other end."

I look up at him, our faces only centimeters apart. He's semi-blurry through my watery eyes. His grip tightens, and I want to speak but . . . how the hell did I get here? I was one birthday away from potentially deeming myself single forever. And now?

My phone blares from across the room. We instantly jump to either side of the couch as if caught in an intimate position by a parent.

I shouldn't get up. I should let it go straight to voicemail and answer this poor man's question. But I need time and potentially need the voice of someone who is on the other end.

When I make it to my phone, the call has been put through again, but it isn't a phone call, it's a Facebook video chat. I click the button to connect, trying my hardest to not watch Everett's frame sinking into the couch.

"Hey guys," I greet.

"Hey!" Kinsley exclaims. "You okay?"

I plaster on a smile, moving the phone just slightly so I can rub both eyes clear of tears. "I'm great!"

My smile grows as Nora and Kinsley both stare at me and then each other before Kinsley starts speaking again. "Perfect idea, you ready?"

Was I ready for more ideas from the bride? Likely not.

"What's up?" I ask, smiling, swallowing my exhaustion.

"Tomorrow,"—Nora starts, and my lungs constrict. Nothing can be added to the bridal shower. Especially in front of Kinsley. If she ruins this at the last moment—"after the bridal shower." I let out a breath, and Nora smirks. She knows what she just did. "We are going to have a game night, and we are going to meet your boy!"

My eyes dart across the room to catch Everett's. He's staring right at me, face straight. I wish I could rewind the past few minutes and immediately answer his question. It will be a "yes," that is, if the option is still available after my foolishness.

"Oh my god, is he there?" Kinsley asks.

"Put him on!" Nora says.

Everett crosses the room and takes the phone from my frozen frame. Maybe a hard seltzer would have been a smart idea to loosen me up and not be so terrified by interactions.

"Hey girls!" They both shriek a hello. "I hear something

256

about a game night? I've heard of these, but I'm officially invited?" His tone is even-keeled, as if I didn't just ruin his confidence.

"Yes!" Nora yells.

"After my bridal shower . . . or, well, actually, we will start after your last boat trip out?"

It's sweet of her to remember his schedule. Between the six of us, it'll be a miracle if we can all get together as time goes on. *The six of us.* I like the sound of that.

"Bring your pretty self, your beverage of choice, and we'll provide the rest," Nora says.

This is all fine. Everything is fine. We'll hang up this call; I'll tell him, "Yes, I'd love to be your girlfriend," and the rest will be history. Evie has not just ruined the boy of her dreams.

"May I bring my favorite game?" Everett questions, and for once Nora, the queen of winning games, is silenced.

He has a favorite game? I should know this, right?

"Absolutely," Nora's fiancé yells in the background.

"Fantastic. Well, we will see you guys tomorrow night, but if you'll excuse us, we have dessert to get to."

They rattle off "ooh, la la's" before Everett is placing my phone on the countertop.

One, this man never mentioned dessert. Two, *Earth to Evie, what the hell is going on in your brain?*

"That sounds fun tomorrow. Should I pick you up, or will I meet you wherever game night is? Shoot, I should have asked." Everett casually speaks as he walks to the fridge and pulls out two slices of turtle chocolate cake.

Of course. It's Friday.

"Y-yes," I whisper.

His brow raises just slightly in question as he pulls two forks out of my silverware drawer.

"Yes, I'll be your girlfriend," I say, only a little louder this time, but he hears it because the forks clank on the counter, and his arms wrap around my waist instantly.

"Hi, girlfriend," he says, his breath brushing against my lips.

"Hi, boyfriend," I whisper, and he connects our lips as if he needs my oxygen to help him breathe, and maybe it's true.

A month ago, I could hold my own, but now? I can still hold my own because I won't get lost in another person—I refuse to—but our lives have intertwined. My plans go through him as his with mine. We aren't separate entities anymore. Well, before a title was placed, we had been operating as two individuals intertwined.

Eight

"You guys are official?!" Nora and Kinsley both squeal, and Willow barks and jumps up onto me.

I've always wanted to be in this position, but I could only imagine how it felt. And now that it is happening? It feels wildly overwhelming. Because what if they didn't like him? What if he didn't vibe with the other guys? We got lucky that Kinsley's and Nora's partners got along well, but adding a third partner into the mix? Was that asking for disaster?

Kinsley had already opened up a Truly Watermelon Cucumber Margarita for me, and the first few sips are starting to settle my low tolerance bloodstream. But he isn't here yet, not that he is late, but the anticipation is killer, and I know the questions aren't going to stop.

"We are, as of last night." I laugh as they give me a massive group hug.

"We are so excited for you!" Kinsley says.

"See! Aren't you happy I responded as you that day?" Nora says.

"Yes, yes, I am." I giggle while balancing it out with a slight eye roll.

Kinsley gestures toward the living room, and we all grab

our drinks. The boys are off playing some video game while we wait for Everett to show up.

"Why are you being so secretive?" Kinsley asks, curling up on the couch under a blanket.

I take the couch across from her, and Willow jumps up onto me, settling to lay her head on my lap. I wonder if Everett likes animals. We have had the weirdest conversations. Some conversations were so intense and personal, and others, like pets and my mother's death, we had barely even spoken about. This is all stuff I should know before committing, right?

"Get out of your head. Stop panicking. He likes you. He's coming to hang out here. He's already spoken to us twice. Love, you're good," Nora says, sitting next to me.

"But I don't know—" There's a panic in my voice that I can't control, and the girls' know by heart.

"You don't need to know everything yet," Kinsley starts. "If you do, what's the point of the future? You'll get bored with him."

I let out a sigh. *I know. I know. I know.* Willow snuggles her head further into me, and I pull her into a hug. She always knows when I need added comfort, and I suppose I'll find out the answer to the pet question tonight.

"What do you want us to grill him on that you're maybe nervous about?" Nora asks, which is nice considering she's usually unfiltered and doesn't care whether or not I'd want her to ask something.

I shrug. My biggest anxiety is going all the way with him. But the dialogue in my head has turned into when the right moment might be, and I think it may be here sooner than I anticipated.

"You really like him," Kinsley observes softly, taking a sip of her mixed gin. "You're afraid you're going to fuck it all up."

I nod and my eyes instantly blur. *Fuck a duck.* I don't have time to be overly emotional right now. If I start crying, I'll air out my fears about the relationship. Fears of letting go. Fears of being vulnerable. Fears of being loved. Do I even deserve it?

A chime rings through the house, and three of us, including Willow, jump at the sound. No one has used the doorbell here since Kinsley and her fiancé bought the house.

I climb off the couch, Willow following excitedly, the moment I realize what is happening. Racing down the stairs, I see him standing outside. His smile widens when he notices me through the glass and he holds up a cake as Willow starts attacking the door. A brand new friend; her favorite.

Also, Everett is my favorite with his dessert heart; I've always needed someone like him.

"Down, down, down," I pre-warn Willow before I open the door.

Kinsley comes chasing down with treats, getting Willow to anxiously sit as I let Everett through the door.

"She'll calm down in a sec," Kinsley welcomes Everett.

He hands me the cake and is immediately on his knees, petting Willow. I almost avoid Kinsley's eyes, but it's evident Everett has already won her over.

"She's so cute. I love animals, but I definitely miss having a dog," Everett offers, and *check!* One more thing I know about him.

"Good, I'm glad. She'll wanna love you all night," Kinsley says before reaching out her hand.

Everett tries to shake it, but Willow sneaks her paw in first, shaking his hands. He chuckles, and leans down to kiss her paw. *Is it too soon to elope?*

"In case you forgot, I'm Kinsley, and this is Willow."

"It's nice to meet you both. I brought, uh, my favorite cake and game. I hope you don't mind?"

I notice his backpack on his shoulder that must contain the game.

"Not at all!" Kinsley grins. "I'll meet you both upstairs." She wiggles her eyebrows at me, takes the cake, and rushes off.

"Hey you." He embraces me, and I sink into his arms.

My overactive brain simmers when he rests his head atop mine. "Hey," I whisper.

It's the first moment today that I feel like I can breathe. I haven't processed that Kinsley's shower is over. Just one more step of getting through tonight.

"Relax," he whispers. His head tilts, pressing a kiss to my neck, and I shiver. "Tonight will be great. And if it isn't? It isn't the end of us."

Everett trails his hands up my arms and interlaces them on the back of my curls, tilting my head back. His deep green eyes gaze into my own, and I believe everything he's saying. This isn't an all-or-nothing event. If he had major red flags, Nora and Kinsley would likely already know. If anything, they have no idea of all the green flags he presents.

I lean up just slightly, pressing my lips against his. We are able to kiss for only a few seconds before Willow jumps up, reminding us she's there. Chuckling, Everett interlaces our fingers, and I lead us all up the stairs.

"Why hello, I'm Nora," Nora offers, looking Everett up and down once we get into the kitchen. "Hot damn, Evie." Her eyes widen and then she winks toward me as if Everett isn't standing right there, watching her every move.

Everett laughs, squeezing my hand before his arm wraps around my waist. Shivers course through my body at his public display. We've been in restaurants, and in front of that group on the boat, but with my friends? It feels way more intimate.

Without missing a beat with Nora, he says, "I think it's more so hot damn, Everett. Not sure how I got so lucky."

And now I'm just melting. I do everything I can to not stumble on my feet or have my face warm or let out an embarrassing giggle. They can read me like a damn book, and now I think I want the focus off of me.

"Ooh," Nora coos, "and he's good with his words. But let's see if he's good with his games."

And insert the awkward squeak of a laugh.

Everett's fingers squeeze my side gently before he lets go and opens his bag up on the kitchen island. He pulls out Ticket to Ride Rails & Sails and then a deck of cards that showcases different sail-boats. Suddenly, I realize I've never stepped foot in his own home.

"Oh! We've been wanting to play this one. It looks dope," Kinsley's fiancé says.

"He's a keeper. We don't have this in our collection yet," Kinsley says.

Everett just beams at me; like he just got accepted into the friend society. Like this is the biggest deal of all time.

I glance over at Nora, who is silently reading the back of the box.

"Oh, got Nora out of her comfort zone. They don't know this one," Kinsley's fiancé points out. Nora and her partner are notorious for kicking our asses in Ticket to Ride games.

Everett pulls out a bottle of wine, Kinsley hands him a wine glass, and just like that, the night is history.

Everett does kick both of the guys' asses. Naturally, I lose, like always. But as a couple, that now means there's competition for all parties, no matter if I'm better at just card games versus board games.

For the next game, we finally play a game I'm ace at; Rummy. It's hard to get this group to play any card games because they all suck at card games and out vote me. But now I have two votes instead of one, so *HA, we're equals now, friends.*

It's quickly clear, though, that I've met my match. Everett claims he's never played the game before, but he takes instruction well. And the damn guy is already beating me.

My hard seltzer helps calm my game frustrations as I was supposed to easily win. Supposed to be impressive. As the game ends, he announces that he's won. But it isn't a shove-in-the-face win. I'll call it beginner's luck for coming to the first game night. Instead, he leans over and kisses me on the lips.

The lips! In front of my friends.

Nora squeals, and I want to turn my head away, but Everett bites my lower lip gently, finishing out the kiss before he separates, but only slightly.

"It's okay. I still love you."

I inhale, and I hear the collective gasps from Nora and Kinsley, and a fucking high-five from the boys.

This can't be real. Can it? Is it possible? Just after a month? After the first night we are official? Is it possible to love that fast?

I lean back, sitting up straight as I study Everett's face, my peripherals blurring. It's just him and me, and Willow shoving her face onto Everett's lap.

"What did you say?" I whisper. My heart rapidly beats in my chest, pressing obnoxiously against my rib cage. This is what I've read about in the books and watched in all my favorite romance movies. But me? I'm worthy of this? He *loves* me?

"Evie," his words are soft and he grabs both of my hands off the table, interlacing our fingers. "I love you. I knew you were different from the moment I met you. I'm so glad you came into my life."

I've never heard Nora be so silent for so long. Not an interruption. A gasp. A laugh. Four sets of eyes burn through the tension building.

His eyes search mine, and *again*, I'm making this poor guy wait for an answer that if I'm honest, I knew days—even weeks—ago. I just wasn't confident of when I should say it.

"I love you too, Everett."

His lips press against mine, and Willow jumps up onto my shoulders, giving me a hug from behind. And just as I'd anticipate, Nora and Kinsley squeal and clap from across the table. If I know anything about them, they are both planning my wedding in their heads.

Nine

Today's the day. I'm no longer twenty-nine. I went to bed in Everett's arms, and then, unfortunately, it starts with a kiss on the lips and a departure from him. He has three boat trips before my sunset birthday cruise. Luckily, I have the best friends who have chosen to celebrate the entire day with me. Well, hopefully not after my birthday cruise, because I have other plans for that.

Because it's a special day, I chose my bomb-ass black dress that has a slit to my upper thigh and shows a good amount of cleavage. It's my fancy dress I like to wear out when I'm looking to feel sexy for myself. It might be a bit revealing once on the boat, but it doesn't matter anymore because I'm *dating* the sailing instructor. And I want said sailing instructor to possibly take it off of me later for the first time.

I giggle and squirm in my bed, kicking the sheets around just at the thought of it. Hello thirty: sexy, thriving, and flirty.

Rolling out of bed, I make it to the kitchen to see a coffee cup sitting on the island with a note beside it. I rush over, hand already over my mouth. Birthday surprises?

Good morning, my love. Happy birthday. I am so excited to be able to treat you on your 30th. It can be such a special birthday, and knowing this birthday is what brought us to meet . . . I'm so grateful. Please enjoy your London Fog and brunch with Nora and Kinsley. I'll be counting down the minutes until I see you for your cruise. I love you.

It's been a week, and I still cannot get over hearing "I love you" or reading it. It almost feels like a fairytale. Like everything is finally falling into place. While I might want to leave my job, I do have a job—a highly regarded position at that—and I have my own place, and now I have my own guy. Not that I needed a man to be complete in any regard. We aren't each other's halves; we are both two wholes, just creating an even fuller life for ourselves.

Best part is he's kept his word. We haven't gone all the way. We've made out. We've felt each other up. We've slept naked. But I haven't been ready, until this moment, to allow him to have that part of me. He's been patient, kind, and a gentleman, and I know it's going to be an excruciating amount of hours until we are both back in this apartment alone.

DURING BRUNCH, Kinsley, Nora, and I make good use of the bottomless mimosas and my free birthday breakfast at my favorite place on the Riverfront. I always have eggs benedict, bacon, fresh fruit, and mimosas. The best part and tradition of my birthday morning.

"I can't wait for this boat ride later!" Kinsley says, shoving waffles into her mouth. "I can't wait to see what this package is."

Of course, my brain is running in seven million directions and turns into a teenage boy—Nora's trained me well—and I giggle at the word "package." I may have seen it already, felt it up against me, but I'm hoping my birthday present has been worth the wait.

Nora glances over at Kinsley, and they both share a look before darting their eyes to me. I take the opportunity to finish off my mimosa.

"Have you . . . are you . . . "

"Oh my god, you're going to have sex!" Nora exclaims.

Thankfully, Kinsley covers Nora's mouth in her own social anxiety as I slouch down in my chair. I had already surveyed the restaurant when we walked in, noting there were no clients, but you can never be too sure.

"Wow. Oh my god. I'm so excited," Kinsley says. "Does he know? Is this planned?"

I look around for the waitress, hoping to refill my glass before I have to answer the interrogations. Thankfully, she nods at me with a smile.

"He doesn't know, but I'm ready," I manage to say, sitting up as the waitress carries over another champagne glass filled to the brim. I'm thirty now. Gotta embrace my body in all ways.

"You should text him. Give him a heads up," Nora says.

The blood drains from my face. I hadn't ever considered the thought that when I was ready, he might not be. He's a guy. . . . Though, he had mentioned he doesn't have much experience. Is it possible that I might not get what I want tonight? I mean, I have to respect his boundaries too. Women aren't the only ones who get to have them, but—

"Whoa, slow your roll, Evie," Kinsley says, reaching her hand across the table. "Nora wants you to start foreplay."

Oh. OH. My eyes shoot between the two of them in a panic. I don't know how to do that.

"Hand it over, girlfriend," Nora says, gesturing her hand in a "gimmie" motion for my phone.

"Oh no. Nope. Absolutely not." I pull my purse that's hanging on my chair closer to my body so Nora can't swipe it.

267

"I appreciate your guidance, and you can talk me through this, but you will not be sending sex messages to my boyfriend."

Kinsley chokes on her mimosas as I finish my statement, and Nora just lets out a laugh.

"Let's do it then!"

Over the next ten minutes, the three of us brainstorm how to start this conversation. I think it should just be letting him know I'm ready. Nora and Kinsley think I should start a sext of sorts, letting something build up throughout the day, making it harder (pun intended, Nora assured) for Everett and me to be on the boat. As if I hadn't been wanting to do this for my thirtieth forever and will now ruin my enjoyment of it because I want to be home in bed. We can be home in bed *whenever*. Just not during the freaking sunset.

We settle on:

Hey you, I can't wait to see you later. After the boat ride, I have an idea for one last gift.

His response is nearly immediate. Doing the math, it looks like we caught him right at his boat change.

Of course, birthday girl. What would you like?

He sends a kiss emoji too, and the mimosas in me want to run down the street and give him a kiss before he takes off again. But I can't do that because one, it's rude to ditch my friends, even if Nora and Kinsley would encourage it. Two, it's unprofessional for him in front of his next party.

You.

Is the only answer I respond with, directed by Nora for being classy and concise.

You've got me, love. I need you to be a bit more specific.

"God, he's a gentleman. Either he honestly doesn't know what you're talking about or he doesn't want to assume. Both are sexy. Go have boat sex!" Nora suggests, wiggling her eyebrows.

I mean, it's not like I haven't thought of that before Everett. And now that I know a guy with a boat? A boat with a cabin? You see, I may not have had sex yet, but I do have a kinky side. At least, I believe I'd seriously enjoy some fantasies I've had. Now, it's having the opportunity to actually role-play them.

Thankfully, for my own comfort and concern, I got myself waxed yesterday. I always get waxed regularly, but it was like my usual lady knew exactly what my plans were going to be too when I asked for a little more than a bikini wax.

Is it written all over my face?!

I respond back:

I'm ready to go all the way.

That isn't exactly what Nora wanted as foreplay sexting, but I'm comfortable.

Fuck.

Is all the man says.

My heart drops, and my hands start to shake.

"Fuck!?" I exclaim, dropping my phone on my table. "What does that mean? Does that mean he doesn't want me? That he isn't ready? Did I just mess it all up?"

Kinsley swivels my phone on the table, dragging it toward her. She's grinning nearly immediately when I would very much like to crawl under a hole in sweatpants and a sweatshirt.

I feel so exposed, especially since my cleavage is the first thing I see when I look down at this dress.

"Evie, you should read the rest."

"The rest?!" I take the phone back and click the screen back on.

Fuck.
Evie, you can't . . . you can't say that while I'm at work.
I . . . I have two more trips before I see you, and now I
want to cancel them both.
Okay, okay. Yes. Tonight. Your place. After we ditch
your friends in a frantic goodbye. I'll make sure it's the
best present yet.

Well now, all I want is to interrupt his next trip and tell his guests that the boat is occupied.

———

SUDDENLY, I'm nervous. I am way out of my element. *Way* out of my element. I mean, for one, I am feeling things in places I didn't know I could feel things in. And I mean, like, of course, during sex, but just through words? Through a phone? Without physical contact? Hours after they were sent? It might be the additional liquor from one of my favorite cocktail bars, Sauced, but there is a part of me that wishes I didn't invite my friends on the sailboat. I find myself wanting it to be like the first night we met.

I couldn't cancel on them, though. I mean, they'd understand. Frankly, they'd probably root for it. But they weren't paying for it, my dad . . .

Oh no.

I immediately freeze. The girls and I are just hanging out by the water. We had gone through the shops; I bought a few outfits, and now we are just having fancy cocktails, waiting for

Everett's boat to come back. Kinsley's and Nora's fiancés are about to meet us, too.

"What's wrong?" Kinsley asks, downing the rest of her cocktail.

"I just realized my dad is going to be on this boat." He had paid for it, the entire thing. It was always going to be my birthday trip, well before Everett came into the picture. He knows about Everett; we don't keep secrets. But he hasn't met him yet.

Nora laughs loudly, leaning back against her chair. "Oh my god. You totally want to just fuck Everett, and your dad is about to cockblock you."

He would. He'd probably find it funny, too. We have a strange relationship. I think it's different from what most people have, and I link it to losing my mother so young. But he's there when I need him, and apparently, there when I really don't need him.

Kinsley joins in on the laughter.

"Who's cockblocking who?" Nora's partner asks as the two guys stroll up, bringing chairs to our table. They look ready for a beach day, in their swim trunks and t-shirts, despite the plan of not getting in the water.

"Evie has been sexting Everett," Nora says.

"Guys!" I exclaim, shooting daggers at both Nora and Kinsley. My face warms, and sweat collects on the back of my neck. Both partners know I haven't had sex yet. But they don't need to be a part of *this* conversation.

The table grows quiet suddenly, and then hands are on my shoulders, squeezing slightly. I've memorized those hands. They send shivers throughout my body, and now, between my legs, tingles in anticipation. But my embarrassment comes from wondering what he could have possibly heard. I didn't see his boat pull in.

"How's the party going, guys?" Everett comes to my side and leans down to press his lips against mine.

Yup. Let's cancel the boat.

"Fantastic!" Kinsley exclaims. Nora just lets out another cackle.

I can't take them anywhere.

"It seems," Everett chuckles. "We may need some life jackets, depending on how you all walk to the boat."

Nora, Kinsley, and I glance at each other. That's not the relaxing sailboat adventure we are looking for.

"I'm joking!" he exclaims. "But can you all walk to the boat? I am ready when you are."

"Of course!" I say, sliding my chair out and standing up. Naturally, my damn shoes cause me to stumble into Everett. "I'm great." I smile.

"I see that." His breathy laugh tickles my neck, and he kisses my cheek, steadying me. "You look absolutely stunning," he whispers in my ear.

It's going to be a long couple of hours.

My dad is already on the boat by the time we all walk over to it. He is stepping away from a tapestry that says, "Happy 30th!" hanging from the back mast. There are even white lit string lights around the deck. The sun is a bit overpowering to see the magic of them, but I can only imagine how they'll look on our sail back.

The table screwed into the middle of the walkway, where Everett presents the charcuterie board for his guests, already has filled wine glasses hanging off the side of the table. He has these cool contraptions that act as cup holders. He showed me one day he can add as many as needed along the edges of the table.

"Happy birthday!" my dad greets me. It's the first year that I've been out of the house for my birthday. We didn't even have a chance to talk on the phone this morning, as I was distracted by Everett and then brunch. To be honest, our daily phone calls have turned into every two to three days since Everett's been around.

"Thank you!" I give him a hug and take in the rest of the boat. I didn't ask for the string lights or the tapestry. My package includes cheese and wine, that's it.

Everett's fingertips on my lower back have me jumping before leaning back against his hand. "Have a seat. We have a surprise," he says.

I glance around and my friends have already taken their seats; we're all going to squeeze on the benches, I guess. I'm sure we'll venture to the front of the boat for more space, but it's tough to eat that way.

My father disappears down in the cabin as if he owns the place. Everett said, "We?" as in him and my father? I have so many questions, but before I can ask, Everett follows my dad down into the cabin.

I take an empty seat next to Kinsley, the seat closest to the captain's chair.

"Do you guys know what's going on?" I ask. There's a nearly empty wine bottle by Everett's steering wheel. It's a winery about an hour away that we've talked about going to this summer. He kept saying that I'd probably love it because they specialized in sweet white wine. But that isn't all; not all the wine glasses have white wine in them. Some are red.

"This is beautiful," Kinsley says.

"I'm so excited!" Nora exclaims, looking around.

Naturally, they ignore my question. I guess I'm not the only one who keeps secrets.

Suddenly, my father and Everett come back up. My dad is holding bags of tacos, and Everett has chips and queso in his hand. I shouldn't be hungry with how much we've consumed today, but my stomach growls as the scent hits my nose.

Everyone helps sort through the tacos once my dad puts the bag down. Everett empties his hands, and starts handing off wine glasses to everyone. Kinsley and her partner have red wine, Nora has a rosé, her partner has a white, my dad has a deep red, and Everett then sits next to me with a white, and hands me a white too.

I'm pretty much in heaven.

"I hope everyone enjoys the wine. I took everyone's suggestions into consideration, but I'm also hoping it's all a new wine for you guys."

Everyone's suggestions? When has he been messaging my friends *and* my father?

"Happy 30th to Evie!" Nora yells. We all cheer our glasses and take a sip of our respective wines.

I moan as I swallow the liquid, closing my eyes to savor the taste.

"Keep doing that, and I'll cancel the trip," Everett whispers in my ear. He presses a kiss against my neck, and I grip my wine glass tightly.

Holy hell, he'll be the death of me.

"Love birds, it's time to eat!" Nora says, and I glance over at everyone as my face warms. Everyone but Everett and I are devouring food.

Everett rests his palm on my thigh, conveniently on the side with the slit. I lean forward, searching for a taco, trying my hardest to ignore the way his hand creeps closer to uncharted territory.

Everett didn't skimp or miss a beat on giving me the perfect birthday sail. I learned throughout the night that Everett and my dad collaborated to make sure my trip was extra special. And that Everett had found Nora and Kinsley on Facebook and asked them about their favorite wines—all before the freaking game night. Apparently, I thought I had been hiding the intensity of our relationship well, but turns out, they basically knew Everett had been spending the night. They were just giving me the space to process my own emotions before filtering in too many outside thoughts. My dad provided commentary when necessary, but for the most part, he kept to himself and just enjoyed the ride. He seemed to approve of Everett, as most of his comments were directed at him, wanting to learn more about the boat itself.

I don't think the trip can get any more perfect, that is, until we are cuddled at the head of the boat, watching the sunset with the bridge in the background. I have been on the boat some weekend mornings, helping Everett stock up for his trips, but it has been a month since the last time I've been in this position.

I could get used to a lifetime of this. A lifetime of soft pecks against my neck, and Everett whispering in my ear, and the way his arms feel, wrapping around me as I snuggle back against him. My loved ones are here with me, showing up on the day I need them the most. Despite our lives being stressful, they are here. They have never left me.

Lights erupt with a crack as the sky dims. We collectively jump, and I twist my head to look at Everett. His grin is so wide, tears brim my eyes.

"Watch," he whispers.

I turn around and watch as pinks, blues, oranges, and white fireworks fizzle above us. The string lights are now serving their purpose. I have a warm buzz still going from the delicious wine.

The show isn't long, but it's absolutely perfect.

"Does anyone know why there were fireworks tonight?" Kinsley asks when silence takes over. Most of us have conglomerated to the front of the boat.

"My buddy Nate lives off to the right." Everett's arm lifts and points into the darkness. It's about a fifteen minute drive from where we are. I haven't met any of his friends yet. "He wanted to do something special for the girl who 'stole me away from him.'"

I laugh; I've had a similar thought process about my

friends' partners coming into their lives. I think we'll get along just great.

"Thank you for the most incredible birthday yet," I whisper, kissing him.

AFTER I'VE HUGGED everyone goodbye, and thanked them immensely for spending the day with me, I turn around nervously. Everett wraps his arms around my waist. Our eyes meet, and I can see the intensity behind them. This is the moment I've been waiting for. The anticipation was just like Kinsley and Nora had warned. Except, now I don't want to be patient anymore.

"How are you feeling?" he asks, brushing his lips across my forehead. "Would you still like to sleep together, or would you like to change your mind?"

"I'm ready," I whisper, stepping just an inch closer to press our bodies together. I caress his cheek with my fingers. Just the fact that he asked makes me even more confident.

"Do you want to go back to your place? Or would you like to go to the boat cabin?"

My mind immediately flashes to *50 Shades of Gray* and my thoughts on wanting to be a bit more adventurous.

"The cabin."

His eyes dance at my words, and in an instant, our hands are interlocked, and he's jogging us back to the boat. He helps me down the narrow few steps of the cabin before he turns and locks the cabin door. I had only admired it briefly when I used the restroom earlier. But there's a small kitchen, bathroom, and then a majority of the space is a queen sized bed that rests up against the front of the boat.

But now, not only are there water bottles on the end tables, he has on two dim lights, string lights surrounding the cabin, and soft music playing. I turn around, and all he does is grin.

"I was a bit delayed coming off the boat because I was hoping you might say you'd want to stay here. I know we've discussed spending the night on the boat, so I was hoping tonight would be that night."

"It's perfect." I walk over to the bed and take a seat, kicking off my shoes. I press my legs down with my hands as the nerves and anticipation start to shake through my system. I want this. I do. But I have zero fucking idea of what I'm doing.

Everett unbuttons his short sleeve collared shirt as he walks over to me. His hands cup my cheeks, tilting my head toward him. "We will go at your pace, okay? At any moment in time, if you want to stop, let me know and we will stop."

I nod.

"Do you want me to take the lead, or do you want to?"

"I trust you," I whisper.

He smiles before connecting our lips. I will myself to be in the moment, to feel the pressure of his lips and the softness of his fingertips trailing down my neck and across my shoulders. The shivers that pass through give me the confidence to reach up and grasp his neck, pulling him over me.

"Evie, I love you," he murmurs against my lips.

"I love you," I say before I end in a fit of giggles as Everett suddenly grasps my waist and tosses me back onto the bed. "Graceful," I laugh, situating myself so I'm laying in the center of the bed.

"You were starting to tense up. Gotta be light and free." His smile is magnetic, and it's like seeing him shirtless for the first time when he peels his shirt off and tosses it to the side. His skin is freshly golden from today's sun. What really turns me on is him crawling up onto the bed, placing a knee between my legs and hovering above me, hands on both sides of my face.

When our lips connect again, I surrender. He interlaces our fingers on both hands and presses them back against the bed, resting his body against mine, so I can feel the rise and fall of his breaths. The body weight helps center me; I consume his energy and start to listen to the way my own body feels and reacts toward him.

My body becomes sensitive to each and every movement. The way his fingers trail my naked skin, dip down and up and in. I wriggle and lift my hips to his movements. I'll never be able to go back. The way this feels. The way he feels. I was always warned that my first time could be a total dud, that it could be just enough to "lose my virginity," and then the second or third go, I'd learn more of what I liked. Honestly, I think not having a good first time is a combination of different factors; one of those being each person not knowing how they like to be pleasured.

By the time that Everett is ready to be in me, I'm begging him for more. He has me at my most vulnerable. He's taken the time to make sure this feels incredible, that I'm close to the edge, that I might nearly orgasm on my very first time, which I read is often impossible for most girls. Again, likely lack of knowledge and shitty partners.

After confirming for the hundredth time, Everett changes my world. He's gentle and slow, and he's holding me in a bear hug as he waits for me to be ready to continue. It's a moment I can't take back, but never want to. I'm safe. I'm happy. I'm terrified to feel the loss the moment we need to disconnect.

As my hips buck up against him, Everett crashes his lips into mine, and we find a pace that has us gripping each other for dear life. It's an unexplainable feeling; but I'm certain he is my first and last. He's nestled his way into the cracks of my heart, sewed them together, and he'll forever be a part of me.

I didn't think it was possible to feel anymore than I already am, but when my name breathlessly leaves his lips, he's not only shaken my world, but I'm forever changed.

"Evie," he softly says.

I glance over at his scattered locks, taking him in. We're

278

sitting in bed, each eating a slice of birthday cake, fueling up. He looks handsome, naked, with just a simple sheet covering our bottom halves, more so acting as a napkin. I always wondered what happened after sex. When you want to be casually lazy. It's not weird or strange to just be sitting here naked in front of him, eating. He sure knows the way to my heart.

"Yes?" I ask, taking a bite of cake.

"I'm all a-boat you." His face is straight as I process his words. As he cracks a smile, I nudge him, rolling my eyes.

"You're cheesy," I laugh.

"You love me." His smile is smug as he puts his empty plate down.

I inhale at his words, allowing a smile to grace my lips as we look at each other. "I do." He takes my plate and puts it on the end table. "I love you, Everett."

His lips press into mine, gently leaning me back onto the pillow.

Happy birthday to me.

Acknowledgments

Thank you to **Ashlyn Drewek**, **D. Allyson Howlett**, and **Danielle Merchant** for joining me in this adventure to create Represent Publishing's 1st anthology. I have loved working with you all and have enjoyed the stories you've created specifically for this anthology. It makes me beyond happy to have had faith from you three. Thank you for trusting me with your work, and I hope this is everything you hoped it would be.

Another incredibly huge thanks, as always, to **Brittany Evans**. Thank you for always creating the most amazing covers and graphics for me! I love being able to tell you I have no idea what I want and somehow you're able to create the vision I barely knew I had. I love how in-sync we are. And I am beyond grateful to call you my friend.

And thank you to all the readers who make anthologies like this possible. You may have picked up this book for one specific author, but I hope you stayed for all. Without our readers, none of this would be possible, so thank you!

I hope this anthology is the first of many anthologies to come!

Love,
Chelsea Lauren

D. Allyson Howlett
"Spirits n' Chai"

Born and raised in the crowded suburbs of Long Island, NY, one thing she never lacked was imagination. Writing screenplays and filming movies with her dad's video camera was her passion and, once college came around, her career. But life doesn't always work out the way we plan it to. All it took was one book about dragons to create the dream of becoming a published writer.

D. Allyson Howlett lives in a New England farm town with her husband, two boys, four house pets, and four crazy cluckers. She loves to be outdoors, is an avid fan of all things' 80s, and enjoys pizza and ice cream Fridays with her family.

Ashlyn Drewek
"Wither"

International best-selling and award-winning dark romance author Ashlyn Drewek has always been a hopeless romantic. She's also fascinated by the dark, macabre things in life (you can blame a love of Halloween and Edgar Allan Poe for that one).

Most of her time is spent making up stories in her head or researching some obscure topic just because she's that much of a nerd. The degree on the wall says she's a historian, but the paycheck says she's a first responder.

Ashlyn lives in Northern Illinois with her patient husband, fearless daughter, and a house full of animals.

Danielle Merchant
"Fairytale Ending?"

Having barely passed an English class in her life, it is ironic that Danielle Merchant is now a published author. Growing up in Minnesota, Danielle was a hyperactive child, an athlete, and a bookworm. She studied Psychology and Health Education in college but really only attended classes for the boys and to be on the swim team.

Danielle now resides in Northern California and lives with her cat, Peanut. She writes fiction romance books. This is her debut publication.

Chelsea Lauren
"All A-Boat You"

Chelsea Lauren is a YA and NA contemporary fiction author. She's an upstate NY native, establishing roots in her hometown with her partner and their dog, Kaiya. When Chelsea isn't writing or working on her business, you can find her devouring books, snuggling with her pup, camping, or having game nights with her friends.

Chelsea is the founder of Represent Publishing, a self-publishing company dedicated to helping authors strengthen their writing, edit, and publish their novels. Her passion lies in helping others accomplish their dreams.

Also by Represent Publishing

Underneath The Whiskey by Chelsea Lauren

Simply An Enigma by Chelsea Lauren and Brittany Evans

Rooted: A Poetry Collection by Cassandra Chaput

Sculpt Yourself by Savy Leiser

'Tis The Effing Season by Chelsea Lauren

Light of Evanora by T.R. Nickel

Theodore's Work In Progress by Chelsea Lauren

Coming Soon:

Apparatus From Aruna by T.R. Nickel

Made in the USA
Middletown, DE
18 July 2022

69351037R00179